Goodnight & Go

Breakaway Book Two

By

Meika Usher

Also by Meika Usher

Breakaway
Something So Sweet
Goodnight & Go
Ready to Run

Watch for more at meikausher.com.

Also by Meika Usher:

Something So Sweet

(Breakaway Book One)

Goodnight & Go

Meika Usher

Copyright © 2018 by Meika Usher

First edition

www.meikausher.com[1]

Cover design by germancreative

Edited by Jessica Snyder

ISBN: 978-0-9991180-2-3

---

1. http://www.meikausher.com

For Ventura—

Thank you for keeping all MY secrets

1: One More Night

I should not have stayed the night.

Sunlight poured in through the window, caressing the bare chest of the sleeping sex god beside me. My lips itched to follow its path. Images of last night flickered through my mind. Maybe I had time for...

No.

Get up, Cat.

Rule number one of a one-night stand: *Never stay the night.*

Why, oh why, had I let him convince me to stay?

The bed shifted beside me and a deep, sleepy groan filled the room. I turned to find a pair of gray-green eyes looking at me. "Morning." The husky, scratchy tone of his voice pulled at all the nerves and muscles in my lower region. My body angled toward him before I caught myself and froze.

"Morning." I pulled my eyes from his. "Listen, last night was great, but—"

"You've got to go." His hand reached for a patch of skin exposed by the crumpled sheet. As his fingers brushed my naked hip, my phone filled the room with a screech.

I rolled away and sat up, the sheet falling to the bed. *Thank you,* I thought as I silenced the noise. "Hello."

"Catharine?" My mother's voice clawed into my ear canal and I immediately regretted picking up. "Are you still asleep?"

Why was I in such a hurry to leave again? Especially considering the fine male specimen beside me, with dimples to die for and abs I could lick for days...

I smiled to myself, reliving last night's finer points. *Mmm...*

"Cat!" Mother Buzzkill said and the smile fell from my lips. "You were supposed to be here half an hour ago."

Fuckshitdamn. Brunch.

"On my way." I ended the call and tossed my phone back onto the nightstand. "Off I go." I glanced over my shoulder, trying not to let my eyes linger too long. No time for a repeat performance. Sadly. I planted my feet on the floor and stood.

Following the trail of clothes strewn all over the floor, I moved across the room, not looking back. Temptation to crawl back into bed would be too strong.

"You can't just be all naked like that and expect me to let you leave," came the sleepy, sexy voice.

"Aww, come on, Jude." I tossed him a look as I pulled my dress over my head. "Just one night, remember?"

"You said that four months ago," was his reply—a reply I chose to ignore as I scooped up my shoes and purse and walked out the door.

———————

"WOULD IT KILL YOU TO make it here on time for once?" my mother asked as I reached her table at the Portside—her restaurant of choice—twenty minutes later.

Every Sunday, we met here for brunch. It was a tradition I would have loved to lay to rest a long time ago, but for some reason unbeknownst to me and the rest of the universe, Nadine Keller-Tobias-Gillette-Bach, or just Nadine Bach for another six to twelve months, depending on how long it'd take her to find her next husband, actually seemed interested in spending time with her only daughter.

"And maybe *not* dressed like a college girl looking for free drinks?" she added, her gray eyes scraping over last night's outfit, a strapless zebra-print dress and six-inch red stilettos.

"Aww, you're sweet." I brushed at a wrinkle in my skirt. "And here I thought I'd started showing my age." I tucked a strand of hair behind my ear, and tried not to notice that Mommy Dearest had taken to wearing her own long, fiery hair in a style very similar to mine. "Or maybe that's just you."

I savored her stillness. There. That'd teach her to yank me out of bed to throw daggers at my life choices.

"Anyway, I'm sorry I was late," I continued, and I meant it. She'd waited a long time for me to show up. "I was up all night...working."

Mom narrowed her eyes on my face and I met them dead-on. *Go ahead*, I thought. *Challenge me. I guarantee you won't like to know what I was* really *up to.*

"I wish you'd stop all this fooling around," she said finally, making an unnervingly accurate assessment. "Don't you think it's time to settle down?"

"Like you did? Three—no, wait—four times?"

Mom didn't even flinch. "It takes time to find the right one."

"Exactly." I picked up my menu. "Which is why I'm in no hurry to rent a limo, pick out flowers and torture my best friend with ugly bridesmaid dresses. Now, what are you going to have?"

Mom scanned the menu, like she was going to order anything other than the California Chicken Salad she ordered every week.

Our waiter, a pimple-faced guy who was probably working the summer to save for college, approached and Mom placed her oh-so-predictable order.

"And for you, Miss?"

And just like that, the kid earned his weight in tips. A girl loved to be called *Miss*.

"I'll have the double cheeseburger."

I graced him with a dazzling smile and enjoyed the blush creeping up his neck. Boys were so easy. "With extra bacon, please. And fries. Lots of 'em." I snapped my menu shut and handed it to him, glancing at his nametag. "Thank you, Johnny. You're a doll."

"Y-you're welcome." He took my mother's menu from her outstretched hand and backed up. "That'll be right up for you, ladies."

Once Johnny was gone, Mom raised her pencil-thin brows at me. "Was that absolutely necessary?"

"What's a little harmless flirting if it'll get me some extra fries?"

Mother shook her head and reached for her water glass. "So, how are things at work?"

I lifted a brow. She wasn't really interested in my job as a junior graphic designer at Eliza, one of the country's top women's magazines. She'd expressed thousands of times over the twenty-nine years of my life her wish that I'd take up something more "suitable" for a woman. Like knitting. Or motherhood. God forbid her only daughter *work* for a living.

But, hey. If she wanted to play pretend, I was game. "Good. We're working on a new design for the website. It's a little tricky. We just upgraded software and it's been a hassle to—"

"Here you go, sir." The hostess brushed passed us, her dog-whistle voice yanking me from my narrative. "Your waiter will be right with you."

At the mention of the waiter, my eyes searched the restaurant for Johnny. I needed those damn fries. Stat.

"Anyway," I continued once the hostess wandered off. "New software. Shit show."

"Must you be so crude?" Mom sipped from her glass. "I did not raise you to speak that way. Especially in a public setting. I mean—"

Mom stopped, mid-lecture, and went dead-body-pale. Her eyes grazed over something behind me, then darted down, gluing themselves to the tablecloth.

I frowned. "What's your deal?" Turning, I scanned the bustling patio. "What are you—"

The ground lurched beneath me. Spinning back around so fast I got dizzy, I leaned in and hissed, *"What's he doing here?"*

Mom blinked. "I-I don't know." Meeting my eye, she straightened. "You didn't invite him?"

"I haven't spoken to the guy in a damn dozen years." I glared. Hard. What kind of question was that? "Of course I didn't invite him."

"I'm sorry. It's just—this is a long way from Hope Falls." She reached for her glass again and her hand shook. I got it. My entire body shook, too.

"I'm sure he's just here for business." I snuck another glance over my shoulder. He was maybe fifteen feet away now, and headed straight for our table.

"Here you are, sir," the hostess said once they arrived.

The dude she'd seated earlier stood. "Arthur. Good to see you."

"You, too, Edward."

From the corner of my eye, I watched them shake hands and take their seats. My entire body knotted up like ramen noodles. Only, before you dropped them into the boiling water. All hard and twisted and...crunchy.

Mom's eyes found mine, gray pools shimmering with a million conflicting thoughts. For a moment—a single, solitary moment—she looked human.

"Let's go." I pushed out my chair and reached for my purse. "We don't have to stay here."

"But...we ordered food. We can't just—"

"We can and we will. Screw the food. We'll pay double." I stood and threw my purse over my shoulder. "Let's just leave."

"Cat?"

I froze. When was the last time I'd heard that voice? Heard it say my name?

I didn't have to think too hard about it. That memory had been cemented into my brain at the tender age of sixteen.

Blowing out a slow breath, I turned to face him. My stepfather. Well, *former* stepfather.

The good one.

You know, until he left.

I took in his features. Same salt and pepper hair. Same brown eyes, framed by new wrinkles and an alien emotion. Nervousness? Caution? A smidge of *Please don't murder me*?

Squashing down the raging tidal of emotions, I blinked slowly. "I'm sorry. Do I know you?"

Surprise flickered over his face but he covered it quickly. Pushing to his feet, he attempted a smile. "Good to see you, kid."

I squinted and tilted my head. "I mean, the back of your head looks familiar. Like someone I saw walk away once."

"Catharine, please." My mother stood, too. She'd replaced the panic with her usual glossed-over demeanor. "Hello, Arthur."

Arthur smiled successfully this time. "Nadine." He reached across the distance and took her hand. "It's so good to see you."

Part of me expected my mother to grip his hand tight and flip him onto the table. Or maybe that was what *I* wanted to do.

"Here you go, ladies." Johnny—sweet, precious Johnny—saved the day, dropping our food off with a grin. "Extra fries, like you requested."

"You're a lifesaver." I reached into my purse and pulled out my wallet. "Can I ask you one more favor?"

"Sure." His eyes lit with the eagerness of a new puppy, and I resisted the urge to scratch behind his ear.

"Can we get this to go?"

"Catharine, I really don't think that's necess—"

"Oh, it's necessary, Mother." I glared in Arthur's direction. "If we stay here, I'm going to lose my appetite."

2: Spaghetti & Soaps

A few days later, I pushed open the door to my grandmother's apartment. "Hazel, I'm here."

"In the kitchen," Hazel called and I followed her voice. She stood at the stove, stirring a pot of magical marinara sauce.

I leaned down and pressed a kiss to her soft cheek. "Smells amazing." I sat the bottle of merlot and a grocery bag on the counter. "I brought you cupcakes."

Hazel stopped stirring and peeked inside the bag. "Ooh. Red velvet." She patted me on the cheek, her warm brown eyes crinkling. "You know me so well, sweetheart."

I smiled. "What kind of granddaughter would I be if I didn't know your favorite dessert?"

Wednesday evenings were *Drama and Dinner* nights—Grandma Hazel would make delicious food and then we'd catch up on her favorite soap opera, *Until the End of Time*.

I considered that part dessert, what with all the hot men parading around in their skivvies.

From somewhere in the apartment, a croaking meow caught my attention. My smile widened. "Peach," I called. "Kitty, kitty, kitty."

A ball of orange fluff came strolling into the kitchen, stopping to rub against my ankles. I bent and scooped her up, careful of her fragile bones. "Hey, baby," I cooed, snuggling her soft fur. "Mama missed you." Her motorboat purr vibrated against my chest and I sighed. Kitty purrs were the best kind of therapy.

Hazel turned back to the stove while I sat at the table. Peach curled up in my lap and gazed up at me with age-wizened green eyes—a cat didn't hang around for nineteen years without learning a thing or two.

"So, how was your weekend?" Hazel asked as I scratched behind Peach's ears.

I thought of Sunday brunch, and the unwelcome memories it had brought. "I've had better." I paused, then added, "I've had worse, too." Because it was true. At least there'd been Dimples McGee.

Putting the lid on the boiling pasta, Hazel crossed the kitchen and joined me at the table. "I spoke to Arthur."

My fingers stilled mid-pet, earning a glare from Peach. "Oh, yeah?"

Hazel reached over to give Peach a chin scratch, and she went back to purring. "He mentioned he saw you."

I narrowed my eyes on a crack in the ceramic-topped table. "Sure did." My stomach burned. It'd taken me days to wash the memory of my former-stepfather's surprise appearance out of my mind. I didn't need to be reminded. Holding Peach to my chest, I stood. "And it was every bit as awkward as you'd imagine."

"He wishes you'd—"

"Hazel." My voice dropped in warning. "We've been over this. And over it, and over it." With my free hand, I swung open the fridge and reached for a soda. "A chance run-in isn't going to change anything. In fact," I gently put Peach down. "If anything, it only reminded me of why we don't speak."

I felt her eyes on me as I cracked open the can and took a swig. I ignored her. "Huh. This tastes *just like* regular soda!"

"He misses you, Kitten."

I sighed. "Yeah, well." I sat the can on the counter and wiped my hands on my jeans. "He kinda gave up the right to miss me when he—"

"When he left. I know." She pushed to her feet and walked to the stove. "You haven't spoken to him since. Maybe now's the time to—"

"Hazel..."

She let out a slow breath. "Fine. I'll let it go." *For now.* She didn't need to say that part aloud. It was implied. It was always implied. "I watched some of our stories without you." She changed the subject like a master as she held the boiling pot over the sink.

"Hazel!" I said, my voice mock angry. "How could you?"

"I'm sorry, baby girl. I needed to know how the hell Loretta faked her death." She looked at me, her brown eyes wide behind her glasses. She plopped the pot back on the stove and piled pasta onto a plate. "I mean, poor Lorenzo, thinking he killed that woman!"

"I guess I can forgive you," I said as I took the plate of spaghetti from her outstretched hand. "But only because you're feeding me."

Hazel smiled and dropped a piece of garlic bread on my plate. "I'm so glad you're easily paid off."

———

FOR THE NEXT HOUR OR so, we ate spaghetti and discussed the complicated and sex-filled lives of our favorite fictional characters. Once we were so stuffed we could barely move, we waddled into the living room and started our weekly marathon.

While Hazel cued up the show, I settled deep into my favorite beat-up recliner, instantly joined by Peach. With a wistful sigh, I ran my hand across the leather. Grandpa Zeke used to sit here every night while he watched the news.

It hadn't been the same since he died three years ago. Hazel was the strongest woman I'd ever met. She survived the worst pain she'd ever felt and was still standing tall. I wanted to be her when I grew up.

As if that would ever happen.

Around twenty minutes into our second episode, Hazel was snoring softly. I smiled to myself and gently scratched the cat's graying chin. Leaning my head back, I closed my eyes and listened to Peach purring, Hazel snoring, and Loretta crying hysterically from the TV. For roughly the one-billionth time, I pondered bringing Peach home with me. She was technically my cat, after all. And it'd be nice to come home to a warm, purr-y companion.

But, no. I glanced at my grandma. The two were a set now. I couldn't break them up after all this time.

Well, that and the whole *being responsible for someone other than me* thing.

Shoving all unpleasant thoughts aside, I snuggled deeper into the chair and closed my eyes.

I'd just begun to doze off when my phone buzzed in my pocket. Peach started then glared. I dug the phone out and opened the message. The number wasn't saved into my contacts, but I knew exactly who it was.

Can't stop thinking about your sexy ass walking out the door last week-end.

A smile touched my lips as I pictured a long, lean, muscled body barely covered by cool white sheets.

Damn, but he was hot.

Of course he was. How else had we ended up here?

Two years ago, we'd crashed into each other like a full-speed Bugatti into a brick wall. One night of hot, uninhibited, toe-curling sex, and that was that. We never spoke again.

Until four months ago.

Seeing him again brought back every dirty fantasy I'd tried to forget, and I couldn't resist reliving those moments. Over and over and over. Damn near every weekend since.

I couldn't resist now, either.

Without thinking further, I responded to his text:

I don't blame you. My ass IS pretty spectacular.

A couple minutes later, my phone buzzed again: *You should bring that spectacular ass on over.*

That brought me pause. It was Wednesday. Jude was a weekend thing—a sporadic, unplanned, hot weekend thing.

No. I wouldn't go down that road.

I rested my head on the back of the chair and closed my eyes. Immediately, my mind skittered to that apartment, that smile, those hands, and...

Well, who couldn't use a mid-week pick-me-up?

Especially after the few days I'd had.

Grabbing my phone, I typed, *Be there in an hour.*

With a glance at Hazel, I shifted in my seat, prompting Peach to take off down the hall, a look of pure disdain tossed in my general direction.

Standing, I tiptoed to the couch and laid a gentle hand on Hazel's shoulder. Her eyes fluttered open.

"What'd I miss?" she asked, looking from me to the TV. "Did Lorenzo find out?"

"Not yet." I laughed. "Almost, though."

"Good. That vile girl needs to get what's coming to her."

"And she will. But in the meantime, I've got to get going."

Hazel nodded. "Get out of here. You've indulged your old grandma long enough." Her eyes sparkled up at me and I felt my chest tighten with warm, tender feelings.

Feelings were reserved for Hazel.

"Thanks for dinner." I squeezed her shoulder. "Do you need help getting around for bed?"

"Nah." She brushed me off. "I'll be all right. Same time next week, right?"

"Of course." I smiled. "We have a standing date, you and I. And Peach," I added as the prissy creature found enough forgiveness to bid me farewell by rubbing her ginger fur all over my black pants.

Hazel snickered and then called the cat to her. I watched Peach jump onto the couch and snuggle with the world's most wonderful grand-ma.

"Love you, Kitten," she said, and she wasn't talking to Peach.

I stuck my tongue out at her, even though I secretly liked the nick-name. Only from Hazel, though. Anyone else who tried it would get a fist in the mouth. "See you next week!"

3: Off With the Pants

J ude's apartment was clear across town. As I drove, I wondered if maybe I shouldn't have just gone home. After all, it was a weekday and I had to work in the morning. Did I really want to drive all the way home in the middle of the night? Because I *definitely* wouldn't be staying the night.

Nope. Not again.

Port Agnes was located on the Hope River, about twenty miles east of Lake Michigan. It was the art and culture hub of western Michigan, with hundreds of restaurants and a killer bar scene. I grew up here and I loved it. I'd heard rumors about people who lived in teensy, tiny towns and actually liked it, but the thought made me shudder. I'd only ever been to one town that small. It was cute, sure, but it sort of creeped me out how everyone knew every one else.

I liked my privacy.

I turned my lime green hatchback down North Pierview Street, and pulled into the space behind Jude's Harley. Yeah. Dude drove a bike. There was a reason I kept coming back. And it wasn't because Jude bought me flowers or made me breakfast in bed. If he tried at any point, I'd probably have to kill him.

Shoving those thoughts aside, I shut the car off and got out. As I headed up the walk to the apartment building, I sent Jude a text letting him know I was here. A couple minutes later, I was in an elevator decorated with mirrors and stainless steel. As I shot upward to the tenth floor, I checked my reflection.

With quick, practiced hands I smoothed my long red hair and tucked a piece behind my ear. Then, I wiped at a smudge of black liner under my eye and applied a coat of pink gloss. Not that it'd last long. I didn't come here to chat.

With two floors left till my destination, I reached into my shirt and gave the girls a quick adjustment. *Not too shabby*, I thought, eyeing my tight black pants and sparkly ballet flats, topped with a simple V-neck purple t-shirt. Probably the most casual outfit Jude had ever seen me in, but I rocked it, dammit.

The elevator dinged and the doors slid open. I exited and made the quick trek to apartment 1003. Before I could knock, the door opened and the breath whooshed from my lungs.

There he was. All six feet four inches of him. I had to look up to see his face. It was easy to forget how tall he was, considering how much time we spent...not talking. There were much better things he could be doing with that mouth.

Speaking of his mouth, his lips were tilted in a sexy smirk that reached all the way to the smeary hazel-gray of his eyes. My tummy did little backflips and my fingers itched to drag through his shaggy brown hair.

"Took you long enough," he said, holding the door wide so I could walk inside. I could feel his eyes on my ass like lasers, so I put a little extra oomph into my walk and threw a grin over my shoulder. "And you're right," he added. "Your ass *is* spectacular."

He shoved the door shut and followed me inside. I sauntered into the spacious living room, running my fingertips along the arm of a decadent leather couch. On the coffee table, a smattering of books caught my eye. *Sense and Sensibility* teetered on top of a well-worn

Stephen King paperback. Beneath them, an open spiral-bound notebook peeked out, its pages covered in neat, small handwriting.

I moved on before I could analyze those details. This wasn't a *Getting To Know You* visit.

Leaning against the counter that separated the living space from the kitchen, I watched as he drew nearer. His walk was almost predatory, the glint in his eyes so hot it had my blood boiling before he even laid a finger on me.

Yes. *This* was why I came.

I allowed my eyes to travel from his bare feet—why was that sexy?—to his jeans-clad legs. I paused at his chest, relishing the subtle way the plain white t-shirt hinted at the muscles beneath it. I couldn't wait to—

My thought was cut off by Jude's lips crashing into mine. He tasted of spearmint and sin and I moaned, gripping his shoulders tight. His fingers burrowed into my hair as the kiss went from zero to a hundred in half a second flat. And just like that, everything melted away, and the only thing that mattered was this moment. Those lips. The anticipation of what would happen next.

I stood on my tiptoes, trying to get closer, as I found the hem of his t-shirt and yanked. My fingertips reached the hot, hard flesh beneath. A low growl filled the room and I wasn't sure who it'd come from.

"Have you gotten shorter?" Jude whispered against my lips before trailing kisses over my jawline and down my neck.

I tossed my head back and laughed. Then, I extended a foot and pointed. "No heels."

"Ahh. Yeah. That explains it." He nodded solemnly. "We may have to do something about that." His hands found my waist and he surprised me by lifting me onto the counter.

"Huh." I looked him in the eye. "So *that's* what your face looks like."

He chuckled, a husky, sensuous sound, before his mouth descended onto mine again. I slid to the edge of the counter and wrapped my legs around his waist, pulling him closer, until I could feel his heat through the layers of clothing between us.

"I'm gonna need you to be more naked," I muttered, nipping his earlobe. He shuddered and obliged, pulling his shirt off. I leaned back then, just to take in the glory before me. Hard muscles? Check. Crisp trail of hair disappearing into the waistband of his jeans? Check. Tattoo? Yum.

I ran a finger over the intricate wing inked over his shoulder and down the back of his arm. "You're ridiculous, you know that?"

"Thanks. I think. Now you." He reached for my shirt and I lifted my arms, helping him dispose of it. He laughed as his eyes traveled over me. "Cute bra."

I glanced down and joined his laughter as I saw what he meant. Each cup of my bra was designed to look like those red and white Pokémon balls. "Eh." I shrugged. "Laundry day."

Jude shook his head, his smile revealing those damn dimples I couldn't stop thinking about. "So damn cute." He lowered his head, dropping hot kisses over my shoulder and across my collarbone. I tossed my head back and sighed as he teased along the lines of my bra.

I dug my nails into his back and he hissed. "Pick up the pace, buddy boy. We ain't got all night."

The words were barely out of my mouth when Jude lifted me off the counter and wrapped his arms around his waist. Without removing his lips from my skin, he carried me to his oversized brown couch and tossed me down.

I laughed and sat up on my elbows. "Off with the pants," I said as I kicked my shoes to the floor.

His lips tilted in a half-smile as he moved closer to me. "You first." He leaned down and looped his thumbs into my waistband. With one swift motion, he had me in nothing but my Pokébra. I ached in anticipation, watching through lust-glazed eyes as he bent to his knees and pulled my leg against his chest, scraping my calf with his teeth.

"Mmm." My eyes closed as his lips moved over the back of my knee and over my thigh.

My heels dug into Jude's back and I closed my eyes just as his mouth reached its destination.

Totally worth the drive.

———————

"*JesusGodAlmighty*," I groaned some time later, collapsing onto Jude's chest. "I feel like I should write you a Thank You card or something."

"I'd prefer a good box of chocolates." He brushed a strand of hair from my forehead, letting his fingertips trail over my shoulder. I shivered. "Maybe some flowers. I like daisies. Orange ones."

"Daisies?" I lifted my head to see his face. "Really?"

He lifted a shoulder. "I'm a simple girl."

I laughed and extricated my limbs from his, reaching for my bra. His eyes followed my every movement as I pulled it on and grabbed my pants.

"Is it just me, or is Wednesday night sex better than Saturday night sex?" I stepped into my pants and glanced at him, keeping my eyes on his face. He hadn't moved an inch since I got up, and the temptation of all that nakedness was too much. "Like. *Way* better."

He laughed, a sexy, husky sound that pulled at my once-satiated muscles. "You may be right," he said as he leveled those sultry gray-green eyes on me and held, warming. "I could get used to it."

Anxiety bubbled inside of me. *No,* I thought, eyes scraping the room for my shirt. *Don't get used to anything.* I fought to hold onto the afterglow brought on by the bone-melting orgasm I'd just had.

I dragged my eyes back to his, the words tumbling from my lips in a quiet request. "Please don't."

The warmth in his eyes dissipated. I winced. "Right." He sat up and reached for his pants. "Got it."

I tore my eyes from him and searched the room, my gut twisting like a dishrag. Time to go. Way passed time to go. "Have you seen my shirt?"

"Counter, I think."

I located the t-shirt on the floor next to the counter. "Thanks." I pulled it on and searched the floor for my shoes, feeling the burn of his eyes on me as I moved across the room.

I wanted to stay. I wanted to discard all the clothes I'd just put on and I wanted to spend the rest of the night with my naked skin against his.

But there was a line. A line that was established from the moment we met: this was a casual fling. Should have been a single night, but somehow we kept ending up here.

Maybe that meant it was time to end it.

I turned to face him. He stood in the middle of the living room, jeans hung low on his hips, drawing my attention to a pair of well-defined, all-too-lickable hip bones. And just like that, my mind went blank.

I forced my eyes away from his waistline and to his face. Bitch of it was, I didn't want to end it. But there were rules. And I'd already broken one. It was time to go.

"Listen—"

"See you around, Cat."

And then he disappeared down the hall, only the rigid line of his back and the memory of the hurt in his eyes to walk me to the door.

4: Lo Mein & Loneliness

———

Two days later, I found myself sitting in a frou-frou bridal shop while my best friend, Tierney, tried on her wedding dress one last time before the I Do's.

"What do you think?" she asked, emerging from the dressing room in a floor length, frothy white thing.

I stood and circled her. She looked beautiful. All dark hair and fair skin. Sort of like Audrey Hepburn, with boobs. "I think that Jack's gonna want to tear that dress right off of you, and everyone else is going to cry from your sheer beauty."

Tierney tucked a strand of hair behind her ear and grinned. "Well, Jack already wants to tear anything I wear off, so..."

"All right. That may be more than I need to know." I tugged at the lace cap sleeve. "You look gorgeous, Tier."

She gazed at her reflection, a smile on her lips. "Thanks." Then, she straightened her shoulders and shook her hair away from her face. "Now, what do you say we go get some dinner?"

At the mention of food, my stomach grumbled. "Thank god."

We'd been at it all day, hopping from place to place, taking care of last minute wedding business. I needed sustenance.

As I waited for Tier to change, I plopped down on the ornate couch and pulled my phone out of my purse. Without much thought, I opened my text messages and read over the last exchange with Jude. I hadn't heard from him since Wednesday night. Which wasn't unusual. We weren't texting buddies. But our last exchange wouldn't stop playing through my mind.

I couldn't pinpoint exactly what was different. I got in, got laid, got out. Nothing new there.

From the moment we slept together a few months ago—well, slept together *again* a few months ago—there'd been rules in place: this was not a relationship. We were not exclusive. Outside of our biweekly, sometimes weekly, hookups, we never even spoke to each other.

Clearly, my accidental sleepover had changed the rules for him.

Well, that couldn't happen.

Everything had an expiration date, and we had reached ours.

"You ready?"

I looked up, shoving all thoughts of Mr. Dimples from my mind. Even out of her blushing bride gear, Tierney glowed. I'd always been jealous of her tall, dark and gorgeousness, always wished she could give me some of her height or boobage, even for a night. Ever since she'd found her happy ever after dude and success in her career, she seemed to be even more beautiful.

It was sickening.

Yet, despite the tinge of bitterness, I was happy for my best friend.

"Of course I'm ready." I stood and pulled my Kelly green cardigan on over my black and white dress. "I've been withering away since breakfast."

I led the way outside and we were greeted by the late spring sun shining on the Hope River. I adored this city. It had such a great mix of charm and beauty, as well as a hopping city life. A person could never get bored.

"So, what sounds good for dinner?" I asked Tierney as we reached my car.

"Chinese." She answered without hesitation, yanking open the passenger door. At my look, she added, "Jack has been on a healthy food kick lately. If I have to eat one more kale salad, I'm going to call off the whole damn wedding."

I laughed as I jammed the key into the ignition. "No, you're not. You'd eat kale salad every day if the dude asked you to."

Tierney passed me a solemn look. "Promise me you won't let that happen."

"I'll sneak you Lo Mein and burgers every day if it comes to that." Putting the car into drive, I eased out onto the street. "No friend of mine is going to eat *healthy*."

ABOUT TWENTY MINUTES later, we were seated at a table in the back corner of Stu's, menus in hand. While Tierney stared at her own menu, I began twisting my straw wrapper. What was it with the women in my life? Just like Mom at brunch last weekend, Tierney knew exactly what she was going to order. Why bother with the menu at all?

Finally, she gave up the show and tossed it aside. "So, did I tell you the latest drama?"

Oh, boy. I folded my hands in front of me and braced myself. Ever since Tierney started shacking up with Jack, it'd been one thing after another. No amount of good lovin' was worth all that crazy. "I don't think so. What's up?"

Tierney rolled her eyes and sat back in her chair. "You know Wes left for a cruise a few months ago, right?" At my nod, she continued. "Well, apparently, he called his mom the other night to tell her he's not going to be home in time for the wedding. Because he met someone and wants to see where it goes." She leaned forward, her elbows on the table. "In Barcelona. "

A laugh burst passed my lips. "Oh, that's amazing." Reclaiming my twisted straw wrapper, I shook my head. "Who'd have thought good ol' Wes had it in him?"

"Right?" Tierney shoved a hand through her hair. "Best part is, Bonnie is *convinced* it's my fault. You know, because I'm marrying his cousin, and it's *just so awkward* that he had to leave the country."

"She has a point." I smiled as she threw me a dark look. "You gotta admit, it's a little weird to marry your ex's cousin." I smiled at the waiter as he sat our water glasses on the table. "Your life is just like *Until the End of Time.*"

Tier let out a strangled denial as our waiter poised his pencil to take our orders. "I resent the accuracy in that statement."

I laughed. "I shall buy you delicious food to make up for it."

She crossed her arms over her chest. "Fine."

Once we placed our order—beef Lo Mein for Tier, Cashew Chicken for me, with a side of Crab Rangoon and egg rolls—Tierney shifted to wedding talk. Again.

"I mean, Mom is thrilled that I'm getting married. I sort of think she'd resigned herself to the idea that I'd be single forever. Of course, that means she wants to be involved in every aspect of the planning."

I tapped my fingernails against my water glass and lifted a shoulder. "Could be worse. I'm pretty sure if I told my mom I was getting married, she'd hire half a dozen wedding planners *and* keep me away from the groom—just so I wouldn't screw it up."

Tierney snorted. "Let's be honest here. You *would* screw it up."

"You kidding? 'Course I would." I sat back in my seat and added, "Assuming I'd ever get that far."

"Which is unlikely."

"Which is never gonna happen." I tossed her a smirk. "Forever alone, remember?"

Tier's green eyes lingered for half a sec. "I'd say you never know, but I know you." She settled into her seat. "I also know you just had brunch with your mom, so you already got the *don't you ever want to settle down?* talk. So, I'll stop now."

"Thanks for the reprieve." I folded down the corner of my paper placemat, Sunday brunch front and center in my mind for the first time today. I hadn't told Tier about Arthur. I looked her way. Maybe now was a good time. "So, guess what—"

Before I could finish, Tier's phone burst into the chorus of "Pour Some Sugar on Me." I rolled my eyes as she shuffled through her purse. "Really?"

She stuck her tongue out as she found her phone. "Sorry, it's Jack. I'll be quick."

I nodded and rested my chin in my hand, my eyes wandering the busy restaurant. It was fine. I didn't need to talk about Arthur's surprise appearance, anyway. It was nothing.

Friday evenings were busy everywhere in Port Agnes, but it seemed that Stu's had lured in more than its usual weekend crowd.

What used to be a little known secret around these parts had blown up a few months back, thanks to a fantastic review in the Port Agnes Press.

I sort of missed when no one knew about it. It'd been so much quieter.

"Jack says hi," Tier said and I looked her way long enough to make a goofy face. She laughed. "Cat sends her love. So, wait. Bonnie thinks we should do *what* at the reception?"

I tuned out as their conversation dissolved into wedding-y stuff. Where was our waiter? I was thirty seconds from gnawing my own arm off. Maybe I could sneak back into the kitchen and—

A couple entering the building caught my attention. My stomach flipped. Of all the restaurants in all the—

"What are you doing?" Tierney pulled the phone away from her ear and glared at the glass in my hand. "You're spilling water everywhere."

"Oh. Sorry." I forced my hands to stop fidgeting as the tall, shaggy-haired guy pulled out a chair for the tiny brunette he'd come in with.

Jude settled in across from his date and I focused hard on my paper placemat. Huh. Apparently, I was a Boar. Who knew?

"Here you go," our waiter said, dropping a plate of delicious food onto my placemat before I could finish reading about my most compatible matches.

Ah, well. Didn't matter.

Even as I thought it, my eyes trailed back to Jude, who was laughing at something his date said, smiling that smile that could melt even the sturdiest of panties. *I wonder what his sign is...*

Shoving that thought aside, I smiled up at the waiter. "You have impeccable timing, sir. You'll be receiving a handsome tip."

He smiled, his dark eyes sparkling. "Thank you, miss," he said before walking away. He'd obviously heard the Miss/Ma'am rule.

Tierney wrapped up her call and tossed her phone back into her purse. "Sorry about that. Bonnie emergency." She unwrapped her chopsticks and reached across the table, digging into my food. "What were you saying?"

I blinked. Oh, yeah. Brunch. Arthur. My stomach knotted. I didn't want to ruin my appetite. "Oh, nothing." I leaned in and twirled a mouthful of Lo Mein onto my fork from Tier's plate. Stu's tradition—we always split our food. "No biggie."

She narrowed her eyes on my face and I shoved my fork into my mouth to avoid further interrogation. After a few seconds of intense staring, she looked away. I breathed an inward sigh. Soul-bearing conversation averted.

As I chewed, my eyes found Jude again. No wonder I hadn't heard from him. He'd found himself a new chick to hang out with. One that would go on dates with him. In public.

Well, good.

Saved me the trouble of ending things myself.

That shouldn't have felt like a fishhook in my intestines.

As if he felt me staring, Jude looked up, his eye catching mine. Even from way over here, I could see the glint of surprise. I mustered up a smile and a wave, then went back to my plate. There. All casual and shit.

Too bad my insides didn't get the memo.

Stabbing a piece of chicken more forcefully than I needed to, I yanked my attention back to Tier. "How's Jack?"

She studied me. "You sure you're all right?"

"I'm fine," I answered around a mouthful of chicken. "Just starving."

Her eyes lingered for a couple more seconds before giving me a slow nod. "Jack's good. He spent the day with his brother, taking care of some last minute things before the wedding." She paused to take a bite. Once she finished, she went on. "I'm so glad he could work things out with his family, ya know? A year ago, I'd have never thought he would ask Luke to be his best man, but here we are."

Ah, yes. The best man. "About that—"

"It'll only be awkward if you make it awkward." Tier drummed her fingertips on the tabletop. "Don't make it awkward, Cat."

I put my hands up in surrender, and she continued talking about the trials and tribulations of the Elliott clan—of which I had banged exactly one. I didn't make a habit out of revisiting the one-nighters. How could I have known he'd be in my best friend's wedding a couple years later?

I jammed a heaping helping of greasy noodles into my mouth and tuned in to Tierney's jabber. She would be a married woman soon. Jack had reconciled with his family. Hell, even Lorenzo would probably forgive Loretta for faking her death.

And then there was me. Shoving my face full of Chinese food while my fuck buddy of the last few months wined and dined a new chick.

Forever alone.

It'd been a joke earlier when I said it, but now it just seemed bleak.

I should've ordered more food.

5: A Tryst at Tryst

———

A week later, I found myself at my usual spot—a popular bar called Tryst—with a few of the girls from work. It used to be Tierney and me, but with her off planning a wedding and boning her fiancé or whatever, I had to improvise.

"And so I took my bra out of his dog's mouth and told him it was over." Beth-Ann, a secretary from accounting with blue eye shadow and fluffy blonde hair, was saying. "I mean, really! That bra cost more than a week's worth of groceries and he was letting his *dog* chew on it?"

As opposed to what? I thought. Would she rather her boyfriend chew on it? Or maybe wear it? And why had it cost so much, anyway? Was it coated in diamonds?

I fought off a massive eye-roll, took a hearty swig of the watered down drink I'd been nursing for the last hour, and willed myself to teleport the hell out of here. To no avail. My super powers must've been on the fritz.

"Like, I totally know what you mean," Kylie, an editorial assistant in the Beauty department, said. "If, like, Mike's dog ever chewed on *my* bra..." She shuddered dramatically, as if it were, like, the worst thing in the world.

"I'm going to get another drink." I shot up from my seat. I couldn't sit there a second longer and listen to this inane conversation. Dogs were cute. Relationships were dumb. Why was it even an issue?

Pushing my way through the crowd I sagged against the bar with a groan. "Can I get a Tree Frog, please?"

The tatted-up bartender tossed me a wink and got to work. I drummed my fingernails on the counter as I waited, watching people circle around each other, grind against each other, avoid each other. Exhaustion trickled through my veins. With Jude no longer an option, I'd need to find a replacement. And nothing sounded more torturous at this moment than participating in the mass-mating dance taking place right before my eyes.

Ugh.

"Come here often, pretty lady?" came a voice from my left.

I turned, already knowing who it was. Jude was a local radio deejay and often broadcasted from various bars in Port Agnes. This was Tryst weekend.

Of course it was.

How had I forgotten that?

I should've had his schedule memorized by now—especially since this was how we kept ending up in a tangle of sheets.

"Hey." I glanced at him from the corner of my eye. I hadn't seen or heard from him since last week at Stu's. Hadn't expected to. Didn't really want to.

Okay. That last part was a lie.

"Looks like you've been having a grand time over there." He closed the distance between us and leaned against the bar. I could feel his body heat, smell the spice of his aftershave.

And it made me tingle.

Biting the inside of my lip, I nodded. "Yep. So fun."

"I find your sarcasm extremely attractive." Jude leaned over just enough to put his face in my peripheral.

He wore a black knit cap over his shaggy hair tonight, and had a nice scruff going, giving him a sort of sexy, grungy look. *Stop it,* I thought. *Stop being so hot.*

"Good to know." I angled my body so that we were facing each other and met his eye. "How was your date last week?"

He didn't even blink. "All right."

"Good. Glad to hear it." The bartender slid my drink across the counter and I caught it.

"Thanks, Sarah." I winked. "You look hot tonight."

Sarah's red lips curved as she grinned over her inked-up shoulder. "Still gotta pay your tab, Cat."

"Damn." I pushed my lip out. "Worth a shot!"

Sarah laughed and moved on to the next customer. I turned away from the bar, hoping Jude had wandered off.

No such luck.

His dimples were on full display as he grinned at me. "You're shameless."

I let my eyes trail over him—all six feet something of him—then back to his eyes. "That makes two of us."

With that, I grabbed my drink and whirled away from him. He followed. "What're you getting at?"

I faced him, hand on my hip. "How would your new girlfriend feel about you hitting on some other girl right now?"

He laughed. "You see me out with someone else one time and suddenly she's my girlfriend?" His eyes glittered. "Jealous?"

I scoffed and washed down the bitterness with a sip of my drink. "Do I strike you as the jealous type?"

"You seem a little jealous." Jude eased just a touch closer and my stupid pulse kicked up a notch. "Ironic, considering our last conversation."

I narrowed my eyes in annoyance. "I fail to see the irony here." After taking a long, fortifying sip of my drink, I added, "And I'm not jealous."

"You are." His gaze dragged over me in a slow, purposeful motion. "And it's sexy as hell."

I looked toward his mouth, then back to his eyes. "Sorry, man. I have a strict *no trespassing* rule."

"Lucky for you, I'm open to the public." As he said it, he frowned.

I laughed. "You didn't think that through very well."

He frowned. "I did not." And then as fast as the frown had appeared, it vanished, replaced by that panty-zapping smile. "You sticking around for a while?"

I gritted my teeth against the urge to lay a hand on his bare forearm, to pull him closer, to bite that spot at the base of his neck, the one that always drove him nuts.

Down girl, I thought, forcing my eyes away. Girlfriend or not, I'd already decided we were done.

"See you around, Jude." I smiled and turned away.

I didn't look back as I made my way back to my table. The girls were *still* talking about the bra-eating-dog incident. I plopped down in my seat and gulped my drink.

"I mean, like, what if it had been your *shoes?*" Kylie's eyes widened. "I just, like, don't think you can risk it, you know?"

Beth-Ann nodded solemnly. "I know. I really do."

"How's the sex?"

I shot off the question before I could think better of it, and everyone swirled to face me. Instead of taking it back, I put on my best nonchalant expression. "It's an important question. Because, I gotta say, I'd put up with a lot more than a dog eating my shoe if the dude knew how to rattle the headboard right."

Beth-Ann's face now matched the cranberry-vodka she'd been drinking. "Well, I...it...was okay?"

"Oh." I waved a hand and sat back, crossing one leg over the other. "In that case, you made the right decision."

Kylie squared her shoulders and nodded. "Right. Right. You *so* did."

Complete vindication from everyone at the table meant Beth-Ann was ready to change the subject. Which, you'd think would be a good thing. Except, what Beth-Ann decided to talk about was...

"Did you guys see the latest episode of *Real Housewives*?"

Everyone had a limit, man. And Beth-Ann had just found mine. Flipping my auditory switch to the "off" position, I sat back and surveyed the pulsating crowd. In the far corner, wrapping up for the night, stood Jude. Beautiful, sexy, *still single* Jude.

Memories, hot, torrid memories, flashed through my mind and caught fire to my veins. Before I thought too much about it, I reached for my phone.

Meet me in the ladies' room?

I watched as Jude felt his phone go off and pulled it out of his pocket. After he read my message, his eyes shot to my face, widened in surprise.

I lifted my eyebrows in a dare and watched as he typed his response. My phone buzzed and I looked down.

Five minutes.

A thrill ran through my entire body. I watched as he finished packing up and bid his crew goodbye. After he passed our table, I pushed my chair away. "Off to the ladies' room."

The girls barely looked up from their in-depth conversation. Good. Meant they wouldn't question me.

The line wove, long and irritating, down the hall leading to the bathrooms. My eyes searched for Jude. I'd bet anything he saw the line and ran the other direction. Damn.

I turned on my heels, ready to head back to my table, when my phone vibrated.

Supply closet, the text read. I smiled, liquid heat zipping through my veins. Even better.

I opened the supply closet door to find Jude already inside. He looked so much taller in this confined space and I tingled at the thought of those big hands of his on my body.

"Hey." I closed the door behind me and moved into the tiny room.

Jude's eyes took a slow journey from my face to my feet, pausing in all the right places. "Hey," he repeated, taking the last couple steps and pulling me into him.

I looked up just in time for his lips to crush into mine. A half-sigh, half-whimper escaped the back of my throat as the kiss went from candlelight to wildfire.

I reached up and disposed of the knit cap, threading my fingers through his hair with one hand, fingertips of the other digging into his shoulder. Kissing him was much easier this time, thanks to the stilettos on my feet. Even so, I stood on tiptoe, trying to get closer.

Without breaking the kiss, Jude backed me toward the door. A sharp, ferocious heat took over my entire body as I found myself pinned between the cold wood and Jude's hot body. My hands traveled over his chest until I reached the hemline of his shirt. The hard, flat muscles of his abs greeted my fingers and I moaned, laying my palms flat against him.

Parting, I looked up at him and slowly lowered my hand, my fingertips just inside the waistband of his jeans. "That's what I like about you," I whispered, meeting his eye. "A man of few words."

Jude laughed, even as he leaned his head back and closed his eyes. Little by little, I slipped my hand into his jeans, until my palm rested against the hard length of him. But before I could do anything about it, Jude was pulling my dress upward, forcing my hand from his jeans.

I pushed my bottom lip out in a pout and he leaned down and took it between his teeth, running his tongue over it. I moaned, leaning into him until my breasts were pressing against those delicious muscles.

"You're so sexy," he whispered, his hands roaming down my sides to cup my ass. I sighed my response, lifting one leg up so that he could slip his hand under my skirt.

He took the hint, his knuckles brushing against the dampness between my legs. A whimper escaped the back of my throat and I arched my hips closer. Slowly, he began a tight circular motion, sending jolts of aching pleasure throughout my entire body. I dug my nails into his shoulders and surrendered myself to the heat. To the passion. To the momentary, the temporary vulnerability of letting another person this close.

And, for these few moments in time, I would not be *forever alone.*

"SO, UH, THANKS." I tugged down my skirt and searched the floor for my panties. "That was fun."

I could feel Jude's eyes follow me, but I kept my gaze low. "Why don't you let me buy you a drink? Maybe a late night dinner?"

I looked up. Warmth pooled in his eyes, bordering on tenderness.

Tenderness?

We just fucked in a supply closet. What was *tender* about that?

I passed a feeble smile his way and fought to keep my tone light. "No can do, man." I spotted my panties near his feet and reached for them. "That's—"

"Against the rules." He pushed away from the wall and scrubbed at the remnants of red lipstick I'd left on his mouth. "Got it." The warmth in his eyes dissipated, leaving tendrils of frustration in its wake.

"Jude." I reached for him as he brushed passed me, but my fingertips merely grazed his shirtsleeve. "I—"

"It's all right, Cat." His hand lingered on the doorknob. A whoosh of cool air rushed into the tiny space as he opened the door. He looked back long enough for our eyes to meet. Long enough for me to glimpse the hollow, hopeless longing in them. "Just thought I'd ask."

6: Places to Bury the Hatchet

———

S unday morning came way too soon. It always did, though, when Mommy Dearest was waiting.

I pulled into the lot behind the Portside and put my car into park, taking a deep breath. I hadn't adequately prepared for the emotional havoc my mother was about to wreak. There wasn't any proper preparation for the onslaught of judgment. Just a fine coating of Teflon and, usually, a hefty drink or two.

Oh, and a round or two of stress-relieving sex with—

Nope. Not going there. Jude was no more.

For the best, really.

The time had come to stop using Jude for loneliness relief. He deserved better. And I deserved...

Well, I deserved the guilt that gnawed at me when he looked at me with those soft, longing eyes.

I hadn't been able to shake the shame since walking away from him last night. And it wasn't the we-just-had-sex-in-a-supply-closet kind of shame. I'd screwed in much more questionable places. It was the I-just-used-a-nice-guy-to-make-myself-feel-better kind of shame.

And it had to stop.

Shaking my hair away from my face, I gave myself one last glance in the rearview before getting out of the car. No time to dwell on Jude. Time to face the mother.

I adjusted the skirt of the silky black dress I'd chosen this morning to curb any snarky comments about my wardrobe. This dress was sure to meet Mom's approval, but the shoes were all for me. Strappy, sexy red high heels that I would wear all the time if I could.

My mind made the trek back home to my overflowing closet. I was mentally pairing my heels with everything I owned when I reached our table.

"Catharine!" Mom's voice grated—or *greeted*—me as soon as I entered. "It is truly remarkable how you can never make it on time."

"Mother." I looked up, snark at the ready. My reply died on my lips, though, when I caught sight of the scene before me.

She'd brought company.

I crossed my arms over my chest and focused on my mother—and only my mother. "What is this?"

"Darling, Arthur decided to join us. I hope that's all right?" Mom's voice melted, soft and sugary sweet, and it made me want to barf. She stood and smoothed the skirt of her perfectly-ironed wrap dress. "We've...reconnected since our run-in." She glanced down at him and they shared a smile. A gross, intimate, sickeningly familiar smile. "Isn't that lovely?"

"Oh, yeah. So lovely." Straightening my purse strap, I took a step back. A rush of reactions raced through me, like a speedboat on a sea of fuckery. I *definitely* hadn't prepared for this. "If you don't mind, I'll leave you to the...reconnecting."

"Please." Arthur stood. "Don't leave on my account."

"That depends." I let my eyes scrape over him, taking joy in the receding hairline and new wrinkles. Outward symbols of all the hell he'd put my insides through. "You staying?"

He looked to my mom, then back to me. "I can go, if you're uncomfortable with me here."

"Why, how could I possibly be uncomfortable?" I glared at my mom. "It's not like I was warned you'd be here or anything."

Mom's lips thinned. "We're all adults, Catharine. I didn't think I needed to *warn* you of anything."

"You didn't tell her?" Arthur's brows lifted toward that hairline I'd been smirking at seconds before. "Nadine..."

Her cheeks pinkened beneath the carefully applied blush. She avoided my eye as she answered him. "She wouldn't have come."

"You're right. I wouldn't have." I took another step back, anger wrestling with anxiety, like King-Kong Vs. Godzilla, in my tummy. "You could've at least saved me the trip."

Before Mother could muster another excuse, I whirled on my heels and walked away. Behind me, the shuffle of chairs cut through the murmur of the crowd. I didn't have to turn to know that Mom followed me. Well, she could try all the guilt-trips/excuses/demands in the book. I would *not* be having lunch with—

"Cat, wait."

Arthur.

I closed my eyes and took a long, deep breath. "So, overt hostility isn't a strong enough hint, huh?" I turned, steeling myself against the current zapping through me. Thirteen years. It'd been thirteen years since he left. It shouldn't still feel like this. But standing here now, in front of the man who'd been the only father I'd ever known, I was sixteen again, watching him drive away. And it was still like a knife through my bones.

"I don't want to do this, Arthur."

My words came out softer than I wanted them to. So much for the bad ass act.

"I know." He put his hands up in surrender—something he was so good at—and added, "And I respect that. I—"

"What are you even doing here? With her?" I waved a hand toward my mother, who had, surprisingly, remained seated. "Didn't do enough damage the first time, so you had to come back for Round Two?"

"It's not like that. I—"

"I don't want to hear what it's like." I gripped my purse straps hard with both hands so he couldn't see them shaking. "I want to hear you say you're going to leave. Now."

His brown eyes found my face. "I can't do that."

"Why not? You're going to do it eventually. Might as well save us all the time." *And the hurt.* But I wasn't going to say that part aloud.

"Cat, I'm sorry—"

"Look." I cut him off, needing to end this now. Needing to leave. Needing to *not* be reliving the worst years of my life. "My mother may believe in second chances and forgiveness and all that burying the hatchet bullshit." My eyes clashed with his as I continued. "But I don't. Only place I want to bury a hatchet would get me locked up."

I took minor satisfaction at the shock on his face and kept talking. "So, go on back to your table and play this game for as long as you need to. We both know it's just temporary."

I spun on my heels before he could contradict me. I'd never claimed to have psychic abilities, but I could see how this would play out.

And, unlike most people, I preferred to look *away* from the car crash.

———————

WEDNESDAY ROLLED AROUND, and I couldn't wait to spend an evening with Hazel, zoning out with *Until the End of Time* and delicious home-cooked food.

I hadn't talked to my mom since Sunday. Didn't want to. If she wanted to relive the past, well, good for her. I would *not* be a part of it.

I shook that train of thought off as I reached Hazel's apartment. The only drama I wanted to think about was purely fictional.

"Hello, dear," Hazel said as she opened the door. Her warm smile instantly soothed the chaos inside me.

I leaned in and gave her a big hug. "Hey, Grams." I entered her apartment and breathed in the delicious smells. "Chili tonight?" My smile widened.

Hazel confirmed it with a nod. "You want to get the cornbread started while the chili simmers?" She motioned to the fixings she already had out on the counter.

"Sure thing, chicken wing." I tugged my jacket off and tossed it over a chair.

Hazel laughed. "You've said that since you were a kid."

I smiled at her over my shoulder. "Some things never change."

Once the cornbread was in the oven and the chili was marinating to delicious perfection on the stove, Hazel and I sat at the table. Peach meandered in a little slower than usual and claimed her spot on my lap. I scratched her chin and smiled as she purred like an engine.

"So, how's your week been?" I asked Hazel, moving my eyes away from the ball of fluff trying to steal my soul with her Cute-Fu.

"Oh, good. You know, the usual. Thelma at church just had her second grandbaby, so that's all she wants to talk about. She brings in pictures every week. Cute little bugger." Hazel gave a soft smile. "Got to get me one of those."

"A baby? Don't you think it's a little...late in life for a new baby?" I asked, sliding my eyes away from hers. I saw where this was going and I wanted none of it.

"I meant great-grandbabies," she said, her eyes twinkling. "My baby-making factory has been out of commission for years."

"Ahh, yeah," I said, laughing. "Well, it's a good thing you've got Peach." I scratched behind the cat's ear and she leaned into my touch. "Fur grandbabies are much better, anyway. Babies require way more..."

"Commitment?" Hazel finished for me, her tone changing ever so slightly.

My eyes jumped to her face. "I was going to say poop and puke."

"Oh, sure. Sure." She patted my hand. "Sure you were, dear." Then she got up to stir the chili and check on the cornbread, leaving me slack-jawed.

What just happened? I felt like I'd just been analyzed by a shrink and found lacking.

Sure, I wasn't actively looking to settle down, but that didn't mean I didn't *want* commitment. I just...preferred to be alone.

As if she were reading my thoughts, Peach looked up and released a croaking *meow*. I avoided her eyes—and the huge dose of guilt that came with it. I could have, at any point in her nineteen years of existence, brought Peach to live with me. So why hadn't I?

Commitment.

"Arthur called this morning." Hazel interrupted my thoughts with an even worse topic. Her tone was light. My limbs stiffened anyway.

I'd rather talk about my commitment issues.

"Hazel." My hand paused mid-pet and Peach glared up at me. Geez. Demanding, much?

"I know, I know. You don't like to talk about him." Her brown eyes met mine and I looked away. "He's serious. About your mother."

"Yeah, well." I shooed Peach from my lap and stood. "Believe it when I see it." I walked to the fridge. "I should have brought some wine with me. Maybe some Tequila."

"I think there's a wine cooler in there somewhere."

"My grandma the lush," I murmured as my hand closed around the Fuzzy Navel in the back of the fridge. I cracked it open and leaned against the counter.

"Did you really threaten to hatchet him?"

My gaze shot to hers. "I...uh...not *technically*..."

"Kitten..."

"I know." I rolled the frigid bottle between my palms. "I know. I just..." My eyes burned, so I squinted to crush any threat of moisture. "It's like I'm back there again, you know?"

Hazel's hand covered mine and I stopped fidgeting.

"He promised." I glanced up, but immediately looked away. The warmth in Hazel's eyes would undo the tenuous control I was clinging to. "He made a promise. He broke it."

"I know, sweetheart." She squeezed my hand. "He didn't want to go."

A laugh sputtered from me, taut and humorless. I pushed away from the counter and lifted the bottle to my lips. "But he did, Hazel. He left and I can't forgive him for that."

"You should give him a chance to explain."

She wanted to push further. I could tell. But after studying me for a few long seconds, she conceded and launched into a regurgitated story about, well, regurgitation.

I sipped on my wine cooler as she talked about Thelma's grandbabies. As she spoke, my mind replayed her words. *He's serious.*

Well, if there was one true thing about Cat Keller, it was that she didn't *do* serious. Serious meant someone was going to get hurt.

And I'd prefer that *someone* wasn't me.

"You okay, Kitten?" Hazel reached over and laid a hand on my arm.

I blinked. Her brown eyes were warm with worry. Mustering a smile, I nodded. "Yeah, I'm good."

I am so going to hell, I thought as we set the table. I just lied to my eighty-three-year-old grandmother.

I was anything but *good.*

7: Girl's Night Gone Bad

———

Saturday arrived, and the idea of spending it with the girls from work sent a shudder of disgust through me. *Real Housewives* recaps and bra-eating pooches held very little appeal. Pulsating music and hormone-charged crowds held even less. Could it be that I was finally growing up? Mother would be so pleased.

The thought almost made me gag.

I had somehow managed to convince Tierney to take a night off from wedding planning, and I was meeting her at their place for a girl's night.

Jack and Tierney shared a tiny house on the west side of town—the side of town filled with, you know, couples and families and whatever. It was this adorable little brick house, complete with flowerboxes on the windows and a big, slobbery dog. Not really the life for me, but she seemed to love it.

I parked my neon green roller skate in the driveway and got out just as the front door swung open. Tierney came down the walk, a wiggly-assed blur of brown following on her heels.

"Mousse, stay," she said, her voice stern. The dog sat his ass on the sidewalk and looked up at her, waiting for her next command.

"Thanks for that." I tossed my purse over my shoulder. "I wasn't in the mood to be mauled today."

Tierney smiled. "Yeah, well that's not really an outfit made for mauling. Unless we're talking about mauling of a different kind."

I glanced down at the outfit in question. Bright red skinny jeans, a silky, flowy black top and my favorite red stilettoes. I shrugged. "Yeah, I'm not really looking to be mauled by a dog. Now, if you know any hot guys..."

As if on cue, Jack joined us, looking all ridiculously attractive in a pair of blue jeans and a Rolling Stones t-shirt. "Hey, Cat," he said as he reached us, his impossible blue eyes finding my face. He graced me with one of those charming smiles. "You ladies ready to party like rock stars?"

I lifted a brow. "Party like..."

"Really, honey?" Tierney said, giving Jack a look resembling embarrassment.

Jack shrugged and started toward the house. "You don't keep me around because I'm cool."

Tierney watched him walk away. "You're right," she called after him. "I keep you around because of that sweet ass of yours."

"You two are absurd."

Tier grinned. "I know. But, really. You ready to party?"

"Please don't add 'like rock stars' to that." I glanced at the dog, who was staring up at me with a hopefulness that bordered on pathetic. Leaning down, I gave him a scratch behind his ear. "I thought we were staying in tonight."

"It's been months since our last proper girl's night," Tierney said, heading toward the house. Mousse got up and followed. "There's a new bar downtown. I figured we could check that out."

Disappointment trickled through me as I mentally waved goodbye to my night of sweats, girl talk, and ice cream. There were a million things I wanted to tell Tier about. Guess they could wait a little longer. "Sounds...great."

———————

WE WALKED INTO THE bar a couple hours later, and I let out a low whistle. High ceilings, exposed beams, a second floor overlooking the stage, lots of dark cherry woods and sexy lighting.

"Nice," I said to Tierney as she looped her arm through mine and led me to a table in the back.

She looked hot tonight in a pair of tight jeans and a sparkly, low-cut teal top. I liked to think I'd taught her a thing or two about fashion during our seven-year friendship.

I took the chair next to her, crossing my legs. While Tierney had chosen to go the sexy-yet-modest look, I had gone the other route—thanks to a stop by my apartment on the way here. The strapless green dress I wore revealed way more skin than it hid, and I rocked the hell out of the leopard print heels and matching belt. I was comfortable in my skin. And I liked showing it off.

Not to mention, I enjoyed the looks I got from people of all sexes when I went out.

Okay, so maybe I was a bit of an attention whore. I was one with it.

"I'm going to grab a drink," Tierney leaned in and shouted over the blaring rock music. "Want anything?"

"Surprise me," I yelled back.

She got up and weaved her way through the crowd. This place was packed. I sat back and studied the sea of bodies before me.

Onstage, a group of guys were just getting their equipment set up. Hot guys. My eyes drank in the toned, sexy arms of the guy I assumed was the drummer, and the long hair and diva-esque air of the lead singer. *Nice.*

I had just moved on to the lead guitarist, all tattoos and cockiness, when another guy walked over and leaned in to say something to him. He smiled, flashing a fierce set of dimples, and my stomach dropped to the gleaming wood floor.

What the *hell* was he doing here?

"Here you go," Tierney said, returning with two drinks in hand. "I hear you like Pina Coladas."

I reached for the glass, not taking my eyes from Jude. He was having an in-depth conversation with the band. At one point, he reached up and took the knit cap off his head, running his fingers through that silky hair of his. My fingers itched to do the same.

"You all right over there?" Tierney waved a hand in front of my face. "You look like you're having a stroke."

"What? Oh. Yeah. Fine." I took a sip of my drink. "Just peachy."

"I mean, I don't blame you." Tierney took a sip of her own drink and looked toward the stage. "Musicians are hot. Especially the one with the smile."

"Yep." I absentmindedly stirred my drink with its straw.

"He's totally your type, too." She leaned forward, chin in palm. "You should totally tap that."

"What?" I choked on the pineapple chunk I'd been chewing. I coughed. "No, no. I'm so good."

"Dude, don't die on me." Tier patted my back. "You know how I hate being the center of attention, and I think your dead body will put me front and center."

I waved her off and sipped my drink. "You're so considerate," I grumbled once I'd recovered. "I'm so glad I came out with you."

I fought the urge to look for Jude in the crowd. Wasn't it just my luck he'd turn up here?

"I know," was all Tierney said as she picked up the menu and studied it. "Now, let's order some greasy bar food and be merry."

There's not enough grease in the free world to make this better, I thought as my eyes found Jude anyway. I slid down in my seat, as if that'd make me invisible, and prayed he wouldn't notice my existence.

Didn't pray hard enough, though. Because he was coming this way.

"On that note." Tierney stood once he reached our table. "I'm going to go say hi to...that person over there." She gave him a slap on the shoulder. "Good luck, buddy."

"Th-thanks." Jude's brows furrowed. "You, too?"

Tierney walked away, turning around just long enough to give me a thumbs up.

I will kill you, I thought, shooting her a death stare. *Kill you dead.*

Jude straddled the chair next to mine, filling the air with his own brand of electricity. "Are you stalking me?"

I dragged my eyes away from my soon-to-be-dead best friend. "Oh, yeah," I said, my voice wooden. "Stalking you so hard."

He smiled and my stomach flipped as his dimples came out to play. *Oomph.* He was so close I could see the flecks of green in his hazel eyes, could smell his cologne. Could lean in and trace every curve of that smile with my tongue.

But I wouldn't. Nope. Not even a little.

"I don't blame you," he continued. "I'm pretty stalkable."

I straightened in my seat and crossed my arms on the tabletop. I refused to be charmed. Re. Fused.

"So." His arms draped over the back of the chair, his eyes landed solidly on my face. "How've you been?" The words held an undertone that sounded an awful lot like *I've missed you.*

Well, this girl didn't do *I miss you's.*

"I've been fine." My voice was stiff, cold. I willed him to leave those unspoken words in the air. To let this thing die a quick death. But I could tell he wasn't going to do that.

"I was thinking," he said. "I want to see you again." Dread tumbled through my belly. *Dammit, Jude.* "Only, the fully-clothed, getting-to-know-each-other kind of seeing you." He smiled, a spark in his smudgy eyes.

I didn't like that spark.

Or, more accurately, I did. But I shouldn't.

Sitting back in my seat, I put on my best don't-give-a-damn air. "I told you. I don't do serious."

"We've been seeing each other for four months, Cat." He didn't even blink. "I think we both know there's something—"

"Listen." Inside, I shook, but I pushed passed it. I knew what had to be done. "I'm not really a getting-to-know-each-other kind of girl."

"So, we can screw in supply closets when you're feeling lonely, but you draw the line at conversation?"

His aim was impressive. The words hit hard, but I didn't flinch. My rules existed for a reason.

But we'd broken one. The rest were bound to crash to the ground, too.

Well, I wasn't going to be buried beneath the rubble. "You got laid." I stood and shoved away from the table. "What does it matter?"

Jude stood, too. "It matters because that's not all I'm looking for."

"It was just sex." I shoved my hair away from my face. "That's all it was ever going to be."

The dim overhead light caught a flicker in his eyes that clawed at something tender in my chest. Ignoring it, I lifted my chin and dared him to contradict me.

Slowly, he nodded. "So that's it, then."

Oxygen lodged in my throat. This was what I wanted—to end it. So why did I feel anything but victorious? I returned his nod. "That's it."

Jude studied my face as if it were the last time he'd see it. And, fingers crossed, it would be. Finally, he nodded. Slow and resigned. "Goodbye, Cat."

Goodbye.

The word rang loud in my ears, sharp and piercing. In its echo, one thought formed: if this was it, if this was the last time I'd be in his orbit, it had to count. This was one goodbye I needed to taste.

My feet pushed me forward before I could think it through. I put my hand on the back of Jude's head. Surprise flashed in his eyes before I pulled his mouth to mine.

He froze for maybe half a second before his hands found my waist. I stepped closer, kissed him deeper, drowning out everything but the heat of his hands on my body, the fire in his kiss.

He tasted of bad decisions and delicious, decadent dessert. And I wanted more. I ran my tongue along his bottom lip and reveled in the shiver that coursed through him. He pulled me closer, until I could feel his pulse beating through my whole body. And we still weren't close enough.

You really should end this, a voice in the back of my mind whispered, but I just held tighter.

Not yet.

"So, yeah," a voice said from just behind Jude. "Not that I don't enjoy watching you cram your tongue down some groupie's throat, but I'm kind of on a time crunch here."

Jude tore his lips from mine and turned. Behind him, a tall, pissed off chick with hair the color of peacock feathers stood, her arms crossed over her chest. Her dark eyes shot between Jude and me. "Seriously. Can we get this shit show on the road?" With that, she turned and stomped her way through the crowd, not waiting for Jude to follow.

Pushing his hands through his hair, he turned back to me. I hadn't moved an inch. Wasn't even sure if I could.

"Y-you should go."

He hesitated. But only for a moment. With a nod, he rubbed the back of his hand across his mouth, wiping away the lipstick I'd left behind.

I swallowed. This was it. The last time I'd leave my mark on him.

"Goodbye, Cat." With half a smile, he stepped backward into the crowd.

I watched him weave his way through the bar to the scary chick near the stage. Once he was out of sight, I closed my eyes. The right decision. This was the right decision.

Right?

8: Groupies & Zombies

M onday morning rolled around bright and early, and I found myself at the office, squinting bleary-eyed at my computer and trying not to obsess about my weekend. Namely, one particular incident.

Namely, one particular person.

Namely, Jude.

Damn him.

I clicked my mouse furiously, opening the photo-editing program we used for most things at the magazine. I'd been tweaking the images for our latest article, "Put Your Best Ass Forward," and I was beyond sick of looking at this particular model's...er, assets.

Perfection could be so boring.

Unless we were talking about abs. Maybe dimples...

"Ugh."

I shoved my chair away from my desk. I needed some coffee. My defenses were low on account of the sleep I hadn't gotten the last couple nights. It was no wonder Jude kept creeping in. I was weak and vulnerable.

That asshole.

In the break room, I grabbed a mug from the cupboard and poured from the pot already made by some kind soul earlier that morning. Suzette, an editorial assistant in the Health and Fitness department, had the radio on as she stirred sugar into her own coffee and microwaved something that smelled like ass.

"What are you listening to?" I made conversation as I waited for her to stop hogging the sugar. I hated the taste of coffee and required lots of additives to mask the flavor. Kind of looked like Suzette wasn't going to save me anything, though.

"Jude Oliver interviewed Lia Frost last weekend." Suzette's blue eyes rounded. "It's coming up after this commercial break!"

I bit back an expletive. I came in here to *escape* Jude. "That's nice," I said as I eyed the ever-emptying sugar container in her hand. If only she'd hurry up. Then, I could be back to my desk before Jude's segment started.

"Yeah! I freaking *love* her." Suzette glanced down and gave the sugar another shake. "I've seen her in concert three times!"

What did I care who Jude interviewed? That was his job. He talked to people all day, every day. I only cared that he *didn't* talk to me.

"You done with that sugar, Suzette?" It came out more bite-y than I intended so I offered an apologetic smile. "It's just, I'm in a hurry."

"Oh. Sure," she said, handing it over.

I tipped it upside down, sending a prayer to the coffee gods that she'd left me enough to cover the bitter taste. On the radio, the commercials came to an end and the morning deejay took over.

"We've got a special treat for you guys this morning," he said as I shook the remaining sugar crystals into my cup. *Almost. There.* "Jude Oliver stopped by this morning with an exciting interview for us." As he launched into the backstory of this Lia person and her brand new solo career, I dug through the fridge for milk or cream or something. Sugar wasn't enough.

My hand closed around a bottle of French vanilla creamer just as Jude's rich voice filled the room, running over me like melted dark chocolate. The man was made of sex. Even his voice made me want to do naughty things to him.

Which was how we'd gotten here in the first place.

I bit the inside of my cheek and straightened. *Here*, of course, being nowhere. Because it didn't matter. *He* didn't matter.

Pouring a huge gulp of creamer into my mug, I ignored the niggling voice in the back of my mind.

I used to be such a good liar.

Especially when it came to lying to myself.

"So, I'm here with Lia Frost," the interview began. I replaced the creamer and turned to leave, but my feet rooted themselves to the dingy gray carpet instead. "Multi-platinum, Grammy-winning recording artist. A few years ago, Lia decided to leave her major label and strike out on her own. She's just released her latest album. How're you tonight, Lia?"

"Oh, great," Lia drawled, her voice smoky, deadpan, familiar. "Probably not as good as you."

"I don't know about that. I'd be feeling pretty awesome if *Power Chord* gave my newest album four stars."

"Oh, come on, man." She dismissed him with a husky laugh. "I'm talking about that groupie you were sucking face with. And I get it. I've had a dozen or two."

Jude chuckled, and I could picture the smile he was probably treating her to. Lucky lady. "It wasn't like that," he started, but Lia interrupted.

"I'll give you credit. That chick was hot." Her voice was wry as she continued. "But I'm not interested in your sex life." She paused briefly, then added, "Well, unless I'm invited."

My ears buzzed as her familiar voice clicked into place. The woman with the techni-colored hair and impatient eyes. The one that had interrupted our goodbye the other night.

Wait.

Groupie?

There was a pause before Jude's throaty laugh filled the airwaves. "I'd be happy to discuss that with you after the show, but for now, how about we stick to the interview questions?"

A *beep* flew from the radio, covering the four-letter-word that fell from Lia's lips. "All right, smart guy. You got it. What do you want to know?"

Jude segued smoothly into the interview. As Lia answered his questions, Suzette popped open the microwave and pulled her stinky breakfast out. She hissed as it singed her fingertips and dropped it to the counter. Her wide eyes found me. "What I wouldn't give to be *that* groupie." She giggled, waving a hand over her food to cool it. "Jude Oliver is *hot*."

My stomach soured. I sat my coffee on the counter and dug through the drawer for a spoon.

Suzette kept talking. "He's probably got women lined around the block for a chance with him."

I rifled through the drawer faster. Why couldn't I find a spoon? There were, like, twenty-seven forks, for crap's sake!

On the radio, Jude's silky voice posed another question. Beside me, Suzette leaned against the counter and dug her spoon—gah! *I* needed that!—into her lumpy breakfast. "I bet he's good in the sack," she said as she chewed.

"He probably has a small di—ah ha!" I held a spoon up triumphantly. Ignoring the weird look from Suzette, I stirred my coffee and tossed the spoon into the sink.

"I don't know." Suzette flinched away from the clatter my spoon caused. "He's, like, ten feet tall. I'd bet everything else is—"

"It's been real nice, Suzette," I interrupted, holding my mug up in farewell. "Chat later."

"Oh. Okay." She blinked and nodded. "Sure. Later."

I turned on my heel and hightailed it right out of the break room, suppressing a long groan.

Suzette was right. Of *course* he'd have groupies. He was hot. He was single. He was famous around here. He probably had an entire cadre of groupies.

Which shouldn't bother me.

It *didn't* bother me. Not even a little. Jude could do what—or who—ever he wanted. Probably, he'd replaced me the moment I left the other night.

As soon as I had the thought, Jude's words echoed in my brain.

It matters because that's not what I'm looking for.

The sex. It hadn't been enough. He'd wanted more.

I plopped heavily into my desk chair and swallowed a gulp of coffee, wincing as it scalded my tongue.

I hadn't been a groupie to him.

A LITTLE *Kill Radius* made everything better.

There was nothing more therapeutic than shooting the shit out of zombies. Maybe some people preferred working out, or watching TV or maybe chowing down on deliciously bad-for-you foods, but this was my preferred method to de-stress.

It helped to picture the faces of the sources of my stress on the zombies.

"Die, die, *die!*" I yelled, showering one particular zombie with bullets from my machine gun. Tonight, every one of them had Jude's face.

It was late. I'd tried the sleep thing for a while, but my mind wouldn't switch off. Every time I began to doze, snippets of my last conversation with Jude would play through my mind, interspersed with Suzette's comments about his groupies.

I *wanted* him to replace me. I did. Because that meant he was okay, and I could move on, guilt-free.

But something in the way he looked at me, the way he kissed me the other night, told me that wouldn't be happening.

It also told me I was an asshole.

And maybe that I owed him an apology. An explanation. Something more than *goodbye and good luck.*

Squinting my eyes, I refocused on the TV screen in front of me. I had just turned a corner to find a street full of undead. Sweet. This would be fun.

As I dismembered two zombies at once, I cast a quick glance at the wall clock. One a.m.

I'd bet Jude was still...

The thought ended abruptly as one feisty zombie tried to bite my face off. "You dirty, rotten *bastard!*" I muttered. "You're going to regret that."

I sought my revenge, but the ticking clock still filled my ears. We both deserved closure, didn't we? Four months was a long time—especially in Cat time. It couldn't hurt to...

Pausing the game, I tossed my controller aside and grabbed my phone. Before I could think better of it, I typed: *You up?*

I didn't expect him to respond. Wouldn't have blamed him if he didn't. Swallowing around a lump of disgust at myself for even texting him in the first place, I tossed my phone back onto the table and grabbed my controller. A few minutes later, a ping filled the air.

I stared at the glowing screen as if it were going to sprout hands long enough to point and laugh. *Ha ha! Just kidding!*

When that didn't happen, I reached across the distance and swiped the screen, fully expecting two simple words to radiate out at me: *Fuck. Off.*

Yep, it read instead. *What's up?*

I eyed the words for a few seconds, wondering if maybe I shouldn't just take a hot shower, drink some warm milk, try to get some damn sleep. I did none of those things, though. Of course I didn't.

Can't sleep, I typed. *Can I see you?*

Weak. I was weak.

And he definitely wasn't going to reply this time.

As if he were *trying* to defy me, Jude texted back: *Sure.*

I blinked and reread the message. Was he messing with me? He was messing with me, right? Like, why would he want to see me? *I* didn't even want to see me right now.

Before I could decide whether or not he was serious, he shot me another text: *Meet me at Shrimpy Dick's in twenty?*

Shrimpy Dick's? The all-night diner on Remington?

Huh. That was new.

Um...if that's in invitation to your place, it's a completely inaccurate code name, I shot back, smiling at my own hilarity.

Funny, his response read. *See you there.*

9: Shrimpy Dick's

───

T he drive to the diner was quick. Not many people were out at one a.m. on a Tuesday. I arrived in about ten minutes, parked and went inside to find Jude already waiting. It was infuriating how good he looked, like, all the time. Tonight was no exception.

He wore a thousand-year-old pair of blue jeans with frayed bottoms and a couple of tears in them, a plain white t-shirt and a navy blue zip-up hoodie. He looked so damn cozy I wanted to snuggle right up to him. Which was more annoying than the whole looking good thing.

I pulled the sleeves of my cozy gray sweater over my hands to discourage any urges and walked toward him. "Hey."

I felt weirdly shy. This guy had seen me naked and in a multitude of compromising positions. This—fully clothed and in public—was nothing.

"Hey," he repeated, shoving his hands into his pockets. "There's a booth toward the back." He led the way before I could respond, and I followed, the quiet of the restaurant closing in on me like fog.

No loud, pulsating music. No crowds to get lost in. No inevitable shedding of clothes in favor of skin-on-skin action.

Yeah, no. This was weird.

What was I thinking?

As we took our seats, a college-aged waitress with wide eyes and a peppy smile, approached the table, menus in hand. "Hi! How are you two tonight? It's a bit chilly out there, isn't it? Can't wait for it to warm up!" she said, setting the menus down on the table.

I nodded, dazed. How many energy drinks had this girl ingested?

"Hi, pretty good, yes, and I agree," I said, answering all of her questions. "Can we get a couple minutes?"

Peppy Pants—her nametag read Penelope, because of course that was her name—nodded and spun on her heel, off to jabber to some other lucky soul. I turned to Jude, mouth agape in awe. "Good God," I said. "I don't think I even had that much energy when I was half her age!"

Jude laughed. "I don't know about that. I've witnessed your energy firsthand." His eyes flickered with a suggestive twinkle, but he quickly clamped it down. "Sorry."

I sat back and twisted the sleeves of my sweater. "S'alright." With a sigh, I dragged my eyes over our surroundings. Across the restaurant, a mob of college students surrounded a table, laughing and talking at distinctly outdoor levels. A few rows away, a couple sat across from each other, hesitant smiles and stilted conversation. Definitely a first date, if their body language was any indicator.

Bringing my attention back to my table, I glanced over at Jude. His shoulders were set in the same tense lines as the dude I'd just assessed. Our atmosphere was filled with the same awkward quiet.

Shit.

"I...uh...this isn't...maybe I shouldn't ha—"

"You guys ready to order?"

My head swiveled toward Penelope. She had her pen poised over her paper, eyes wide and waiting.

"I'll have the turkey burger," Jude said, his menu closing with a slap. "Extra pickles on the side."

"You got it." Her ponytail swayed as she turned to me. "And for you?"

A time machine, so I can go back to half an hour ago and not *text Jude,* I thought. "Um...just some fries, please." I closed my menu and handed it to her. "And a chocolate milkshake."

There. That way when I left, Jude would still have a full meal.

Because I *would* be leaving. I shouldn't have come in the first place.

"So," Jude started once Penelope had trounced off to place our orders. "Why couldn't you sleep?"

The condensation on my water glass captivated me. I wiped at it with my thumb and avoided the burn of Jude's eyes. *To apologize. To explain myself. For closure,* I thought. I didn't say any of it aloud, of course. Instead, I shrugged. "No reason."

His eyes lingered on me for a few seconds before he nodded. "Fair enough."

Relief hissed from my lungs. I sat back and reached for a straw. "So. Did you take her up on it?"

Jude's hand hovered near his water glass and he frowned. "Did I take who up on what?"

I threw a smile his way, trying hard to channel my usual self. Feelings, schmeelings. "That crabby singer chick and her offer of a groupie threesome."

An ever-so-slight flush crept over his face. *Shut up,* I thought. *That is not adorable.*

"You heard that?"

"Not intentionally." Pulling my legs up, I stretched them across the booth. "A co-worker had the radio on in the break room."

"Of course." Jude put an elbow on the tabletop. "You wouldn't be caught dead listening to my show."

"Exactly." I unwrapped my straw and stuck it into my glass. "It's not like I'm a *groupie* or something."

At that, Jude threw his head back, releasing a hearty, beautiful laugh that pulled hard at my insides. Once he recovered, he treated me to one of those straight-to-the-eyes smiles. "Trust me, you are anything but a groupie."

As he said it, all the thoughts from earlier stood for an encore in my head. The cadre of groupies, the hope that he'd replaced me with one, the hunch—the now confirmed hunch—that I'd meant more to him.

In a moment of unwanted vulnerability, I met his eyes. "It'd be better if I were."

The smile withered on his lips. "I know."

Before either of us could say anything more, Peppy Penelope crashed through the silence—literally. We looked over in time to see her hands fly to her cheeks as the tray of food she'd been carrying clattered to the floor.

"Oh, I'm sorry!" She knelt down and scrambled to clean up the food crime scene from the floor. "I'm so, so sorry!"

I jumped to my feet and joined her. "It's all right," I said, gathering up rogue fries.

She looked up at me, her eyes wide. "You don't have to help. I've got it. I—"

"Hey, no worries," I cut in with a smile. "I've got this if you want to grab a mop."

She blinked. "O-okay."

As she disappeared, Jude joined me on the floor. We worked together silently to clean up the bulk of the mess before Penelope arrived with the mop. Mess taken care off, she vanished with a promise to be back soon with our food—again—and profuse apologies.

We settled back into our seats, and I glanced over at Jude. His lips were tilted in a warm smile.

"What?"

"You're a fraud, Cat Keller."

"Well, that's a mean thing to say." My brow furrowed. "What are you talking about?"

"You and your spiky, scary armor. It's all a show." He took a sip from his water glass and eyed me. "You're all mush inside."

"What? Why?" I scoffed. "Because I helped some waitress clean up a mess? Please. Anyone would do that."

His eyes left mine to take a slow, pointed journey around the room. "Mmm hmm." Settling deeper into his seat, he smiled. He didn't say another word. Just gave me an all-knowing, all-squishy look.

"*Anyway,*" I grumbled, crossing my arms tight over my chest. "About that threesome."

About fifteen minutes later, once Jude was pink and flustered from my interrogation, Penelope arrived with our food. "Here we are, guys," she said as she plopped the plates down on the table between us. "I'm so sorry about the wait. If you need anything else, let me know."

How about a stone mason, I thought, clamoring to straighten the bricks that had threatened to tip from the top of my wall. Clearly, it had fallen into disrepair.

Ignoring the twinge somewhere inside my chest, I thanked the waitress and pulled my plate of fries closer. "Mmm, grease-soaked death sticks."

"Grease-soaked death sticks?" Jude repeated, his brows raised. He took the top off his burger and added a squirt of ketchup before offering the bottle to me.

I took it and sat it aside. "That's what my mother calls them." I divided my fries into two piles and drizzled ketchup all over one heaping mountain, my tummy grumbling at the sight.

"Well, that's just wrong." Jude reached across the table, grabbing a fry. I watched through narrowed eyes as he took a bite and licked the ketchup from his bottom lip. "Fries are more like little slices of potato heaven."

"Agreed," I said slowly. I grabbed a ketchup-less fry and dipped it into my chocolate shake. "But my mother hates all things good and right in the world."

"I'm sorry." Jude reassembled his sandwich. "My mom is pretty awesome."

I glanced at him, mid-bite. This was unfamiliar territory. I mean, what else did we need to know about each other outside of the bedroom?

"Both my parents are great, really," he continued, clueless to my reaction. "I'm actually heading home this weekend to celebrate their thirty-seventh wedding anniversary."

"Wait, what?" I asked around a mouthful of potato-y goodness. "*How long* have they been married?"

"Thirty-seven years. Married right out of high school." There was a touch of pride in Jude's voice as he said it. I briefly flashed back to the stack of books on his coffee table. Jane Austen. This dude had a romantic side.

"Wow." I bit into a fry. "People actually stay together for that long?"

"Right?" Jude took a bite of his sandwich and continued once he'd swallowed. "Pretty cool."

"So, where's 'home'?" I instantly wished I could take it back. *This is not casual conversation,* I thought. *Do not get to know this boy.*

Too late, though. The question was out there, buzzing around between us like a fat, clumsy bumblebee. I wanted to swat it away, pretend it didn't exist, but Jude was already answering.

"A little town up north. No place special." He grabbed another fry from my plate. "My parents grew up there, and then raised my sisters and me there, too."

"Small town boy." My nose wrinkled. "That's...sweet."

Jude laughed. "City girl to the bone, huh?" His smile lingered. "I don't blame you. I love my hometown, but there's a reason I don't live there anymore." He reached for another fry, and before I could think it through, I slapped his hand away.

"Hey!" He pulled his hand back, eyes wide. "What was that?"

"Cat doesn't share food." I shrugged and bit into a fry.

"Point taken." He picked up his sandwich and treated me to the most pitiful puppy dog eyes I had ever seen.

"Oh, come on," I groaned. "Don't look at me like that!"

"Like what?" he asked, raising his eyebrows, his smoky eyes softening. Then, he pushed his bottom lip out pitifully.

"Dude, really?" I laughed, shoving my plate toward him. "Help yourself."

The pout was replaced with a dimpled grin as he reached for the plate, grabbing a few ketchup-covered fries. "Thanks, you're too kind."

"That was pathetic. You know that, right?" I shook my head, trying to fight off a smile.

He grinned around a mouthful of fries and nodded. "It worked, though," he said once he swallowed.

The smile won out, and it was accompanied by laughter. "I may have to add that to my repertoire," I said. "Puppy dog eyes: the most effective way to get what you want."

Jude slid his plate across the table. "Sandwich?"

"And I didn't even have to give you the eyes," I said as I picked it up and took a bite.

"God help the world if you ever master the eyes." Jude shook his head with a smile. "You're already dangerously convincing without them."

My cheeks heated and I suddenly found my milkshake terribly fascinating. "Thanks," I murmured, swirling a fry in my shake.

As we finished our meal, we continued to chat. I learned a few more things about Jude that I hadn't known before. Like, he had a dog named Crowley when he was a kid, and his favorite movie was *An Affair to Remember*.

Yes, *An Affair to Remember*.

"But, dude. *Die Hard*," I said as we paid our bill—the waitress had lumped it all together, and Jude insisted on taking care of it. "It doesn't get better than *Die Hard*."

"Eh." He held the door open for me. "We'll have to agree to disagree."

I narrowed my eyes as I passed him. "Fine. Continue being wrong. See if I care."

We walked in silence to our cars. As I dug my keys out of my pocket, I glanced up at him. "Hey, thanks for the fries."

"I ate half. It was the least I could do."

"And thanks for meeting up with me," I said. "I'll be dead on my feet tomorrow, but I had a good time."

"Me, too," he said.

Shifting my keys from hand to hand, I stared at the cracked pavement. This next part would be harder.

Forcing my eyes to his, I added, "And I'm sorry for the other night."

The air around us stilled. After a beat of silence, Jude said, "You weren't wrong. You told me you didn't do serious months ago. I was the one that—"

"I know. But I didn't have to be so...harsh about it." I squeezed my keys hard in my palm. "I don't want anyone to get hurt."

Jude covered my hand with his and I loosened my grip. "No one ever got hurt sharing a meal or two," he said. "Unless, of course, they tried to steal a fry."

I laughed and stepped toward my car, our hands dropping to our sides. "Next time you'll know better."

As soon as I said it, I wanted to take it back. Next time? There couldn't be a next time. This felt an awful lot like—

"So, there'll be a second date." He grinned. "Good to know."

I opened my mouth, denial at the ready, but he'd already started across the parking lot. "Later, Cat."

10: Tainted Pastries

―――

"It was *not* a date," I announced, as I plopped into Tierney's car the next evening. "Not even a little bit."

"Oh...kay." Tier pushed her sunglasses up, greeting me with confused eyes. "I believe you."

I yanked on my seatbelt and ignored the mocking tilt of her lips. Today, it was *my* turn to try on pretty dresses. Well, pretty *dress*. Well...whatever Tier decided to put me into for her wedding.

Which I couldn't even focus on right now. I'd been so in knots over the not-date that I would probably end up in the world's ugliest bridesmaid dress without realizing it.

Stupid Jude.

"We just met up, had some food, and went our separate ways. That doesn't make it a date."

"Oh, no." Tier replaced her sunglasses and readjusted her rearview mirror. "That doesn't sound like a date at all." Her voice was laced with sarcasm. "It's not really a date unless you share your food, anyway. And we both know you don't share food."

My stomach clenched as I recalled Jude's hand reaching across the table for my fries. "Bite me."

Tierney's mouth dropped open. "You didn't," she said. "You shared your food with this guy!"

Ignoring her, I grabbed the bag of whatever she'd been snacking on when I interrupted her. "What the hell is this?"

"Trail mix," she said, taking the bag back. "Get your own."

"I don't want it anyway. Looks like bird food." I shuddered. "Why can't you eat real food? Like donuts? Or pizza?"

Tierney rolled her eyes. "You eat like a teenage boy." She took a bite of her trail mix before zeroing back in on the original topic. "So, why wasn't this a date? And who didn't you go on this date with?" As she asked, she put the car in drive and pulled away from the curb.

I groaned and covered my face with my hands. I probably shouldn't have said anything. Tierney wouldn't let it drop until she'd wrenched every detail from me.

I hadn't been able to sleep much more than an hour last night.

I couldn't stop thinking about that jerkoff. I couldn't stop thinking about our conversation and how I'd learned more about him in a couple hours than I had over months of sleeping together.

It sucked.

I should have stayed home.

"It's the dude, isn't it?" Tierney said, interrupting my internal tirade. "The one you nearly choked to death over the other night?"

I didn't answer. Just groaned into my hands again.

"Why don't you want to date him?" I could hear her set her breakfast aside. "I mean, you like the guy. The sex is obviously pretty good, or you wouldn't keep going back. He's super cute. Why don't you want to date him?"

"I don't do relationships." I shoved my hair out of my face and looked at her. "You know this." We'd been friends for seven years. I hadn't been in a relationship the entire time. Casual flings? Sure. The occasional one night stand? Maybe. But relationship? Nope.

Tierney shook her head, her expression genuinely baffled as she stopped at a red light. "Dating the dude doesn't mean you have to marry him. You're not your mom."

At that, I glared. Hard. "No shit."

A pair of green eyes narrowed in on my face and I squirmed under their scrutiny. "What?" I squeaked. "Why should I buy the cow when I can get the—"

"For the love of all that is good and holy, do not finish that sentence." Tierney held up a hand to silence me as the light turned green. "I'm still eating breakfast."

"Serves you right." I stuck out my tongue. "Now, can we please hit up a drive-thru? I need a donut."

———

THE DONUT WAS TAINTED.

I couldn't enjoy the sugar-loaded treat, or the hot, caffeinated beverage that accompanied it. I couldn't even enjoy the look on Tierney's face when I suggested I walk down the aisle wearing a squirrel costume.

"I could hold a sign saying *Jack is Nuts About Tierney*." I grinned as she went white.

"That's not funny."

"I mean, it's kind of funny." I stepped out of the strapless blue thing I'd just tried on. "Jack would be amused."

Tier rolled her eyes. "That's because both of you have the sense of humor of a couple of five-year-olds." She picked up the dress and shook it out. "What do you think?"

"It's your wedding, lady." I reached into my bra and readjusted the girls. "I'll wear whatever you want me to."

Her gaze dropped to the dress in her hands. Her thumb ran across the fabric. "It's the same shade of blue as Jack's eyes..."

"Oh, gag." I yanked my own dress off the hook and pulled it over my head.

"I think it's perfect." Tier opened the dressing room door. "I'll be right back."

"Okay," I replied from inside my dress. The door clicked behind her just as my head emerged from the head hole. Ahh, alone time. However brief it might be.

Sitting on the bench, I reached for my shoes. As I pulled them on, my mind resurrected the memories I'd been avoiding all day. Jude laughing. Jude sharing my fries. Jude telling me about his family.

And me, soaking it all in.

Me, sharing personal stories *and* food.

"That's it," I grumbled as I buckled the ankle strap on my stiletto. "I'm broken."

"What are you in here mumbling about?" Tierney swung the door open with a bang, scaring the bejeezus out of me.

"What is *wrong* with you?" I glared, willing my heart rate to slow.

"That's a loaded question," she said, her face serious. "You ready to get out of here?"

"Yep." I stood and threw my purse over my shoulder. "You want to go for a drink?" My mother had called this morning to "warn" me that she'd be bringing Arthur to brunch Sunday. In all the Jude drama, I'd been able to shove that tidbit far, far into the back of my mind. It'd taken all day to creep back into the forefront, and I needed Tier to tell me I wasn't being dramatic. That this was crazy, my mother was selfish, and this wasn't normal.

I needed my best friend.

"Can't." Tier pushed open the door and waited as I exited. "Jack's aunt wants to have dinner. So, you know, I might die tonight."

I ignored the sharp stab of disappointment and rolled my eyes at Tierney. "If Bonnie was going to kill you, you'd have been dead the *first* time you dated one of her family members."

"Not helping." Tier threw a glare over her shoulder. "Not helping at all."

"I know." I caught up to her, and we left the shop side-by-side. "But I've got a point."

"So, hey." She bumped her shoulder into mine. "Has he texted you yet? The guy you went on a date with last night?"

I stopped walking. Tier turned long enough to give me a patronizing smile. "You know your wedding invite is a plus-one, right?"

I snarled. "Just because you're happily engaged and about to sell your soul to another human being, doesn't mean I'm going to have a change of heart." I stomped up the sidewalk. "I don't have one, any-way."

"A heart? Please." Tierney tucked a strand of dark hair behind her ear. "You barricade it behind barbed wire and brick, but it's there."

"Yeah, well. Behind the barbed wire and brick it's gonna stay."

Especially now that Arthur's back around.

Pointing her keys toward her car, Tierney unlocked the doors. "I'd lecture you on the unhealthy and depressing state of your life, but I'm too busy pondering the ways in which my future aunt-in-law is going to end *mine* tonight. You're on your own."

I scowled in her general direction before getting in the car. "You're not gonna have to worry about Bonnie if you keep it up."

"What was that?" Tier called as she pulled open her door.

"You're pretty," I called back as she settled in.

Her eyes swept over me, wry disbelief in them. "Uh huh." Sticking the key in the ignition, she added, "Bitterness is not a flattering shade on you."

"Yeah, well smug ain't so good on you, either."

She started the car and looked my way. "Fair enough."

As we shot through the streets of Port Agnes, my mind became a revolving door of Jude-ness.

I don't do relationships.

There would not be a second date, because there wasn't a first date.

Because it was not a date.

By the time Tier dropped me off at my place, I had one single train of thought:

Jude needed to be set straight.

11: Boundaries, Man

———

Jude's neighborhood looked different in the middle of the day. Nicer. Less shifty. Kids played on the sidewalk, an old woman sat on the stoop with a lapful of yarn, and a tiny kitten peered at me from a first story window.

Kinda made all of our late-night hangouts seem even dirtier.

Shaking the thought away, I started up the stairs. As I passed the old woman, I discreetly tugged down the hem of my dress.

She took notice. Her shrewd eyes skittered over me. I braced myself for the judgment. "I can knit you a cozy for your downstairs bits, if you like." She held up her knitting needles and grinned. "It's a bit breezy today."

A surprised laugh shot from my lips. "That's not a bad idea." I scrutinized the multi-colored yarn in her lap. "Can I get it in red?"

"I've probably got some yarn leftover from my grandbaby's Santa hat." She grinned as her knitting needles clinked together. "Just let me know."

"Will do." I tossed a wave over my shoulder and pulled open the door, still smiling. Hazel's church friends all clucked their tongues at my short skirts, but Hazel always shushed them with a glare. Maybe I should introduce her to Stoop Lady.

My heels clicked loudly on the tile floor, bringing me back to the moment and I stopped.

What was I doing here? This could easily be settled over the phone. One text message. *Dude, we ain't dating.* Done.

I didn't need to see him. In fact, it was probably best if I *didn't* see him. Bad things happened when we occupied the same space.

Well, not *bad* things. They were actually quite good. But that wasn't the point.

My fingertips brushed over the door handle. *I should go.*

The elevator door slid open and, almost without thinking, I stepped inside.

My reflection blinked at me from the mirrored interior, as if I'd just betrayed it in the worst way. And maybe I had. Maybe this was a line I shouldn't cross. I'd never ended things with anyone in person. No one had meant enough for it.

Jude didn't mean enough.

Reaching into my purse, I grabbed my phone. I stared at Jude's number.

And stared.

And stared.

The elevator shuddered to a stop and a couple people joined me inside. They lost themselves in chatter about a movie they were going to see, and I kept my eyes on my phone. Touching the text icon, I stared at the blinking cursor. *Hey, so about the other night,* I started before backspacing through the words. With a growl, I tried again. *Maybe we shouldn't—*

The elevator halted and the couple walked out.

"This is the last floor," the girl said. She was gracious enough to only say the word *creeper* with her eyes.

I shot her a tight smile and a silent *bite me*, and got out. "Thanks."

To my left and four doors down, Jude was probably sprawled out on that decadent couch. Maybe he was shirtless. Maybe we could—

"Shut it down." I tossed my hair over my shoulder and straightened my spine. "Shut it way the fuck down. That's not what you're here for."

You shouldn't be here at all, a voice sang and I had to acknowledge it was right. Tone deaf, but right.

Absently, I meandered down the hall while I took another stab at that kiss-off text. *Listen,* I started. *It's been fun and all, but I told you. I don't share food.*

Yeah. That's it. The food.

I should really make that one of my rules...

"I think it's that weird neighbor kid," a voice to my right said just as a door swung open.

I turned to find a tiny brunette in a red plaid shirt and black leggings scowling at me. I blinked and took a step back. Her heavily-lined eyes scraped over me, from my surprised face to my six-inch stilettos. Curling her lip, she slammed the door.

"What the fu—" I started just as the gold-plated numbers on the door caught my eye. 1003. "Shit."

I couldn't tell if the burn in my gut was because this was Jude's place or because he had a woman inside.

I told myself it was the first. Because what did I care about the second? I'd come to tell him we were—

"Cat?"

I turned and the air hissed from my lungs. It really wasn't fair of him to look so good.

"Sorry about..." he waved a hand toward his apartment. "What's up?"

I tore my eyes from him and backed up. Distance. I needed distance. "Sorry, I didn't mean to..." I trailed off, shifting my phone from hand to hand. "Um. I'm gonna go."

"You came over to tell me you're leaving?" Jude laid a skeptical glance on me. "Doesn't seem very efficient."

Exhaling all the oxygen in my lungs in one breath, I lifted my chin. *Get it over with.* "It wasn't a date."

His brows lifted. "What—"

"Shrimpy Dick's. It wasn't a date." I gripped my phone tighter. "Just two people eating food. Which, by the way, I don't share. Boundaries, man."

A chuckle worked its way from Jude's throat. I glared and he fought to erase the amusement from his face. "There's nothing funny about this."

Tilting his head, he conceded. "Okay. Sorry. So. It wasn't a date. And you don't share food." He caught my eye. "Anything else I should know?"

"No. I...uh, I think that's it." I stepped backward. Behind him, the apartment numbers glittered in the light. Oh, yeah. There was a girl in there. "Oh, and, hey. Sorry for interrupting your date." My throat burned as I said the words, but I pretended not to notice. With a smile that felt more like a scowl, I waved. "Enjoy—"

Behind him, the door opened.

"Come on, man." The chick gave Jude a shove as she spoke. "I'm starving, and I'm not above murdering you for withholding the goods."

Jude laughed. "We both know Mom and Dad would kill you if you murdered me."

"Well, yeah. You're their favorite. Of course they would." She paused, a contemplative look on her face. "But then they'd be down two children, so maybe not."

My eyes ping-ponged between them, words flitting in and out of my mind. *Mom, Dad, children...*

That meant cranky girl was Jude's siste—

Which meant nothing to me. Nothing at all.

"How about we put that creepy thought on the backburner and get moving?" Jude said as he reached behind his sister to pull the door shut. "How's Olaf's sound?"

"Miraculous." As she said it, her eyes skimmed over me. "What's up with the groupie? I thought we discussed *not* giving them your home address."

Jude looked my way. "Oh, no. She's not—" He paused, a frown dropping his brows. "She's a...friend."

"Friend?" she asked, her voice dripping with skepticism. "Really, Jude."

"Well, I mean, we've boned," I supplied helpfully.

Beside me, Jude let out a surprised scoff. I looked his way, brows raised. "Well, we have."

She narrowed in on my face for a few seconds. "Right on," she said, finally, extending her hand. "I'm Sunny. This doofus's sister."

I started to reply, but she'd already shifted her focus. "You coming with us? I'm so freaking hungry I could eat an entire hippo."

I looked from Jude to Sunny. Dinner was one thing. Dinner with a family member? Well, that was *definitely* a rule-breaker. Rule number three, in fact. *Family is verboten.*

"I'm, uh, not hungry," I told Sunny. "But thanks."

Sunny linked her arm through mine. "Please. There's no such thing as *not hungry*," she said as she propelled me forward. "Now, I don't know if you've ever been to Olaf's, but they've got the best dessert menu."

Shooting a glance behind us, she added, "Besides, Jude is buying, so, you know. Free food."

I laughed as Jude fell into step beside us. "I mean, how can I say no to free food?"

Jude smirked as he hit the elevator button. "It might mean you have to share."

"Pssh. No." Sunny ushered me into the elevator and sneered at Jude. "Don't listen to him. There will be no food-sharing."

12: Bad Liar

M y insides told me this was a bad idea. That I should make up an excuse once we hit the sidewalk and leave. But then Sunny mentioned jalapeno cheese dip, and, well, my self-control took a nosedive.

And, as it turned out, it wasn't the worst decision I'd ever made.

Over appetizers—Jude watched us eat the jalapeno cheese dip through wide eyes—I learned that the siblings were three years apart, and that it was "super annoying to be related to someone so absurdly good-looking. Especially when all your friends wanted to bang him." Over entrees, it was revealed that Sunny had tried out for the cheerleading squad in ninth grade, and had been passed over for a "sophomore with a blonde ponytail and huge tits."

Overall, I found myself having a good time. Sunny was cranky, sardonic, bitter...completely opposite her name. Plus, she didn't make me share food. I dug it.

As the waitress cleared away our dinner plates, Sunny reached for the dessert menu. "Ahh, and now for the highlight of my evening." She paused and looked from me to Jude. "No offense."

I laughed. "None taken. In fact, if you like sweets, I know a guy that—"

"Just in time for dessert." A dark-haired, scruffy guy nabbed the menu from Sunny's hand as he sat down beside her.

"Really? You felt like that was an okay thing to do?" Sunny glared. "Here, why don't you *snatch* my purse while you're at it?" She bent down and fished her purse from the floor, thrusting it at the new-comer.

"Aww, don't be like that, Sunshine. You know I love you," the guy said, his brown eyes trying and failing to pull off sincerity.

"Dick," Sunny mumbled, dropping her purse to the floor. "You invite this jerkoff to dinner?" she asked Jude, her tone accusing.

Jude shrugged. "You know Ben. He has a nose like a hellhound. I'm sure he sniffed us out."

"Hey! I find that offensive. I saw your car outside, so I figured...hey, who's the hottie?"

"You are so classy," Sunny drawled, snatching the menu back. "Way to make a good first impression."

"I *am* classy. Thanks for noticing. And I was talking about the guy sitting *next* to the fiery little vixen. Hey, baby." He winked at Jude. "Is it hot in here, or is it just you?"

"Oh, you," Jude said, tossing his hair back. "Such a charmer."

Sunny looked from one guy to the other, her nose curling. "You two are so fucking weird."

"If by 'weird,' you mean 'awesome,'" the guy said. "Then, yes. We are weird. I'm Ben, by the way." He extended his hand to me, treating me to a lopsided grin. "This guy's other woman."

"Also known as my best friend," Jude said, shaking his head. "Regrettably, at times. I really can't take you anywhere, man."

"Hey, you knew what this was," Ben said, narrowing his dark eyes on Jude. "Don't try to act all innocent. No one at this table is buying it."

Laughing, I took Ben's hand. "I'm Cat. This guy's...friend."

"She means fuck buddy," Sunny cut in. "She's Jude's fuck buddy."

Ben shook my hand, his eyes taking me in, then shooting to Jude. "Nicely done, man," he said, his thumb stroking my knuckles. "She's a looker."

"All right, creeper." Jude removed my hand from Ben's. "Don't mind him, really."

I glanced down at his hand still resting on mine. *I should move away.*

Jude read my mind. He pulled his hand back, and I smushed down the disappointment he left behind.

"You two have issues," I said, focusing hard on the dude across the table. The one that *wasn't* hacking at my brick wall with a sledgehammer and a smile. "Like, a lot of them."

"Thank you!" Sunny tossed her hands in the air. "I've been saying that for *years!* Now, if we're done with the Jude and Ben Freak Show, can we please get some dessert up in this piece?"

"Yes, yes we can." Jude's gaze was laser-focused on the menu. "Lemon cream cake, peanut butter chocolate pie, double chocolate brownie sundae." Each dessert sounded more amazing than the last. "Apple raspberry pie? One of each?"

"My god, man!" I grabbed the menu from his hand. "Are you trying to kill us?"

Ben laughed. "Nah, this is normal. Jude's got a sweet tooth the size of my dangler."

"So, like, this big?" Sunny shot back, holding her fingers about an inch apart.

"Have you been spying on me, Sunshine?" Ben asked, flashing a crooked grin her way.

"Yes. Yes, I have." Her voice was dull. "Because I have nothing better to do than use my microscope to look at your wiener."

"Yeah, so...new person at the table," Jude interjected, his expression slightly mortified. "Could we not freak her out with all the wiener talk, please?"

"As long as no one whips out their wieners, we're good," I said, leaning into Jude to peek at the menu. His scent tickled my nose and I nearly buried my face in his long-sleeve t-shirt. We'd spent an entire meal not touching. A whole ninety-something minutes. It had to be a record. "I think I want the apple raspberry pie."

"Good choice," Jude said, and I looked up in time to meet his gaze. "Brownie sundae for me, though the pie was a close second."

My gaze traveled from his eyes down the slope of his nose, to his lips, tilted in a half-smile. "If you're nice to me, maybe I'll share."

Yeah. I heard the words. So much for *not sharing food*.

"And by 'nice' you mean, if I share my sundae, right?"

"Exactly." I smiled, finding his eyes again. My heart thumped hard against my ribs. Oomph.

"Give me that menu," Sunny said, and I flew back into my own personal space bubble. "I want dessert, too, dammit."

As if sensing her impending doom if she did not deliver the goods to Sunny, our waitress appeared at our table and took our dessert orders.

While Sunny placed her order—the lemon cream cake *and* the brownie sundae—Ben leaned forward, planting his elbows on the tabletop, his eyes narrowed on my face. "I know you."

I sat back and studied him, a brief moment of panic rushing through me. Had we dated?

I put the thought to rest almost as soon as it formed. Nope. He wasn't my type. So, how did he know me?

"I don't think so, man," I replied, noting that Sunny had started paying close attention, her blue eyes taking in everything. "You've got to be thinking of someone else."

Ben looked at Jude. "This is her, right? The chick who—"

"I don't think I told you about the thing that happened at work last night." Jude leaned in and slapped a hand on the table. "Crazy story."

"Wait, wait." I faced Jude, not willing to let him change the subject so easily. His cheeks tinged with red. He looked the most uncomfortable I'd ever seen him. A nicer girl might've taken pity and moved on. But we all knew I wasn't a nice girl. "The chick who what?"

"It's nothing," he said, shooting Ben an eyes-wide, shut-your-trap look.

Interesting.

I rested my chin on my hand. "Doesn't seem like it's nothing, man."

He glared my way. "Remember how I was going to share my sundae with you?"

I winced. "Hit me right where it hurts, why don't you?" I muttered as I straightened in my seat. "Story time's over, Ben."

He looked from me to Jude, then shrugged. "All right." Picking up a stray straw wrapper, he rolled it between his fingers. "It's a good story, though."

Seconds later, Ben and Sunny dissolved into a bickering match, and I looked to Jude. The flush had dissipated, but he still hadn't returned to his usual easy demeanor. I bumped my shoulder into his. "You told Ben about me, huh?" I said so only he could hear.

His lips tilted, but he didn't look up. "Nothing but good things, I swear."

"How boring." I tossed him one of my trademark smiles and ignored the flashing warning signs. So he told his best friend about me. So what? Didn't mean anything.

Except that when Jude finally met my eye, something flickered back at me. Something sweet and hopeful and...terrifying. "Nothing about you is boring, Cat."

I looked away. I'd been right earlier.

This had to end.

———

DESSERT CAME AND IT was delicious—rumor had it, anyway. I robotically shoveled pie into my mouth, not tasting a thing.

By the time we returned to Jude's place, I had transformed fully back into my usual self. On the outside, at least. Inside...oh, I was a wreck.

Not that anyone could see it. After years of plastering on this carefree façade, I'd become a master at make-believe.

"So, what's going on in there?" Jude asked as we stood next to my car. He tapped a finger against my temple, his eyes warm on my face.

Or, at least, I *used* to be a master.

Tossing my hair over my shoulder, I smiled. *Nothing to see here.* "Food. Sex. Video games." I shrugged. "The usual."

Leaning against my car, his expression turned somber. "You're a bad liar, Cat."

I ignored the shudder against my ribs and maintained eye contact. "Then tell me what I'm thinking, smart guy."

"You're thinking that this was fun. That the other night was fun. Maybe even better than the sex. And you're thinking that it's scary. Which is why you showed up at my place tonight—to slap a few more bricks onto that wall of yours."

I blinked. "You don't know what you're talking about."

He did not blink. "Don't you ever want more than just—"

"No." Taking a step back, I straightened my shoulders. The shudder turned into a rattle and I refused to let it become a boom. "I don't want more. That's why I told you—"

"It wasn't a date." He pushed away from the car. "I know." His voice was heavy with resignation. "Got it."

Guilt gnawed at me. What was I doing here? This guy liked me. I could tell. And here I was, letting him. I knew he wasn't going to get anything more from me. I didn't *have* anything more to give. There were a million parts of my soul that I could never bare.

No, a little voice whispered. *But you can bare everything else.*

I ignored the voice—and the stab of hurt that it brought with it—and forced myself to look Jude in the eye. "I'm sorry."

"Don't be sorry, Cat. *Do* something about it."

"Like what?" I pulled my hair over my shoulder and twisted it. "What do you want me to do here?"

"Make a decision." His eyes flashed hot. "Either you're in or you're out. But this in-between, *I don't do serious, but let's get to know each other anyway,* shit you're doing isn't cool."

I opened my mouth to respond, but he kept going. "I like you. You're brash and outspoken and, frankly, a little terrifying, and I like you. But you've got to pick a lane. I can't keep up."

"What about friends?"

The words fell from my lips before I thought them through. Jude looked just as surprised as I felt.

Irritation replaced surprise in his eyes. He held my stare. "What makes you think we have anything here that could become a success-ful friendship? You don't know anything about me."

Okay, not what I expected him to say. I lifted my chin. "I...I know you like desserts."

"No." He shook his head. "You don't know anything *real* about me."

"I—" I stopped. He was right. We'd only scratched the surface. There wasn't much you needed to know about a fuck buddy, beyond their skill level in the sack.

But I wanted to know more.

The thought struck me hard. I snapped my mouth shut and took a step back. *Maybe now would be a good time to retreat.*

"Maybe now's a good time to start."

Fuckshitdamn. My brain and mouth were *not* cooperating with each other today.

Jude narrowed his eyes, studying me hard, giving me the chance to take it back. And I knew it'd be in my best interest to take him up on it.

I didn't.

Instead, I held his eye in challenge.

"It would mean no more wild monkey sex," he said finally.

"When did we ever have wild monkey sex?" I shot back, enjoying the look of hurt/surprise/amusement on his face.

"Well...uh...there was that one time..." he stammered, and I couldn't tamp down the laughter bubbling up in my throat.

"I can't say I've ever done friends with a dude before." I tilted my head and studied him. Two options here: friends or nothing. I could walk away now and never see him again. Never hear his voice, see his face. Nothing.

I could do it.

But did I want to?

The thought left a hollow thump inside me.

I extended a hand. The decision was made.

Jude looked at my hand, then back to my face. Slowly, his hand grasped mine. "Friends, it is," he said.

I nodded. "Just don't make it weird."

13: Flimsy Menu Forts

———

The rain pounded hard against my windshield as I parked my car outside the Portside on Sunday. It'd been a busy few days, between work and Maid of Honor duties and the constant doubting voice ringing in my head:

Are you sure you can be friends with him? it asked. *You've already seen each other naked. You can't unsee that.*

Yeah. The voice sounded an awful lot like Tierney. Mostly because she'd said those exact words to me Thursday night over frozen pizza and seating charts.

"Seriously," she'd said as she snatched a piece of pineapple from my plate. "Cat Keller doesn't *do* friends."

"I don't know," I replied. "I could do friends. I've never tried."

Tier leveled her green glare on me. "Maybe because that's, like, one step away from commitment." Refilling her glass of wine, she took a sip and added, "Which we both know you don't do."

My stomach somersaulted. *Commitment.*

Ugh. First Hazel, now Tier. Did I really reek of commitment issues that badly?

"Either way," I said, grabbing the wine bottle from her hand. "We're gonna give it a go."

"Mmm hmm." Leaning forward, Tier shifted a pushpin to the left on the seating chart. "Just in case."

I looked at her handiwork. She'd emptied the seat next to mine.

Ignoring her giggles, I took a swig straight from the bottle.

Now, as I sat back in my seat, watching fat drops of rain assault my car, I rolled the memory around in my mind. Maybe Tier had a point...

My phone screeched to life, ripping me from my thoughts. Fumbling through my purse, my fingers closed around it. *Mommy Dearest,* my screen read. Swallowing a few choice swears, I picked up.

"I'm right outside, Mother. Literally in the parking lot. I'll be there in—"

"Sorry, dear," Mom interrupted. "I'm actually running late this morning. I had a last minute meeting with a client that ran over." *Oh, yeah,* I thought. Mom *did* have a job other than harassing her only child. "Please just hold our regular table, and I'll be there shortly."

Before I could confirm or deny her—or even give her shit about running late—she hung up. Jamming my phone into my purse, I got out of the car and ran for the entrance.

The host recognized me immediately, despite my drowned-rat appearance. With a polite smile, he led the way to our table.

Which was not empty.

"This isn't his table," I said to the host, ignoring the single occupant's eyes on my face.

"Oh, I'm sorry." He looked from Arthur to me. "Ms. Bach informed me there would be three of you today. I can—"

"She's kidding." Arthur stood and smiled at the guy. "Ms. Bach will be along shortly. In the meantime, can we get some drinks?"

"Absolutely, sir. I'll send the waiter right over."

Arthur smiled his thanks and re-seated. I remained standing. "I think I'm going to wait for my mother outside."

"Cat, please." He gestured to the chair across from him. "It's pouring out. Sit."

I adjusted my purse strap and looked over his shoulder. Rain slammed in sheets against the windows. I could choose my pride and wait out there. Or I could sit. In here. With Arthur.

Around us, people were staring. Not really something that usually bothered me, but today, their eyes felt like daggers. Judgy, pointy daggers.

Huffing out a breath, I yanked the seat away from the table. "Fine. But we're not speaking."

Arthur's lips tilted ever-so-slightly upward. "Deal." Sitting back, he drummed his fingers on the tabletop, but he said no more.

The restaurant bustled with the clink of dishes and the murmur of conversation, yet the silence at our table nearly drowned it out. I crossed my legs and reached for a menu. Maybe they'd updated it since last Sunday...

Across from me, Arthur cleared his throat and shifted. I glared and propped my menu up in front of me, like my very own fortress of fooditude.

"Hey there." Our waiter smashed through the silence. "Your usual today, Miss?"

Oh, Johnny. I gave him a smashing smile. "You are my favorite person of today. Maybe ever."

He preened under the attention, straightening his tie. "Thank you."

"You are so welcome. So, listen. Can I deviate from the usual this morning and start with dessert? What do you have for me today?"

As Johnny listed off the desserts, I covertly searched the restaurant for my mother. No sign. If I didn't know better, I'd swear this was intentional. But she wouldn't do that. She valued her existence, after all.

"...topped with fresh summer berries," Johnny finished and I dragged my gaze back to him.

"That one sounds perfect," I said, resting my chin on my hand. "And maybe a glass of Moscato?"

"Sure thing." He scribbled down my order and turned to that dude sitting across from me.

Once he finished taking Arthur's order, he reached for my menu. "No!" I gripped it tighter than maybe I needed to. "I mean, can I keep this for a while longer?"

He blinked in surprise but nodded. "Sure. I'll be back with your wine."

As he walked away, I readjusted my menu fort and narrowed my eyes on the appetizers list. *Three Cheese Crostini, Blue Cheese and Pear Tartlets, Fig and Olive—*

"Cat, can we talk?"

I glared over my menu. "Why?"

"Because there's a lot to be said." He reached over and flattened my protective barrier. Before I could protest, he continued. "I tried to reach you after I left. For three years."

I shrugged and reached for the menu. He held firm. I snarled. "It doesn't matter."

"It matters to me." He paused, and I thought he was done. I opened my mouth, ready to fire off another snarky remark, when he added, "And I think it still matters to you."

"See, that's where you're wrong." I sat back in my seat and met his eye. "I don't give a fuck about whether or not you tried to reach me thirteen damn years ago. I've moved on."

"Thirteen years may have passed, but I think I still know you a little," he said, undeterred by my hostility. "And you're still hiding behind walls and...menus, to avoid real life."

His assessment sent a jolt right to my marrow. I stiffened my spine. "I'm not hiding from anything."

"Really?" His brown eyes didn't waver. "So tell me why you never answered my calls."

My mind sputtered back to sixteen-year-old me, hiding out in my room while my mother begged Arthur to stay. Peering out my window while he climbed into his Lincoln and drove away. Comforting my crying mother for days, weeks, months.

Dodging phone calls and emails and any mention Hazel made of Arthur for years and years after.

And each memory hurt just as sharply as it had in real-time.

"I don't owe you an explanation." Pushing away from the table, I tossed my napkin down and stood. "I don't owe you a goddamn thing."

He was on his feet before I could escape, his hand on my arm. "Cat, wait. I—"

"You left me."

I didn't mean to say it. I didn't mean to say anything. But there it was. No point in going back now. I met his eye dead-on, the pain inside stealing all oxygen from my lungs. "You said you'd never, and you did."

His eyes shone with sincerity, but it was too late for that. "I tried, Kit-Kat."

I ignored the nickname that used to make me feel special. Loved. Like someone worth sticking around for. "You didn't try hard enough."

Before he could sputter another syllable, I was already weaving through the crowded restaurant, my eyes trained on the Exit sign.

"Catharine, dear." My mother's hand closed around my elbow just as I reached the door. "I'm sorry I'm late. Is Arthur already here? What's wro—"

I tore my arm from her grasp. "Do me a favor, Mother," I said between clenched teeth. "And let me know when you're done with him."

Her gray eyes widened, but I didn't wait for her reply. Yanking the door open, I stepped into the storm.

Better out here than in there, anyway.

14: I Now Pronounce You, Couch & Cat

———

I didn't know where to go.

Sitting in my car outside the restaurant, I rested my head against the seat and watched the rain sluice down the windshield. Overhead, thunder rumbled and I willed it to scare away the memories that still hovered like ghosts.

I'd spent years barricading those memories far, far in the back of my mind. Years piling on emotional Band-Aids so I would never have to feel those things again. And in a matter of seconds, Arthur ripped them all away.

My eyes burned. I swallowed and squeezed them shut. I would not cry. Not a single tear. He didn't deserve that.

Clearing my throat, I straightened in my seat and reached into my purse. With shaky hands, I fumbled with my keys, trying to jam them into the ignition. After the third failed attempt, I tossed them onto the passenger seat.

"Dammit!"

I rested my head against the steering wheel and breathed deep, counting each breath. *One...two...three...*

"Okay." I sat up and grabbed my keys. "Okay."

The key entered the ignition easily this time and I nearly cried in relief. Starting the car, I kept my focus on a single task at a time. Put the car in drive. Pull out of the parking lot. Drive home.

Home.

The word left a hollow feeling inside my chest.

I'd be alone at home. Just me and my empty apartment and the memories threatening to creep back into consciousness at any moment. I didn't want that. Couldn't handle that. Not right now.

Without thinking, I reached for my phone and dialed.

"Well, this is unexpected," Jude said after the third ring.

"Yeah, I know. Weird, right?" I closed my eyes and laughed. Absurd. This was absurd. I should've called Tierney. I should've just sucked it up and went home. "I...just thought I'd call, see what's up."

"Nothing much. Just watching some TV." He paused. "Everything okay?"

"Yeah, fine." I squeezed my eyes shut as the next words fell out. "So...uh. We're friends, right?"

"That's the plan."

"Can...can we put that to use today?" Ugh. Weak. I was weak.

A few seconds of quiet ticked by. Just the sound of the rain and my idiot brain trying to justify this phone call. When Jude didn't say anything, I spoke up. "Never mind. You're probably busy and it's last minute and—"

"Cat," he said, his voice level. Calm. "Come on over."

Relief whooshed through my veins. For the second time in, like, five minutes, my eyes threatened to spill tears. "Thank you. I'll be there soon."

Before I could change my mind, I hung up and put the car in reverse.

And though he wasn't the person I maybe should've reached for, I already felt a little better.

———————

MINUTES LATER, I STOOD outside Jude's apartment, knocking on the door. The rain hadn't let up for a second, so the walk from my car to his building had been adventurous, to say the least. My poor stilettos were soaked.

I'd just started wringing excess water from my hair when the door swung open. The Jude that greeted me was not what I expected. He wore a pair of low-slung navy blue sweats and a white t-shirt with a cartoon pig on it that read, *Bacon makes everything better.*

"Huh," I said, taking it all in. "Bacon *does* make everything better."

"What?" Confusion wrinkled his brow. I tilted my head toward his shirt and he looked down. "Oh. Right. *Right*?"

I laughed and Jude stepped aside to let me into his apartment. There was a savory smell clinging to the air and I inhaled, my tummy rumbling. "Popcorn?"

He shrugged. "Can't watch TV without popcorn." He walked toward the kitchen and I followed, feeling drawn to the delicious treasure inside.

"You're all dressed up," Jude said, his eyes taking in my dress and heels. "Special occasion?"

I shrugged, my nose wrinkling in disgust. "Brunch with the mother. It sucked."

"I see." He watched a droplet of water fall from my hair to the floor. "You need a towel. Hold on." He rifled through a drawer and tossed me a hand towel. "That'll get you started. I'll be right back."

He disappeared down the hall and returned a few seconds later with a full-size towel and a wad of clothing. "Sunny's always leaving things behind. I thought you might want to get out of that wet dress."

Huh, I thought as I took the offered items. *Not usually how I lose my clothes here.*

But friends didn't lose their clothes the *other* way.

I shook the thought away and smiled. "Thank you. I'll just...bathroom's this way, right?"

His head tilted in agreement. I kicked off my heels and walked to the bathroom. Once inside, I sat the pile of clothes on the sink and began toweling off. As I pulled my damp dress over my head, I waved away the wisps of memory that threatened to remind me of all the other times I'd been here. This was not that, and it'd be a good idea to remember it.

Scrubbing away those thoughts along with the raindrops that clung to my skin, I made quick work of drying off and dressing. As I yanked my borrowed shirt on, I glanced down and laughed. *Zombies Hate Fast Food,* it read. I knew I liked that girl.

With a cursory glance in the mirror to ensure I didn't have mascara dripping down my face—the dude might be a friend, but I didn't even treat Tierney to a face like that—I left the bathroom.

"I'm beginning to think I shacked up with the wrong Oliver," I said as I entered the kitchen.

Jude's hand stilled as he reached for a giant bowl. "What?"

I motioned to the shirt. "Zombies, food whore, snark. A girl after my own heart, really."

"I see." Jude reached into the microwave, pulling out a bloated, aromatic bag. "I've got popcorn."

"You sure do." I eye-banged the snack in question—really, to avoid eye-banging the dude holding it—and grinned. "It's kinda all you've got going for you at this point."

He laughed as he emptied the bag onto the bowl. "Well, feel free to pursue my sister. Though I'm not sure you're her type."

"Never underestimate my persuasive powers." I winked as I walked into the living room, leaving Jude chuckling behind me. "What are you watching?" I asked, picking up the remote.

"What?" He glanced up from the popcorn. "Oh." Before I could press Play, he'd ninja'd his way into the living room, removing the remote from my grasp. "Nothing."

I raised a brow. "Listen, if it's porn, I'm cool with it." With a smirk, I added, "Might even watch it with you."

"Really?"

I shrugged. "We had sex in a public bathroom. Do you really think I'd draw the line at porn?"

"Huh." His mind was obviously drawing a very clear picture for him. While he was distracted, I snatched the remote back and hit Play.

Familiar theme music filled the room as the screen displayed a pocket watch with wonky hands. "Dude!" My eyes shot to his face. "You watch *Until the End of Time?*"

His cheeks pinkened in the most adorable way. "N-no. Must have recorded the wrong thing."

Pointing the remote at the TV, I pulled up his DVR list. "You have a series recording set for the show, man. This is no accident."

His eyes darted from the TV to my face and back again. "Okay, fine," he finally said. "I watch a soap opera. Let the laughter commence."

My lips lifted in a smile, but I didn't laugh. I thought I would. It *was* funny. But he looked so...endearing that I found myself pausing the show and tossing the remote aside. "Throw in some beer, and I'll watch with you."

"You serious?"

"Yeah. I watch with my grandma every week. No shame in it." I paused, pensive as I thought about all the screaming, crying, sex and murder that happened in an hour's time. "Well, maybe a little shame."

Jude crossed the room and reached into the fridge. While he procured the beer, I grabbed the popcorn. Then, we went back into the living room and settled in.

"I want to marry your couch," I said, leaning my head back into the delicious leather.

"I don't think that's legal." He joined me on the couch. "Although, you two do look really good together."

I smiled and extended a hand. "Popcorn me."

Jude obliged, tilting the bowl so I could delve in. I tossed a few kernels into my mouth and closed my eyes. "Mmm, so good," I mumbled, relishing the melty, salty goodness on my tongue.

I could feel him watching, so I looked over. "What?"

"Nothing." He shook his head. "You're just really enjoying that popcorn." He glanced at my lips as my tongue darted out to lick the butter away.

Out of habit, I angled my body toward him, looking at him through lowered lashes. "You know what else I enjoy?"

His eyes flashed and my pulse picked up pace. In my mind, he closed the remaining distance between us, pushed me back onto this delectable couch and kissed me until I couldn't think straight.

In reality, he handed me a cold beer. "You look thirsty."

I took the bottle, blinking to dispel the last vestiges of desire from my brain. *We're friends. Friends don't do that,* I reminded myself.

Beside me, Jude clinked his own bottle with mine before taking a swig. Clearly, I wasn't the only one fighting with our new dynamic. "You ready for this?" he asked as he pointed the remote at the TV.

Ready for what? I wanted to ask. I didn't, though. I shoved the rest of my popcorn in my mouth and nodded, even as my body betrayed me.

Cat Keller doesn't do friends, I heard Tierney say. And, watching from the corner of my eye as Jude settled his long, muscular frame into the couch, I wondered if maybe she was right.

15: Like a Piñata

———

"Wow," Jude murmured later as our second episode wound to a close. "If I ever complain about my boring life, remind me about poor Lorenzo."

I laughed and pulled my feet onto the couch. I had successfully maintained a healthy distance for the entire afternoon. It had to be a record of some kind. "Your life? Boring?" I rested my elbow on the back of the couch and propped my chin in my hand. "What about the hordes of groupies, and the celebrity threesomes?"

He shot me a side-glare. "Groupies are overrated."

"And the threesomes?" I smirked as he shifted and cleared his throat. Uncomfortable Jude was appealing as fuck. Which was no good. "Are those overrated, too?"

"Closest I've ever come to a threesome is using the bathroom on Plethora of Daves' tour bus while the band waited outside." He shuddered. "Someone left their, uh, battery operated friend on the sink."

I leaned forward, intrigued. "Who's was it? Drummer Dave? He seems kind of kinky."

"I didn't ask." Dusting popcorn crumbs from his shirt, he pulled his leg up and turned toward me. "Some things are better left unknown."

"Party pooper."

He didn't respond, merely smiled. He moved the popcorn bowl onto the coffee table and stretched his arms high above his head. I ignored the flash of tummy his shirt lifted to reveal and pulled my legs closer to my body.

Down girl.

"So," he said once his stretch was finished. "What made you call today?"

Like a flood, it all came back. Arthur and his too-familiar eyes. Every memory and feeling and...

Well, I didn't feel very handsy anymore.

Suddenly claustrophobic, I stood and stacked the dishes from the coffee table. "No reason."

Jude watched as I walked to the kitchen and deposited them into the sink. "Okay."

I stopped, my hand half to the faucet. "Really? That's it?" Leaning against the counter, I studied him from across the room.

"Well, yeah. If you don't want to talk about it, that's fine."

"You're bad at this friend thing," I declared, turning to rinse out our glasses. "Tierney would be whacking at me like a piñata right about now."

Well, not lately, I thought, instantly feeling guilty. *She's busy with wedding stuff. Things will be back to normal soon.*

"Yeah, well." Jude joined me at the sink. "I prefer a different approach."

I watched as he took the dishes from my hands and deposited them into the dishwasher. "Besides," he continued as he kneed it closed. "I've known you long enough to know you ain't that easy to crack."

"Good call." I ignored the tiny chorus of *aww's* inside me and lifted my chin. "What about you?"

"What *about* me?" He reached into the fridge, pulled out a couple bottled waters and offered one to me.

I took it and unscrewed the cap. "You're alone on a Sunday afternoon, eating popcorn and watching soap operas. Classic signs of self-pity, man."

His bottle paused halfway to his mouth. A short laugh left his throat. Shaking his head, he resumed sipping. "You're good, you know that?" he said once he finished.

"That's not the first time you've said that to me," I said before I thought better of it. Pressing my lips together, I winced. "Sorry."

"It's okay," Jude said as he walked back into the living room. "It'd be impossible to ignore that we have history."

Oh, but I wish I could, I thought as I followed. "Okay, so." I plopped down on the couch. "What're you moping about?"

"I wouldn't call it moping..." He joined me on the couch and acknowledged my glare. "Okay, fine. Maybe a little moping."

"Why?" I uncapped my water and sipped. "You're hot and successful and worshipped around these parts. You're living the dream."

"I'm living *somebody's* dream," he said as he stretched his long legs out in front of him, resting his feet on the coffee table.

"Not yours?"

"Not mine." His eyes fell to the bottle in his hand. He picked at the label and I waited for him to continue.

I leaned closer, ready to drink in whatever Jude wanted to tell me. *What are you doing?* a voice asked. The less I asked, the less I knew. The less I knew, the less I wanted to stick around.

"What's yours?"

Looking briefly my way, he lifted a shoulder. "A new position just opened at the station. I want it. Bad. But..." He trailed off, leaving the sentence dangling between us.

"But what?" I shifted closer, curiosity pulling at me from the inside. "You don't think you'll get it."

"It's almost a certainty I won't." His eyes focused on something across the room. "There are people that would prefer me to stay right where I'm at."

"But, why?" My fingers itched to calm his fidgeting hand, but I stayed put. Not a friendly gesture. "You're great at your job. Why wouldn't they want to promote you?"

"Because it's not a promotion." He glanced my way again. "It's a completely different job." When I didn't say anything, he went on. "It's in the marketing department. Behind the scenes."

"But you're so good...in front of the scenes. Why would you want to—"

"I took this job as an in for what I really wanted to be doing. I didn't think it'd go so well."

"Ooh, color me intrigued." And I was. Jude always seemed to be in his element when he was at his shows every weekend. And I'd heard him on the radio—he was good. To think that this wasn't what he wanted to be doing...well, I needed to know more.

"What's the job you really wanted?"

"I want to be the promotions director." His eyes lit as he said it. "It's what I went to school for, what I love doing. The backstage stuff—planning events and promotions and..." He trailed off with a shy smile. "Well, anyway. A position opened up. Entry level, but it'd be a start."

"But the station doesn't want to consider you for it because you're doing so well in your current position."

He nodded.

"That is fucked up."

"Yeah." A hefty sigh left his lungs. Picking up the remote, he looked my way. "What do you say we forget about all *our* heavy shit for now and get into *theirs* instead?"

"If it means that I won't have to talk about my heavy shit, yes, please."

Jude shook his head, a smile touching his lips. "I'll crack you open one of these days, Cat Keller," he said as he hit Play on the remote.

Not in this lifetime, man, I thought as the theme music filled the room.

Maybe not even in the next one.

THE NEXT THING I KNEW, I was waking up to an infomercial blaring on the TV. I blinked, disoriented, and looked around the room, then to the arm hanging over my waist. Craning my neck, I took in the situation.

We were lying on Jude's couch, my back against his chest, his breath stirring my hair. I looked over at his face. He slept soundly, his features peaceful. The warmth of his body against mine, the weight of his arm around me, tugged at something inside me, beckoning me back to dreamland. I snuggled in closer and closed my eyes.

I started to drift back to sleep when a shock of realization ran through me. I jolted fully awake, jumping to my feet like a kitten that'd fallen into a bathtub full of water. He didn't wake, just shifted slightly and released a small snore.

My eyes traveled back to his sleeping face and the temptation to join him was strong.

"Shit," I whispered, my heart slamming erratically inside me. *"Fuckshitdamn."*

Fuck Buddies: 1, Friends: 0.

16: BFFs

The next day, I was hunched over my desk hard at work on our latest feature, when Kylie popped her head into my cubicle.

"Hey, Cat! How was your weekend? We missed you Friday night!" I could practically feel the exclamation points, and I wanted to stab her with them.

I kept my eyes on my computer screen. "Oh, yeah. Missed you too." *Go away,* I added silently. *Go away now.*

My patience—or what masqueraded as patience most of the time—was rice paper thin this morning. Which had nothing to do with a certain incident last night. Nope. If anything, my crankiness could be blamed on the lack of cream cheese for my bagel. Or because I ran out of conditioner mid-shower. But not because of—

"You'll have to come out with us this weekend, for sure!"

"Yeah, maybe." I cradled my head in my hand and gave her my best attempt at a smile. Placated, she turned on her heel and started down the hall.

Thank God. I sagged into my chair with relief.

"Oh! I almost forgot!" Her voice gnawed at my last thread of civility.

"*Yeeeees?*" I said, covering my face with my hands. *Woosah.*

"Someone is here to see you. He's down in the lobby. Patty said to tell you."

Patty the front desk receptionist. Why didn't she just call me? Oh, these people. They'd be the death of my patience as I knew it.

"Who is it?" I said, pushing my chair back. No one came to see me at work. Ever. "Did Patty say?"

"That guy. The radio guy. The hot one, not the bald one. Did you win a prize or something?"

"No. No I did not." I pushed away from my desk and stood, shoving my phone into my pocket.

"I mean, unless *he's* the prize." Kylie stepped to the side, letting me pass her. "That'd be a pretty awesome prize."

I ignored her—and the stab of jealousy in my gut—and started down the hall.

I thought leaving in the middle of the night would be a crystal clear indicator that I didn't want to see him. But I should've known better. Dude was terrible at taking hints.

As the elevator reached the lobby, I took a deep breath. I'd just have to tell him. This friends thing wasn't going to work. Shit got weird last night, and the best option was to cut our losses and—

I lost my train of thought as the elevator doors slid open, revealing Jude on the other side of the lobby.

He stood near the wall of windows, silhouetted by the late-morning sun. I hung back for a few seconds, taking him in, from his black leather shoes, to his dark blue jeans and gray button-down. He wore a black leather jacket over his shirt and my hands itched to wriggle their way inside it, soaking in his body heat.

Stop it, I told myself, tossing my hair back. *This is exactly why we can't be friends.*

With a big, deep breath, I started across the lobby, the click of my heels echoing loudly. Jude turned my way, eyes scraping over me.

Trouble.

Jude Oliver reeked of it.

"What're you doing here?" I asked, shoving anything resembling happy-to-see-him way, way down. Because I wasn't happy to see him. I wanted him to go away. For all the livelong day.

"You vanished last night." He raised his brows. "Kinda weird."

My lips twisted. "No, what's *kinda weird* is couch-snuggling with a dude you used to shag but are now 'just friends' with."

I air-quoted the friends bit, then crossed my arms over my chest. "I woke up to find your hand in a distinctly *un*-friendly place."

Jude's cheeks reddened. He shoved his hands in his pockets and rocked on his heels. "I'm sorry. Habit?"

I took a step away. In my back pocket, my phone vibrated. I ignored it. "It's a habit you've got to break, man."

"I know. It won't happen again."

He looked so earnest, I wanted to believe him. I *did* believe him. It was me I didn't believe. Grabbing my still-vibrating phone from my pocket, I glanced down. Hazel's warm brown eyes shone up at me. Weird.

"Listen." Shoving the phone back into my pocket, I faced Jude. I'd call her back. "I don't think this whole *friends* thing is gonna work."

Giving him a smile to soften my words, I added, "But, hey. We tried, right?"

I turned toward the elevator before I could catch the look on his face. I couldn't deal with the puppy dog eyes right now. I'd cave for sure.

"Wait a damn minute." He stepped in front of me, and I slid to a stop. I winced. Not puppy dog in the least. More like an angry bull about to charge. "So, what? You've gotten everything you need out of this arrangement, and now you're done?"

I blinked. "I—"

"I don't know how everyone else in your life responds to the *puppet master* thing, but it doesn't work on me."

"What—"

"You said you wanted to be friends, but I don't think you know how friendship works. You make selfish decisions to keep yourself safe. I get that." His eyes flared with frustration. "But aren't you at all curious how *I* feel about this?"

Guilt simmered hot in my stomach. I hadn't thought to ask.

"I'm sorry, Jude. I didn't—"

"It's fine." He took a step back, shoulders lifting in a deceptively casual shrug. "I should've known you were never going to give us a chance."

I opened my mouth to defend myself, but my phone vibrated against my backside. Pulling it from my pocket, I glimpsed Hazel's face again. What could be so important? She knew I was working.

Lifting it to my ear, I raised a finger to stop Jude. We weren't done here. "Hazel, hey. I'm sorry, I'm sort of in the middle of something. Can I call you—"

"Cat, sweetie, I've got some bad news." Hazel's voice sounded small and teary.

Immediately, my entire body stiffened. "What's wrong?"

Jude watched as Hazel spoke again.

"Sweetheart, it's Peach."

My stomach dropped.

Hazel kept talking. "She's...she's not doing so well. I'm with her at the vet's office. They're saying there's not much we can do. I..." she trailed off, the words she didn't say hanging on the line.

Tears filled my eyes. I blinked them back. "I'll be right there."

I hung up the phone and closed the ten feet between the elevator and me in record time. Jamming my thumb into the Up button, I swallowed the surge of tears that threatened to break free. "Shit," I whispered. "*Shitshitshit.*"

"Are you okay?"

I turned to find Jude's worried eyes on my face. "No." I pushed the Up button three more times. "I...I need to..."

He put a gentle hand on my shoulder. "What can I do?"

Every semblance of strength I'd been clinging to tumbled to the ground. I stepped forward and threw my arms around him. "I need to get to Peach," I murmured against his jacket.

"Okay," he said. And he put his arm around my waist and led me outside. "Where are we going?"

———

WE FOUND HAZEL IN AN exam room, sitting next to a table. Peach lay there, eyes half-closed, as Hazel stroked her head.

My stomach tumbled to my toes, bringing my steps to a halt. Jude's fingertips lingered on my back, and he gently urged me forward.

"Hey," I whispered, moving to Hazel's side. I put one hand on her shoulder and the other on Peach's soft fur. I petted her, watching as she breathed, slow and heavy.

"Hey," Hazel returned, her hand coming up to give mine a squeeze.

"Dr. Hewitt said there's nothing to do but wait. She's an old girl, lived a long life, and it's finally caught up to her." Her voice cracked on the last word and she reached up to stroke Peach.

I blinked rapidly, Hazel's words like a punch to the gut. This cat...she was my best friend. I'd spend weekends with Hazel and Zeke, and Peach would curl up in bed with me, listening as I told her all about my life. My mom and her latest husband, some boy I liked at school, the latest video game I'd become obsessed with. And Peach would listen patiently, looking at me with her big green eyes.

And I knew she'd done the same for Hazel. Curling up in her lap on the long, lonely nights after Zeke's passing, lending her ever-patient ear and soothing purr.

At that thought, my fragile reserve broke and tears flowed. I took the seat next to Hazel and scratched Peach under her chin. She'd always loved that. A slow, melodic purr emanated from her throat and I smiled. "Sweet girl," I whispered. "Sweet, beautiful Peach."

Jude came up behind me and put his hand on my shoulder. I glanced at him and his eyes warmed.

"I should give you some time alone," he said, his voice soft. "I'll be right outside if you need me."

I nodded numbly, not taking my eyes from Peach. Her breathing had slowed, her eyes narrow slits. It wouldn't be much longer. My heart clenched and cracked. I laid my head on the table, my hand still petting the cat's soft fur.

"I think I'll join you, dear," Hazel said, getting to her feet. She smoothed a hand over my hair. "I've had years alone with her. I got all my words out. It's your turn."

I listened to them walk across the room and open the door. I heard the door click shut behind them. And then I lost it.

I wasn't a crier. I always held my emotions firmly in check, all neat and tidy on the inside of my body. But sitting here now, listening to the labored breathing of my beloved cat, knowing she was minutes away from leaving me forever, every ounce of emotion tore from my body.

Tears fell from my eyes in rapid succession, spattering on the faded linoleum floor. I watched them for a few seconds before lifting my head to look at Peach.

"I don't know if I ever thanked you," I whispered, my throat closing over more tears. "You really have been my best friend. You know all my secrets, and you've never told a soul."

I scratched behind her ear and leaned in to kiss her head. "Not even about the time I raided Zeke's liquor cabinet before that Mathlete competition and spent the entire night leaned over a trash can."

As if she understood what I was saying, Peach raised her head the teensiest bit and meowed, a hoarse, crackling sound. I ran my finger along her nose, waiting for her motorboat purr. What came was much weaker, like a toy racecar. My heart twisted, but I kept petting her.

"I should've been the one taking care of you all these years," I said, watching as her eyes drifted closed. "I just..." Closing my own eyes, I rested my forehead against hers. My chest ached from the unspoken words. I thought I could protect myself from this. From the pain.

Jude's voice rang in my mind. *You make selfish decisions to keep yourself safe.*

Raising my head, I looked at Peach's tired face. I'd been so selfish. She spent years loving me unconditionally, and I kept my distance. Distance meant safety. Safety meant no getting hurt.

Somewhere beneath my ribcage, my heart struggled for each painful beat. So much for that.

"He's right, you know," I whispered, and Peach opened her eyes. "I haven't been a very good friend. To him, or to you."

I blew out the breath I'd been holding and continued to stroke her paw. "I'm sorry I haven't been a very good kitty mama." She watched me, her emerald eyes unfocused. "I love you, sweet girl." I leaned in and kissed the top of her head. "Thank you for everything."

At that, Peach gave one last, rasping meow and closed her eyes. Her breaths became shallow and further apart. I watched, tears rolling down my cheeks, gently petting her, until finally she took her last breath.

I felt like my breath went with her. I continued to stroke her soft fur, even though she couldn't feel it anymore, and, for the first time in a long time, I let myself fall apart.

17: Friends are Not Boys

———

"You don't have to come in," I said to Jude as the cab approached my building a couple hours later.

We'd taken the cab to Hazel's apartment, and, after her endless insisting that she'd be okay alone, we headed to my place. On the way there, I called my boss to let her know what was up. Getting fired didn't sound like a good finish to the day, after all. She told me to take the rest of the day, and I hung up, relieved. I'd have been useless, anyway.

I leaned against the cool window and closed my eyes. My head was pounding, my eyes burned and my heart wouldn't stop aching. All I wanted to do was cry until I couldn't cry anymore. Which I would not—could not do—in front of Jude. And, yet...I didn't want to be alone.

As if he sensed my thoughts, Jude squeezed my knee. "I'm not going anywhere," he said, leaning forward to pay the driver.

When we reached my door, I fumbled for my keys. Realization settled in—Jude was about to enter my apartment. My sanctuary.

No man's land.

Rule number two, my mind whispered. *Never Bring a Boy home.*

But this wasn't a boy. This was Jude. Jude, who I was no longer boning. Jude, my friend.

Friends were not boys.

Rule number two could remain unbroken.

I jammed the key in the lock and took a deep breath..

As we walked into my place, I glanced around, seeing it through new eyes.

My favorite throw was draped over the back of the couch and last night's empty popcorn bowl and soda can still sat on the coffee table. Tossing my keys and purse on the counter, I entered the living room and began tidying up.

"Sorry." I glanced at Jude as I headed into the kitchen. "Wasn't expecting company."

Jude stood just inside the apartment, looking all big and out of place. He dragged a hand through his hair and gave me a smile. "You don't have to clean up on my account." He uprooted his feet from the floor to join me in the kitchen.

I turned on the faucet and filled the sink with sudsy water, thankful for the menial task to distract me. From Jude. From Peach. From everything.

"You think this is for you? Please. I just don't want rodents wandering in." Glancing in his direction, I submersed the bowl in the water and began washing.

"Noted," he said, taking the clean bowl from my hand. I watched as he rinsed it and put it in the dish drainer. "What else you got?"

"What?" I frowned up at him, baffled.

"You didn't fill the sink just to wash one bowl." He moved around me and gathered the smattering of dishes on the counter, putting them in the soapy water.

"You're not here to help with the housekeeping."

"Well, I'm not here to watch *you* do it, either." Reaching in front of me, he unplugged the sink, filling the room with the slurpy sound of water going down the drain. Then, he put his arm around my waist and led me away from the kitchen. "Come on. Sit down."

I didn't have the energy to argue. Once in the living room, I plopped down on the couch. The sigh that left my lungs felt dangerously close to a sob. Looking at Jude through carefully neutral eyes, I said, "I'm probably just going to go lay down. You don't have to stay."

I didn't want him to see me like this. I was fun Cat. Happy Cat. Casual, laid back Cat. So far today, Jude had seen me angry, vulnerable and sad. I didn't really want to add a sobbing wreck to that.

Jude sat next to me and put his fingertip under my chin, tilting my head up. His smeary gray-green eyes were warm and pulled at something deep inside me that I'd spent years hiding behind a brick wall. *Please, please just go,* I thought. *I can't deal with this right now.*

Almost as if he could read my thoughts, he nodded. "All right. I'll give Ben a call and see if he'll come get me, take me back to my bike."

"Okay." But something inside me sunk as I thought about him walking out that door. The empty apartment would echo around me. The distance between us would feel safe. But the pain would still be just as real. Looking up to find him hovering in the middle of the room, I said, "But...maybe in a little bit?"

He studied me for a few quiet seconds before nodding. "You got it." Kicking off his shoes, he reclined next to me, his arms behind his head. "Want to watch a little *Until the End of Time*?"

I smiled and disposed of my own shoes. "Sure. But we need ice cream first."

Jude nodded solemnly. "Ice cream is nature's Band-Aid. Makes everything better."

Standing, I walked into the kitchen. "I don't think that's how Band-Aids work, man."

He joined me, leaning his hip against the counter. "Whatever. Ice cream is magical, is what I'm saying."

I pulled open the freezer and grabbed the quart of Moose Tracks. Setting it on the counter, I looked Jude's way. "Bowls are in the middle cupboard, bottom shelf. Do you want anything on your ice cream? Chocolate syrup? Whipped cream? Potato chips?"

"Potato chips?" Jude repeated, brows raised. "Really?"

"Hey, don't knock it before you try it." I pulled the lid off the ice cream. "It's delicious. That whole salty and sweet thing."

"Huh." He located the silverware drawer. "So, the same idea as chocolate-covered pretzels."

"Exactly." I grinned. "See? You get it."

"I mean, kind of. Still weird, though."

I stuck my tongue out at him and turned to pull a bag of ruffled potato chips from the cupboard. "You're going to try this. And you're going to like it."

"That's...what she said?" Jude said, looking pleased with himself.

"How *old* are you?" I shook my head, even as laughter spilled from my lips.

"Thirty-two," he deadpanned. "How old are *you*?" He reached for the ice cream carton and began scooping.

"Didn't your mother ever tell you that it's impolite to ask a lady her age?"

"I don't see any ladies here," he shot back, bracing himself as I half-heartedly socked him on the arm. "Yeah, okay. I deserved that."

"Yeah, you did." I opened the chips and crumpled a handful on top of Jude's ice cream, then did the same for mine.

"Shouldn't you have done one, just in case?" He cast a worried look my way. "I mean, what if I don't like it?"

"You'll like it." I picked up the bowls and headed into the living room. "Will you put that ice cream back in the freezer, please?"

"Yes, ma'am," he called after me.

I spun to face him. "Don't call me ma'am. Do I *look* like a ma'am?" I held my arms out, a bowl of ice cream in each hand.

"Right now, you look like my most favorite person ever," Jude replied, coming toward me. "I mean, you've got dessert. Even if you've tainted it with potato chips."

"I did not taint it. I *improved* it. You'll see." I moved out of his reach and headed to the couch. He followed, then sat right in the middle.

"Here." I handed him a bowl and sat mine down on the coffee table. Then, I grabbed the remote and plopped down next to him, watching as he took a spoonful of ice cream, avoiding the potato chip topping.

"Really, dude?" I scooped up a big bite of my own ice cream, with plenty of chips, and held it out. "Eat."

"That's what she—" he started, but I stuck the spoon in his mouth before he could finish.

He gave me angry eyes as he chewed. "Not cool," he mumbled around the ice cream. Then, as all the flavors mingled and melted in his mouth, his expression changed.

"Mmm hmm, see?" I said, nodding in satisfaction. "What'd I tell you?"

He finished the bite then lifted a shoulder. "S'alright," he said as he took the spoon from my hand and took another bite.

"S'alright?" I laughed. "You're officially the world's worst liar." I dug my spoon into my ice cream. "I mean, I'm not going to say 'I told you so,' but it's clearly implied."

I pulled my feet onto the couch and flipped on the TV. "You ready to find out whether the jury convicts Loretta of murder?"

Jude turned sideways and stretched his legs across my lap, my couch dwarfed beneath his long frame. I glanced his way, surprised by the familiarity of his gesture. "She's *so* guilty," he said as he dug into his ice cream.

I mentally shrugged and pointed the remote at the TV. *No big deal.*

We fell into silence as I scrolled through my DVR for the soap opera. My thumb hovered over the Play button, but I didn't press it. "I ever tell you how Peach and I met?"

I didn't know why I said it. It'd be much easier to let the fictional world on the screen pull me in, distract me, make me forget about the piece of my heart that was now missing. But once the words were out, I felt the fierce need to talk about it. About her.

"I don't think so." He stopped spooning his ice cream and looked up. "But I'd like to hear it."

I sighed and rested my head against the back of the couch. Memories swirled through my mind like spun sugar in a cotton candy maker. Closing my eyes, I began speaking. "My stepfather brought her home for me when I was eleven." I pictured the tiny ball of fluff huddled in the cardboard pet carrier, my heart aching. "She was so small, and so scared, but the moment I pulled her out of the box and held her to my chest, she started to purr." My voice caught as I recalled that detail. I could almost feel her tiny purr vibrating against my heart.

I swallowed the threat of tears and cleared my throat. "My mother had a conniption. *It's going to get hair everywhere,* she said. *And what about the litter box?* She absolutely refused to let me keep her." Memories, vivid and alive, flickered through my mind. "Arthur jumped into action so fast." I glanced at Jude, a smile on my lips. "He convinced my grandparents to take Peach in, so I could visit her whenever I stayed with them."

The smile faltered. I looked down at the ice cream in my hands. I'd buried that memory—along with millions of others starring Arthur—deep in the back of my brain. It was easier to focus on the bad. Arthur was bad. He promised he wouldn't leave, and he did. As a broken sixteen-year-old, I had needed to remember that.

The good memories had hurt too much.

But Peach was the one good thing Arthur hadn't taken with him. The thing that soothed the broken places he'd left behind.

And now she was gone, too.

My throat tightened. I squeezed my eyes shut and forced myself to breathe. I wouldn't cry. Not now. Not with Jude sitting beside me, comforting and kind and...

No.

Shaking my hair away from my face, I looked over, smile at the ready. *Moving on.*

Jude reached over, his hand covering mine. "I'm sorry, Cat."

The smile never made it to my lips. I looked down at our hands. *You should move away,* I told myself. *Distance is good.*

I didn't listen. Instead, I flipped my hand over and let our fingers intertwine. He gave them a squeeze, and my heart echoed the motion. I looked up. Tears blurred my vision, and I blinked them back.

"That cat was my best friend." My voice cracked on the last word, and with it, my resolve. A single tear slid down my cheeks. Jude swung his feet to the floor and took my barely-touched ice cream from me, setting both bowls aside. Then, he put his arm around my shoulder and pulled me close. My head found his chest, and I leaned in.

That was it. No overblown sentiments about how she was in a better place, or at least I had nineteen years with her.

I didn't know until that moment that it was exactly what I needed.

But I knew it wasn't what I *wanted* to need.

As the thought settled in, I straightened and reached for the abandoned bowls on the coffee table. "Here," I said, avoiding his eye as I handed him his bowl. "Ice cream's melting."

18: The Hug of Ultimate Comfort

———

Two hours and nearly three episodes of *Until the End of Time* later, there was a knock on the door. I jolted upright from my half-awake position on the couch and looked at Jude.

He peered at me from one eye and my lips twitched. I wasn't the only one on my way to Sleepy Town. "It's not me," he grumbled, pushing himself into an upright position.

I pushed his legs off of my lap and stood. "It's probably Tierney. I'm sure Hazel called her."

"Tell her to go away." He burrowed deeper into the couch, snuggling a throw pillow tight. "I've already got the comforting friend thing taken care of."

A smile touched my lips. He really *had* come through. In between episodes of the soap, I'd told him more stories about Peach. He, in turn, told me about losing his dog, Crowley, when he was a teenager.

"It was the hardest thing I'd ever been through," he'd said, picking at the fringe on his throw pillow. "So, I get it."

My insides, though still ravaged with heartbreak, were soothed by his presence. It'd been much better than crying alone all night.

"Sorry, man," I said to him now as I reached for the doorknob. "As my oldest friend, Tierney's got first dibs. You might have to make room on the couch for her." Pulling open the door, I filled Tierney in. "I've already had ice cream and bad TV. I hope you brought the booze."

"Uh, no." Arthur took a step back, a frown creasing his forehead. "I didn't realize that was a requirement."

My already-raw insides twisted painfully. Gripping the doorknob tight, I met Arthur's eye. "What are you doing here?"

"I tried calling." He ran a hand over his salt-and-pepper hair. "Hazel told me about Peach. I'm so sorry, Cat." His face warmed with sympathy, and I bit back the sting of fresh tears.

I straightened my spine and swallowed the sharp reply on my tongue. I didn't have the energy to argue right now. "Thank you," I said, my tone cool. "Now, if you don't mind, I've—"

"I'm thinking about ordering a pizza," Jude called from behind me. "Does Tierney have any topping preferences?"

"Sorry, I didn't mean to interrupt." Arthur shifted. "I just wanted to express my condolences. I know how much you loved Peach. You did from the moment I brought her home."

Memories teased at the corners of my mind for the second time that night, and I blinked hard to clear them away. "Yeah, well. At least you've got that in your Win column." I glanced behind me. Jude had rustled up a pizza menu from the stack on my coffee table. Looking back to Arthur, I continued. "Thanks for stopping by, but I'm not in the mood to play *Remember When* with you."

"Right. Sorry." Arthur tilted his head in apology. "I should let you get back to your boyfriend."

"He's not my boyf—" I rested my head against the door. Didn't matter. "Goodnight, Arthur."

"Goodnight," he replied. He got two steps away from the door when he turned around. "Oh. Right." Backtracking, he added, "I actually came to give you this."

I looked down to find a plain white gift box about the size of a paperback novel in his hand. "Thank you, but I don't need your gifts."

"It's not a gift. Just...something I've had lying around. I thought you might like to have it." He edged the box closer, and I took it. The faster I wrapped this conversation up, the faster he would leave.

"Thank you."

He looked like he wanted to say something else, but the expression on my face must've made him think better of it. Instead, he nodded and walked away.

I watched as he disappeared down the hall, then closed the door behind him. Heading back inside, I crossed the room to join Jude, dropping the package, unopened, on the coffee table.

"Not Tierney?" Jude asked as I sat next to him.

"Not Tierney." I reached for the menu in his hand and studied the toppings list.

"Who was it, then?"

My shoulder lifted. I fought hard for nonchalance. "Nobody important." And, before Jude could question me further, I added, "What do you like on your pizza?"

TURNED OUT, MY FAVORITE pizza toppings paired perfectly with Jude's.

Over slices of the most delicious pizza I'd ever eaten, we theorized about the upcoming episodes of our soap opera. During cleanup time, Jude called Ben for a ride. And while we waited for Ben to show up, we talked about Jude's job, and whether or not he would apply for the new position we had talked about before—mostly because I didn't want to linger on my own life right now.

"I don't know." He shrugged. "I think they've already made up their minds."

"So make them change them." I rinsed our plates as I spoke. "You can be awfully persuasive, you know."

"Can I?" He leaned on the counter next to me and I glanced his way. A tiny frown had settled between his brows.

"Uh. Yeah." Setting the dishes in the drainer, I dried my hands and leaned next to him. "You persuaded me to give this friends thing a go."

His eyes darted to mine. Our earlier fight flashed through the air between us. "I did, huh?" His cheek dimpled. "You *were* a pretty hard sell."

"Don't count your chickens, man." I crossed my arms over my chest and sent him a stern look. "I'm still not entirely convinced."

"Ahh." He pushed away from the counter and faced me. "That's because you haven't experienced the Jude Oliver Hug of Ultimate Comfort." He lifted a brow and added, "TM."

I snorted. "Did you just trademark yourself?"

"Sure did." He opened his arms wide. "Now, come on. Bring it in."

"Sorry." My lips twitched with a smile I refused to let go. "I don't hug dorks."

Jude opened his mouth with a comeback, but a knock at the door cut him off.

I lost the smile battle, but hid it from Jude as I crossed the room and opened the door.

"Hey, Foxy. Good to see you."

My smile widened in response to Ben's contagious grin. "You, too. Your man is inside." I tilted my head to indicate Jude, still standing in the kitchen.

Ben entered my apartment, but instead of addressing Jude, he threw his arm around my shoulder. "Sorry about your cat," he said as he squeezed me tight.

Thrown off by his gesture—and his kindness—I stumbled into him, a hot rush of grief slicing into me. "Th-thank you."

"I thought you didn't hug dorks."

I separated myself from Ben to find Jude standing in front of us. I cleared my throat and straightened. "I made an exception."

"Hey." Ben attempted an outraged expression, but failed epically. Instead, he conceded with a nod. "All right." Then, he drifted away from us to study my bookcase. "Whenever you're ready, man."

Dragging my eyes back to Jude, I smoothed my hands over my shirt. The realization that he'd be leaving settled heavy in my gut—or maybe that was the fourth slice of pizza. "So...thanks," I said, quiet so Ben wouldn't overhear. "For, you know, everything."

He smiled softly. "You're welcome."

"And..." I dragged my eyes away to watch my toes trail across the carpet. "About earlier. The whole 'selfish jerk, puppet master' thing." I looked up. "I'm sorry."

Jude's eyes flickered. He cleared his throat and shoved his hair back. "Thank you. That means—"

"*Oh, my God!*" Ben shouted, making us both jump. I spun to find him standing at my TV, a video game in his hand. "You play *Kill Radius?*"

"Um, yeah. It's only the best game ever." I joined him. "I mean, what other game allows you to blast zombies in the face with giant bazookas?"

"Right?" Ben's eyes widened. "Or chop their heads off with those badass machetes?"

"Dude, so much blood!"

"I know. Awesome, right?"

"Uh...so, you two are kind of scaring me," Jude said, bringing an end to our bonding. "Remind me never to cross you in a dark alley."

"Relax." I crossed the room to link my arm with his. "You're perfectly safe. Unless, of course, the zombie apocalypse starts. Then, it's on."

"Oh, yeah," Ben said, setting the game back down. "Just don't become a zombie, or slow us down while running from zombies, and we promise not to kill you."

"And on that note," Jude said, patting my arm. "I think I'm going to head home. You need anything?"

I smiled, despite the wave of panic rushing through me. "No, thanks. I'm good. You've been awesome."

"All right. Well, you know where to find me." And then he stood there, his eyes steady on my face. Could he sense my hesitance to let him leave?

Ben cleared his throat. "I'll be outside when you're ready. Bye, Cat."

I waved his direction, then pulled my ponytail over my shoulder. Once the door clicked shut behind him, I turned my attention back to Jude. "Did you, uh, want to take the leftover pizza home?"

"Nah, you keep it." His gaze didn't leave mine. "You sure you're gonna be okay?"

"Me? Pssh. Please." I lifted my chin. "You kidding? I got this."

"It's okay if you don't, you know."

His voice was so soft, words so simple, that my eyes filled. Blinking, I looked away. I wanted to say something pithy. Something to reassure him that I'd be okay. But I knew that if I tried to speak, I'd lose my fragile hold on these tears.

I didn't need to say anything, though. Jude stepped forward and wrapped his arms around me. I hesitated, holding steady, but he was just as stubborn. My body made the next move before my mind could stop it. With a sigh, I moved in closer, my arms circling his waist.

The warmth from his body seeped right into my bones. In a rush, every ounce of tension left my body, and with it, the tears I'd been fighting off for hours.

"It's all right," Jude whispered, his hand smoothing over my hair. "I got you."

Burying my face in his leather jacket, I cried. And cried, and cried. Inside my chest, my heart ached like a giant fist gripped it. On the outside, Jude held me just as tight.

I didn't know how long we stood there, but he held me till the tears died down to a mere trickle. Sniffling, I stepped back and wiped at my face. "S-sorry. I snotted all over you." I couldn't look at him, so I stared at the ground instead.

"Don't worry about it," was all he said. He reached out and touched my arm, and I raised my eyes to his. "I can hang around longer if you need me to."

I shook my head, my heart aching again, but with something much scarier this time. "Th-that's all right. I'll be okay."

He scrutinized me for a few seconds, like he wasn't sure if he could believe me. "Okay. I'm only a call or text away if you need me."

"Thank you." I tried for a smile, but only got halfway. "For everything."

Jude smiled back and stepped toward the door. "That's what friends are for."

I watched as he headed for the door. His hand had just touched the knob when I spoke again. "Hey."

He turned. "Yeah?"

You were right about that hug."

19: Expiration Schmexpiration

―――

"I'm so sorry, hon," Tierney said the next night, eyes warm with sympathy as she handed me a glass of wine. "I know how much you loved that cat."

I sat on her couch, munching on a bowl of popcorn while she perched on the arm, within reach of our shared snack. "Thanks," I said, holding the bowl out to her. "I'm going to miss her."

She gave my knee a squeeze, a soft smile on her lips. "Wanna do ice cream and TV? I can kick Jack out for the night and— "

"I already did the ice cream and TV thing," I said around a mouthful of popcorn. "Last night. With Jude."

Tierney's eyes widened. "Ooh!" she squealed, sliding from the arm of the couch to squeeze in next to me. "Details. Now."

I shook my head, stuffing another handful in my mouth. "Not a whole lot to tell. I was with him when Hazel called, so he took me to the vet's office, and then took us home. He stayed with me for a while. We ate ice cream and watched *Until the End of Time* for a couple hours."

And then he held me while I cried.

But I didn't say that part aloud.

Jude's presence last night had been the perfect distraction. I'd needed that. And, after he left, I'd let the tears flow. I needed that, too.

But I could still feel his arms around me, his hand on my hair. The soothing sound of his voice still hummed in my ear. That, I didn't need.

"I don't know if I should be jealous or not." Tierney took a handful of popcorn from the bowl and tossed a few pieces into her mouth. "I mean, the guy totally stole my best friend thunder." She sipped her wine. "On the other hand," she said once she finished. "You let him hang out at your place. That's a pretty big deal."

I shrugged, staring intently into the half-empty bowl. "Wasn't that big a deal."

"What?" Tierney snatched the popcorn from my hand and sat it on the coffee table. "Rule Number Two: Never Bring a Boy Home."

I winced under the reminder of my rules. "Jude's not a boy. He's just a friend." Leaning forward, I grabbed the popcorn. "It doesn't count."

"Bullshit." She took the popcorn again. "Total bullshit."

"Hey." I snatched it back and scooted away from her. "It's not bullshit. *We're* friends. You come over all the time."

"Yeah, but you haven't slept with *me*."

"I mean, there was that one time—"

"Nope." Tierney raised her hand to silence me. "Getting drunk on daiquiris and almost making out is not the same as boning a guy for months."

"We did more than *almost* make out," I grumbled, aware that it was *not* her point. I got her point. Loud and clear. In fact, it was the very point that had kept me up when crying for hours should have had me comatose.

Tier lifted her brows. "I fell forward and *accidentally* touched your boob." She smirked as she added, "Unless Jude's penis *accidentally*—"

"You are so done." I sat the popcorn bowl aside and got up. "Where's your man? I'd much rather be talking to him right now."

She laughed. "He took Mousse for a walk. Sorry, you're stuck with me." Pushing away from the couch, she added, "I gotta say, I'm a little miffed that some guy gets to be your therapist instead of me."

I waved her—and the voice in my head that agreed with her—off. "Trust me, my next crisis is *all* yours."

As I said it, Arthur's face popped into my mind. I hadn't told Tierney about his reappearance yet.

"In fact," I started, my stomach twisting in knots. "I've already got one for you."

"Is it the whole *I don't want to walk down the aisle with Luke* thing again? Because I told you—he's Jack's best man. There's nothing I can do about it."

"Ugh." At the mention of Tier's wedding, and the best man I'd shacked up with, all thoughts of Arthur dissipated. Some other time. I'd tell her some other time. "I still think you could let us fly solo down the aisle. Why do we have to go together?"

"Because my mother would like a semblance of tradition, and this is a small thing I can give her." Tierney pushed her hair away from her face and sighed. "It's either that, or the cotton candy machine."

"Ahh, yes. I see your dilemma." I returned to the couch and plopped down. "I, too, would choose cotton candy over my best friend's peace of mind."

"You're being dramatic." Tier rested her feet across the middle of the couch. "Besides, if it's really that big a deal, bring a date. That way, you'll have someone to hang out with while you're avoiding Luke."

Pausing, she reached for the TV remote. "Even better if this date is, you know, a *friend*. Then, at least you'd actually like him."

I rolled my eyes. "You're so subtle."

"Hey, man. At least consider it. I bet he'd look great in a suit."

"I don't care what he looks like. He's my *friend,* remember?" Even as I said it, my mind started a game of dress-up, starring one Jude Oliver. And, Tier was right. He'd look stunning in a suit...

But, no. I would not be asking him to Tier's wedding. Even as a friend. It'd be too weird.

Wouldn't it?

———

HAZEL'S APARTMENT FELT different. Quiet. Empty.

I didn't like it.

Tapping my fingers on the table, I glanced at Hazel, who stood at the stove, stirring copious amounts of butter into her famous mashed potatoes. "Need any help?"

"I've got it under control," she replied. "Unless you want to set the table?"

I leapt from my chair, glad to have something, anything to do. The longer I sat there, the more I felt the hollow place Peach had left behind. And I did not want to cry today. Mostly because I already had. Plenty. But also because I wanted to be strong for Hazel. *She* was the one who raised my kitten, after all. She was the one who'd spent every day, for years and years, with her. It had to be harder on her.

And so I threw myself into the menial task, rifling through the cupboards for plates and napkins and whatever else we could possibly need to devour Hazel's mashed potatoes and fried chicken. By the time Hazel put the finishing touches on the food, I'd set the table to the nines.

"Goodness," she said as she turned around, chicken platter in hand. "Are we expecting company?"

"What? No." I shrugged and looked at the place settings. Three different forks, cloth napkins, a turkey-shaped centerpiece I'd made for Hazel when I was eight. "I just...thought it'd be nice."

Hazel smiled, wrinkles showcasing the warmth in her brown eyes. "It *is* nice." She sat the chicken on the table and turned for the bowl of potatoes. "You should have invited that friend of yours."

"Who? Tierney?" I waved a hand. "She's busy with wedding stuff right now."

"No, dear. That fella from last week. The tall, good-looking one?"

"Oh, *him*." I gave Hazel a sly look. "You think he's good-looking, eh?"

She slapped my arm with a dishtowel, even as a light flush crept into her cheeks. "In an overt kind of way, yes."

"Well, I have it on good authority that he's single." I winked. "Want me to give him your number?"

"Oh, no." Hazel laughed and took her seat. "But it *would* be nice to invite him for dinner. As a thank-you for his help last week." She began scooping potatoes onto our plates, but paused long enough to give me a look. "If you're still speaking to him."

I paused, a forked chicken leg halfway to her plate. "What do you mean?"

"You don't keep many people around." She shrugged. "Just me and Tierney. I assumed this one had an expiration date."

My mouth opened, but no sharp retort could be found. Hazel patted my hand and shook out her napkin. "I don't mean anything by it, Kitten."

I tried to tamp down the hurt her assumption stirred up. Tried real hard. Hazel knew my reasons for keeping my distance—she knew better than anyone. I didn't need to defend myself.

And yet...

"There's no expiration date," I said, dropping the chicken leg onto her plate. "In fact, we've been friends for months now."

Or, something *like* friends, anyway...

"Well, that's good, dear." Hazel expertly hid her surprise. "So you'll have no problem inviting him to dinner? Next week?"

No problem except for Rule Number Three—*Family is Forbidden.*

But I'd already met his sister.

He was a friend, though. The rules did not apply to him.

Before Tierney's voice replayed in my mind, questioning that very concept, I nodded. "Sure. I'll call him tonight."

20: Melodrama & Sex

―――

Jude was on board for Hazel dinner. In fact, he seemed excited about it. I tried not to notice how adorable he sounded when I told him Hazel wanted to make his favorite food.

"She doesn't have to do that," he'd said, an *aww shucks* tone in his voice. "I'm just honored to be invited."

"Either make a choice, or I tell her your favorite is grilled cheese. Because I could really go for a grilled cheese, and Hazel's are the best."

Seconds ticked by. I could picture his contemplative expression as he thought about the plethora of food options he had in front of him. "I could go for grilled cheese, too," he said finally.

And so grilled cheese it was.

I almost texted him no less than eighty-three times all through the week to cancel. I dreamed up a surplus of excuses, each one worse than the last. I was coming down with something. Hazel was coming down with something. My mother had been in a horrible accident and I had to rush to her side. I was having a bad hair day.

In the end, I did nothing. Which meant Jude showed up at my place at seven on the dot.

I took a huge breath and pulled open the door.

"Hey."

"Hey, back." He rocked on his heels and I let my eyes quickly scrape over him—in a totally platonic way.

He'd actually dressed up a little. Gone were the faded blue jeans and casually un-tucked button-ups and t-shirts. Instead, he wore a pair of black dress pants and a black sweater, a blue plaid shirt peeking out from beneath it. The color in his shirt picked up sparks of blue in his kaleidoscope eyes, and I caught myself staring.

"You look...um...nice," I said, tugging self-consciously at my t-shirt.

Jude's eyes fell to my chest. *"I put the 'hot' in Psychotic,"* he read. "Huh. Good to know." Then, he smoothed a hand over his sweater. "I'm sorry. I just figured, dinner with a grandparent, should probably dress nicely."

"That's cute." I patted his shoulder. "We should get going. Hazel hates it when I'm late." Closing the door behind me, I threw a grin his way. "But only because it delays her soap opera time."

"I like her already," Jude said as he followed me down the stairs.

And I like you.

The thought came out of nowhere, and I stopped abruptly, Jude bumping into me. "Sorry," I muttered, forcing myself forward.

This was going to be a long night.

HAZEL GREETED US AT the door, a grin on her weathered face. "There you are! It's good to see you again, young man." Stepping forward, she took Jude's hand. "We haven't formally met. I'm Hazel."

"Jude." He treated her to a smile. "It's so nice to meet you, Hazel."

"Well, aren't you polite?" she said with a grin. "And a looker, too. Good job, granddaughter." She winked at me and I threw a horrified look her way.

Jude laughed. "I almost feel like you've got a high five coming," he said, and Hazel cocked her head.

"He's right." She raised her hand. "Come on, Kitten, don't leave your grandmother hanging."

"Oh, my God," I muttered, giving my eighty-three year old grandma a high five. "What have I done?"

"Oh, pssh," Hazel said, her brown eyes twinkling. "Come on in, you two. Dinner is about ready."

It smelled glorious inside Hazel's apartment. Like grilled cheese and homemade chicken soup heaven. "Mmm," I groaned, following her into the kitchen. "Do you need help with anything?"

"No, no," she said. "Why don't you give your boy a tour of the place? I'm sure I've got a photo album or two we could show him."

"Don't you dare," I said under my breath, my eyes widening. Hazel had good, solid proof of my nerdiness from ages nine to fifteen. Proof I'd rather not show Jude. I had a reputation to maintain, dammit.

"Calm down." Hazel patted my cheek. "I would never. At least not while you're awake."

"Oh, so your plan is to stuff me so full of delicious food that I pass out, and while I'm in a food coma, you'll reveal my embarrassing and traumatizing childhood to the hot guy I brought with me?"

"Exactly," Hazel said. "How does that sound, Jude?"

Oh, right. He was standing right behind me.

"Sounds great. Especially the part about Cat's embarrassing and traumatizing childhood. We should do that."

I shot him an evil look, which only made him laugh. "Let's go take a tour." I grabbed his arm and lead him out of the kitchen. "You're an ass," I said once we were out of earshot.

"What?" he asked, his eyes widening. "I'm just being polite."

"Right, sure you are." I pointed straight ahead. "Look, that's the living room. Bathroom is down there. A couple of bedrooms, and whatever. There's your tour."

"I think you missed your calling as a tour guide," he said, trying and failing to look sincere. "Tell me again. What's this room right here?" About three steps into the living room, he paused. "Huh," he said, and I turned to see what had caught his interest.

A wall full of picture frames greeted me and I winced, moving past them. "Have you seen the chair yet? It's a good chair."

Jude grabbed my hand and pulled me back to him. "Is this you?" He pointed to a picture of a grinning fire-haired ten-year-old sandwiched between a much younger Hazel and Zeke.

"Yep." I crossed my arms over my chest and stared at the faded area rug.

"You look like Hazel."

"Thanks." I laughed. "But that's not really possible." I moved into the living room and plopped down on the couch.

"What do you mean?" Jude sat beside me and I glanced over, feeling very much like I'd been stripped naked.

"I...Hazel's my step-grandma. Or, she used to be. Until my mom divorced Hazel's son. Now, she's just my Hazel." I shrugged and studied my frayed jeans.

"So the guy in that other picture. He's your stepdad?"

I flinched. "Arthur. Yeah. We don't talk anymore."

"Why not?"

The whole story sat on the tip of my tongue, waiting to dive out. The hurt I'd felt when Arthur left. The wound that he'd reopened when he showed up at the restaurant that day. How he'd stopped by the other night to offer his condolences. It was all *right there*.

I blinked, my eyes suddenly burning. I stood before Jude noticed. Before I could say another word. "I'm going to see if Hazel needs help."

But I didn't go to the kitchen. I ducked into the hall and sagged against the wall, taking deep, slow breaths. If he had prodded, I knew I would have told him more. And I couldn't have that. I'd spent years building up the wall between me and the rest of the world. That dude out there...he didn't even have to *try* and I wanted to spill my secrets.

That's it, I thought, pushing away from the wall to go help Hazel. *This has got to end.*

———

"SO, HOW DID YOU TWO meet?" Hazel asked as we settled in at the table a while later. Her brown eyes landed on my face, filled with curiosity. Not surprising, really. I had never brought a guy over for Hazel to meet. *Historic* didn't quite cover it.

"I...uh..." I stammered. I couldn't really tell my grandmother that I met this guy at the club, went home with him and screwed his brains out. And continued to do so for months.

No, Grandma Hazel would not approve.

Luckily, Jude jumped in. "I work for a local radio station," he said as he sat his sandwich down. "And Cat's company had an event party—the one millionth issue or something—and they just so happened to have the party the same night I was doing a show at the club."

I reached for my wine glass to hide my smile. *Nice save.*

"I'd been having a bad day," he continued, and my eyes shot to him. Oh, so he wasn't done. "Real rough one. I'm talking cranky, foulmouthed, and generally unpleasant to be around."

"Now, I find that hard to believe," Hazel chimed in, passing him a smile. "You're positively charming."

"Thank you." Jude laughed—and blushed—and my insides got a little mushy. Dammit. "But I assure you, there was nothing charming about me on this day." He looked at me. "And Cat noticed."

My eyes narrowed. Was he still making this up?

His lips twitched. He knew I couldn't tell.

"I'd been minding my own business, when Cat marched up to me and said..."

I've been watching you all night, I'd said. *And you're real cute. But—*

I straightened in my seat as the memory wriggled free.

"'Your sad sack face is bringing me down,'" he said.

Across from him, Hazel let out an incredulous sound. A laugh spilled from my lips. "I did not say that!"

"Oh, you did." Amusement danced in his eyes. "You definitely did."

"All right, all right." I waved my grilled cheese through the air. "*Maybe.*"

Hazel leaned in, entranced. She loved a good story. And, the way Jude was telling it, this was a *really* good one. "What happened next?"

Jude sat back in his seat, his gaze holding mine. "She declared that it was her mission to cheer me up."

The details rushed in. Jude, mopey and unsmiling. Me, watching from a distance. I'd seen him before, admired him from afar, but we never spoke. He was always too busy, too surrounded by other girls, too...everything. But then, that night...

"How'd she do it?" Hazel crushed a handful of crackers into her soup. "How'd she cheer you up?"

Jude looked my way, his cheek dimpling. It came into complete focus then. The pulsating music, the sweaty, riled-up crowd, the chill of my glass against my fingertips. Jude's eyes drinking me in, warming me from the inside out. The challenge I'd issued before walking away.

I leaned in, our gazes locking across the table. "Keep your eyes on me."

The warmth in his smile sent chills over my skin. "Yeah."

I turned to Hazel. "Every time he caught my eye for the rest of the night, it was my mission to make him laugh." Hazel's eyes twinkled as she looked between us. I kept talking. "Whether it was a wave or a smile, or—"

"One of these—" Jude stuck out his tongue and held his hands up to his head, making moose antlers.

I laughed and grabbed his hand, killing his moose impression. He let his fingers tangle with mine, a smile clinging to his mouth. "It worked." His eyes warmed, and my heart tripped over itself. "By the end of the night, I was significantly less cranky."

Hazel laughed, and I yanked my hand from his. "Oh, that's adorable!" she said. "What'd you do next?"

We went back to his place, where I fucked his brains out.

"We went out for pancakes and talked all night."

I took a long sip of wine to drown my laugh.

"I must say, I love middle-of-the-night pancakes." Hazel dunked her sandwich into her steaming bowl of soup, looking my way. "Your grandpa and I used to spent all our time at that all night diner in Hope Falls." Her gaze drifted briefly to a far away place, and I stomped down the immediate and traumatizing question: did Hazel realize that *pancakes* was code for...

"So, tell me, Jude." Hazel tossed her napkin onto the table. "Do you like melodrama and sex?"

That. Did she know *pancakes* was code for that?

Jude opened his mouth, but nothing came out. I buried my face in my hands, partly amused, partly disturbed.

Thankfully, Hazel put us both out of our misery fast. *"Until the End of Time."*

"Oh. Oh, yeah." Jude tilted his chair back. "I mean, what is this show you speak of? I'm a manly man. I watch NASCAR and...football, and hockey." He pounded his chest and pushed out his bottom lip. "Me caveman."

"Please." I laughed and pushed away from the table, shoving off any lingering warmth Jude's story time had foisted upon me. "Hazel, don't let him fool you. He's a total soap opera junkie."

"Well, I think that's very manly," Hazel said, getting up. "It takes a very secure man to admit he's into such things."

"Oh, well in that case," Jude said with a smile. "Can you believe the whole Loretta and Lorenzo thing? I mean, that poor guy. Why would she fake her own death just when he had fallen in love with her?"

"Well, the thing you must understand about Loretta," Hazel replied, her eyes lit. "Is that everything is about her. She killed Otha and didn't want to go to prison, and so she staged that horrific death and let poor Lorenzo mourn for her for months..."

The two of them talked business while we cleared the table. Who knew there was so much to debate about Loretta's character? I'd always just thought she was a skeezy skank, but apparently she had *layers*.

Once the table was cleaned up, we headed into the living room. In a not-so-subtle move, Hazel took my usual spot, leaving the couch empty for Jude and me.

I shot her a dirty look and took the corner furthest from her. Jude plopped down in the middle. I felt suddenly like an awkward high-schooler on a chaperoned date.

Not gonna work, I telepathed to her. *I've already made up my mind.*

21: Charlotte's Cobweb

"Thank you for a delicious dinner, Hazel," Jude said a while later.

"Oh, you're welcome, dear." She leaned forward and gave his hand a squeeze. "And thank *you* for your eye-opening insight on Loretta's character."

I fought back a snicker. All evening, the two of them paused the show periodically to discuss scenes and dialogue and even acting chops. I had to admit, it was kind of cute.

"Do you need any help cleaning up?" Jude leaned forward, eyes steady on Hazel. He was good at that—making you feel like you were the only one in the room. And Hazel definitely noticed.

"Oh, no," she said, a soft flush filling her cheeks. "I can take care of it."

"You sure? I don't mind."

Casting a quick glance my way, Hazel reconsidered. "Actually...you're quite tall. Can I ask you for a favor?"

He grinned—the knock-a-girl's-shoes-off kind of grin—and said, "Anything for you."

A girlish giggle escaped Hazel's lips. Sitting back in her chair, she pointed toward the dining room. "There's a pesky cobweb in the corner I haven't been able to get to. Do you mind?"

I snorted, then covered my mouth with my hand. *Really, Hazel?*

"You got it." Jude stood and I lounged in his place, watching as Hazel directed him to the dust rag and cleaner.

"You're shameless," I said to her as she settled back into her seat.

"There's a very important lesson to be learned here, Kitten." I peeked out of one eye and she finished. "I'm not as limber as I used to be, but I can still take advantage of a man like *that*."

"Hazel!"

"What?" She laughed. "One of us ought to."

"Uh, Cat?" Jude called from the next room before I could further chastise my grandmother. "Can you come here for a second?"

Pushing myself off the couch, I ignored Hazel's wink and headed into the dining room. "What's up?"

Jude stood in the middle of the room, dust rag in one hand, spray can in the other, horror on his face. "I don't mean to alarm you," he started. "But that cobweb is...uh...inhabited."

"Okay." I glanced toward the far corner, where he'd managed to clear away most of the dusty web mess. "Enlighten me."

"Spider." His eyes doubled in size. "Huge, disgusting spider."

"Oh." Squinting, I moved closer. Sure enough, a hairy black thing crept lower on the wall. "Yuck."

Without another word, I headed into the kitchen.

"Wh-where are you going?" Jude called behind me.

"You and Charlotte look like you could use some alone time," I said as I took another couple steps backward.

"Wait, what?" he asked, his voice hitching up a notch. "Uh...Charlotte really isn't my type."

"Just keep your eye on her for two seconds," I called back. Once in the kitchen, I searched the cupboard. With a triumphant fist pump, I headed back into the dining room to find Jude still stuck to the floor.

"I got this," I said to him, tiptoeing over to the spider, which hadn't moved an inch. I put the plastic dish I'd scrounged up close to it and waited as it crawled in. Then, I covered the dish with its lid and went back into the kitchen.

I could feel Jude's wary eyes on me as I leaned over the sink and cracked open the window.

Once the little terror was set free, I returned to the dining room and found a sheepish look on Jude's face. It was so stinking cute, I wanted to punch him. "All gone," I said, waving my empty hands in the air.

"I promise, someone tries to burgle you or get frisky, I've got you. I just...don't do bugs."

I laughed. "No worries, man," I said, bumping my shoulder into him. "Now. What do you say you finish up that dusting?"

He looked at the corner, wary. "Okay, but if I find another spider, I'm out."

———————————

"SO THAT WAS HAZEL," Jude said as we reached my car a while later. He'd finished dusting without incident, and we said our goodbyes to Hazel and walked downstairs in silence.

I hit the Unlock button on my keys, and he opened the driver's side door for me. "Yep."

"You're a lot like her." He draped his arm over the open car door. "Feisty, funny...flirty."

I laughed. "I'm so sorry about that! I didn't think she'd be so blatant."

He shrugged, lips tilting in a cute little smirk. "I figure, I've got a backup now. You know, since we're just friends." Pushing away from the car, he headed to the passenger side. "I'm even thinking about proposing."

I climbed into the car and pulled the door shut. Jude got in beside me and I looked over, momentarily caught off guard by his closeness. "You can try, but I don't think Hazel's the marrying kind."

"Something else you two have in common, huh?" He shifted away from me and pulled on his seatbelt. "What a shame."

I let the comment slide into the darkness and started the car. As we pulled onto the road, I glanced over. "It was really nice of you to help clean up."

After the Spider Incident, Jude had volunteered to wash dishes as Hazel and I tidied up the kitchen. As we cleaned, I stayed quiet, just listening to them talk—about food, soap operas, family...everything.

I let it all swirl around me, valiantly trying to remain unaffected. But then my mind drifted back to the dinner table, and Jude's retelling of how we met.

How had I forgotten?

No, I *knew* how I'd forgotten. Because it hadn't mattered. We were never supposed to see each other again. We *definitely* weren't supposed to sleep together again.

Time had passed and I'd moved on, but the moment I saw him again two years later...well, I needed to feel his touch again.

And we'd tumbled headfirst into this long, satisfying, rule-breaking thing.

I wanted to regret it. I wanted to *end* it. But as I watched Jude hug Hazel goodbye a while later—a real, genuine hug—everything inside me begged to reconsider.

"Don't let this one get away," Hazel had whispered to me when it was my turn for goodbyes. Almost as if she'd been reading my thoughts. Before I could say a word, she patted me on the cheek and said goodnight.

Now, with the streetlights illuminating Jude's profile, his presence filling up the small cab of my car, I wondered if Hazel was right. Maybe I was being hasty earlier, thinking it was time to break things off.

"I had a really good time," Jude said as we pulled to a stop outside my building. "Thank you for letting me meet your Hazel."

I smiled through the chaos inside me. "You're welcome."

His fingers hovered over the seatbelt release, his eyes lingering on mine. In my mind, I watched him get out of the car, mount his bike, and drive away. It'd be so easy to put an end to things then, when he wasn't sitting in front of me. It'd be so easy to repair the damage he'd caused to my protective wall.

But that wasn't what I wanted. What I wanted was Jude in my life.

In whatever way I could get him.

"Well, goodnight, Cat." He reached for the door handle but I stopped him with a hand on his arm.

"So, hey." Words tumbled from me like clumsy toddlers on a sugar high. "Next weekend. My friend is getting married. Tierney. You met her. She likes you."

"That's awesome." Jude's brows furrowed. "Tell her I said congrats."

"Yeah, I will." I gulped in a breath. "Anyway. You wanna go?"

He blinked and I rushed to continue. "As friends, of course. You want to go to Tierney's wedding as my friend? There'll be cake."

A smile cracked through the darkness. "Well, if there's going to be cake."

22: Bitches Get Handsy

———

"**Y**ou don't have to come if you don't want to," I said for the billionth time the following weekend. My car was parked in front of Jude's apartment, where he stood, overnight bag in hand.

The wedding wasn't until Sunday, but as I'd been asking Jude to go last week, it hit me that this wedding was a weekend shindig. There was a last-minute get-shit-ready party tonight, rehearsal dinner tomorrow and then the wedding Sunday evening. All of that came out in one babbling, nonsensical sentence, and the next thing I knew, he was agreeing to come to June Lake with me. For the whole weekend.

What the hell had I done?

"I mean, you can just meet me in June Lake on Sunday, and go to the wedding. The rest of it...you don't need to be there. In fact, you'll probably be bored out of your mind. Not to mention, you don't know anybody. And, man, small towns are weird. The people there..."

"Cat, stop." Jude stood in front of me, shushing me with a look. "It's fine. I knew what I was getting into when I agreed to come. Besides," he said with a grin. "I'm from a small town, remember? I know how weird they can be."

"If you're sure..." I raised a skeptical brow.

"I'm sure." He tossed his bag in the backseat and stood to face me. "Let's talk about what's really bugging you here. You thought I was going to change my mind, and now you're second-guessing the whole thing. I mean, this feels an awful lot like a date, right? That's gotta be freaking you out."

I sagged against the car, releasing a huge breath. "You have *no* idea. I already want to jump out of the car on our way out of town."

"Tuck and roll, baby," he said, opening the car door. "We're just friends, right? Two friends going to a wedding together." He paused long enough to smirk my way. "As friends."

"Okay, okay." I shoved him—or tried to. The dude was like a tree. Didn't even budge. "I get it."

He smiled. "Good. Now, we better get going if we're going to make it to that party on time."

I dug the keys out of my pocket and rounded the car. "Driver picks the music," I said, grinning. "Hope you like boy bands."

Jude's eyes widened. "Please tell me you've got *Boy Toyz*"

"It frightens me on so many levels that you even know who they are." I shuddered as he got in the car next to me. "Your man card has been revoked."

"I didn't realize I had gotten it back after the spider incident," he replied, pulling on his seatbelt.

"Eh. Spiders are creepy. I get it." I turned on the radio and glanced his way. "Just don't sing along. *That* damage cannot be undone."

"Duly noted." He crossed his arms over his chest and stared out the window, pouting like a kindergartener as the music filled the space between us. From the corner of my eye, I could see his fingers tapping along with the beat.

I fought the smile pulling at the corners of my mouth and focused my eyes straight ahead. We got about three miles down the road when I caved. "*Fine*. Go for it."

Jude grinned at me and then cranked the volume on the next song, a super cheesy number about a girl who didn't know she was beautiful.

Any control I had was gone in that moment. I laughed as he did a not-so-bad impression of the lead singer's falsetto, and then I started to sing along, too.

This trip might not be so scary after all.

———————

THE LAST MINUTE GET-shit-done party was at Tierney's parents' house. Amid all the other wedding-y stuff, a few tiny tasks had fallen through the cracks. It was Tierney's mom's idea to host a get-together to wrap everything up. We'd spend the evening finishing centerpieces or whatever.

I was staying in Tier's old room back at the house, but before we headed over, we stopped at the motel to get Jude checked in.

When I pulled into the Chandlers' driveway, I turned to Jude. "Okay, fair warning: Tierney's mom is..." I paused, searching for the right words. "A handful. And by handful, I mean, she'll probably grope you."

Jude grinned. "If you think I can't handle a little groping, clearly you've never paid attention to the Saturday night crowd at Tryst. I've been touched, squeezed, stroked, fondled..."

"All right. I get it. Bitches get handsy," I muttered, fighting off the flicker of white-hot envy biting at me. Friends did *not* get jealous. "And so will Tierney's mom." With that, I got out of the car and opened the hatchback.

Laughing, Jude joined me at the back of the car. I yanked my bag out of the car and dropped it at his feet, narrowly missing his toes, which did nothing to kill his amusement.

"Cat, sweetheart!" Tierney's mom called from the doorway. "It's *so* good to see you! How have you...who's this?" Charla Chandler, a near mirror image of her gorgeous daughter, with dark curls and curves to die for, stopped cold in front of Jude, eyes drinking him in.

I turned to find Jude holding my suitcase in front of him like a shield, his eyes widened in mock-terror. Laughter burst from my lips as I reached out to lower the suitcase. "This is Jude," I said, struggling to keep a straight face.

Jude stepped forward, hand extended. "Nice to meet you, Mrs..." he trailed off, glancing at me.

Chandler, I mouthed.

"Mrs. Chandler," he finished, taking her hand.

"Call me Charla," she said, giving Jude a coquettish look. "Cat didn't tell me she was bringing someone with her." Call-Me-Charla was the nicest woman ever—right behind Hazel. She adored her husband, but boy did she like to flirt.

"Last minute change of plans," I jumped in. "Don't worry, though. He's all checked in at the motel."

"That's probably for the best, dear," she said, leading us to the stairs. "I doubt there would have been enough room on that futon for..." Her gray eyes roved over Jude, from top to bottom. "All that."

"That's what I figured." We followed Charla up the stairs, to my temporary quarters. "Thanks again for letting me crash here." The words rushed from my mouth as I brushed passed her, taking Jude's hand and pulling him into the room.

"Anytime, darling," Charla called behind us. "Tierney should be here soon."

"Don't say I didn't warn you," I said once she disappeared down the stairs.

Jude shuddered. "I feel like I need a shower. And a cigarette."

"You might want to get both those things now." I peeked out the second story window. "Because it's about to get a lot worse."

He joined me in time to see a long line of chattering females enter the house. Eyes wide, he looked back at me. "What have you done?"

23: Sugar Seduction

J ude had reason to be scared.

Women got weird during wedding season. If you added in the small town thing, factored in Jude's eligibility, and, well, that face of his...I'd basically sentenced him to an evening of inappropriate fawning and overly enthusiastic come-ons.

At first, I was amused as a tiny, shriveled woman named Dottie sidled in nice and close to him and batted her geriatric eyes. "Tell me, honey," she said. "Are you into older women?"

I sat across from them, putting the finishing touches on a centerpiece comprised of carnival prizes, unable to hide my amusement.

He cleared his throat and eased ever so slightly away from her. Catching my eye, he raised his brows. *Help. Me.* his expression said.

Sorry, I mouthed, tearing apart prize tickets.

"My apologies, dear," Dottie said as she caught our exchange. "Is this your fellow?"

"Oh, no." I waved her off with a wink. "He's not taken."

If bringing him here in the first place was my first mistake, my second was telling Dottie he was single.

The moment the younger crowd caught wind, all my amusement disappeared. Especially when some lip-glossed harpy stole Dottie's seat when she got up. Her exceedingly manicured fingertips brushed against Jude's knee as she leaned in to whisper something to him.

On the other side, a cute blond sent furtive glances his way, her cheeks pinkening. I'd bet anything that after her first wine cooler, she'd have a hand on his knee, too.

But it didn't matter, I reminded myself. We were friends. He could talk to whomever he wanted. He could flirt with whomever he wanted. He could take anyone back to his motel room and—

I stood abruptly, dropping the centerpiece I'd been working on to the table. "I'll be right back."

No one even looked up as I left the room, heading straight for the kitchen. Taking a deep breath, I leaned against the wall and closed my eyes. Mistakes were made. I shouldn't have brought him here. I shouldn't have believed we could do this. I shouldn't—

"You okay?"

I opened my eyes to find Jack standing on the other side of the kitchen island.

I huffed out a breath and shoved my hair out of my face. "Yeah. Fine," I said, ignoring the stupid tears that had filled my eyes.

Seeing the tears, Jack came around the counter. "Here, sit," he said, his blue eyes narrowed—with concern or fear, I couldn't really tell. But it looked more like fear. I would probably be a little scared if a crying girl showed up out of nowhere, too.

"Sorry, I don't mean to interr—" I said as he closed the kitchen door behind him. "I just...I just need a...um...is that pie?" I trailed off, eyes falling to the counter.

"It is." Jack was right behind me. "Have a seat. I'll grab you a piece."

I climbed onto one of the stools at the counter and watched him slice into a gorgeous cherry pie.

"Thank you," I said as he sat the pie in front of me.

"It's a bit crazy out there, huh?" He wiped his hands on a dishtowel. "That's why I'm hiding out in here."

I nodded, distracted by the explosion of sweet and tart on my tongue. "I'm, like, ninety-nine percent sure Tierney is with you for this pie," I mumbled.

"Well, that and the cookies." He moved to the stove. I watched him from the corner of my eye as he pulled a sheet of cookies from the oven, then got another batch ready to go in. "I have no illusions."

I dropped my fork and leaned forward. "D-did you say cookies?"

Without answering, he crossed to the fridge and pulled out a carton of milk, then grabbed a glass from the cupboard. Then, he put a plate of two cookies in front of me. I slid the empty pie plate away and inhaled the sweet aroma.

"Mmm," I sighed. "You're the best."

His lips tilted in a crooked grin. "Thanks. That's a new recipe. Maple pecan. Let me know what you think," he said, turning to mix the batter for another batch.

"You don't have to ask me twice," I said, already shoving a cookie into my mouth. My eyes widened as the flavors revealed themselves. Sweet and salty and heaven-sent. "Oh, God," I groaned. "Are you trying to seduce me?"

Jack stopped mid-stir and looked at me, puzzlement scrawled all over his face. "N-no," he said slowly.

I raised an eyebrow and picked up another cookie. "Are you sure about that? Because this here," I wiggled the cookie, "is what I like to call Cat-nip."

A smile slid onto Jack's lips. "You caught me. Secretly, my type is sugared-up redheads with crazy eyes."

Laughing, I took a sip of milk. "Well, it ain't gonna work, buddy, but that doesn't mean you have to stop trying." I slid my now-empty plate toward him and waggled my brows.

"You're shameless," he said, but he dropped another cookie onto my plate anyway.

"And you're my favorite," I replied with a grin as I took a bite.

I ate my cookie while Jack continued working. Laughter and chatter drifted in from the next room. I ignored it, ignored thoughts of Jude sitting between two women fawning over him like a piece of meat. Ignored the heavy, hot feeling inside my chest.

He's not mine, I reminded myself. *He's not mine, and that's what I wanted.*

But was it?

My heart stuttered and I dropped the rest of my cookie onto the plate and pushed it away. I *liked* him. I liked his smile and his arms and his own special brand of goofy and—

"Want to talk about it?" Jack asked, jolting me from my thoughts.

I looked up to find him standing across from me. He had his eyes trained on the cookie sheets in front of him, but I could tell he was paying attention.

Sitting back in my seat, I crossed my arms over my chest and sighed. "I don't know."

"Fair enough," he said, glancing at me. "Want another cookie?"

I liked this dude. He wasn't pushy *and* he supplied sweets. "Chocolate chip?"

"Coming right up." He swung around and grabbed a couple still-warm cookies from the far counter then dropped them onto my plate.

"Still not getting into my pants, though," I mumbled, stuffing a whole cookie into my mouth.

"Oh, darn," he muttered, his face deadpan. "You have crushed my dreams." The timer dinged on his latest batch and he turned to get them.

I studied Jack as I chewed, the wheels in my mind turning. He loved Tierney. Tierney loved him. Clearly, since they were getting married the day after tomorrow. How did that work? What would Tierney do if he pulled an Arthur? How would she survive that?

Recalling the way he'd looked at her my last visit, how his eyes warmed with absolute adoration, I had my answer: she wouldn't have to survive, because it'd never happen.

"You're not going anywhere, are you?"

The question fell from my lips before I realized that, to a normal person not inside my wild, junk heap head, it didn't make any sense.

Jack stopped what he was doing and cocked an eyebrow. "You've had too much sugar. I'm cutting you off," he said, reaching for my plate.

I caught his hand with my ninja-like reflexes. "Don't you dare," I snarled and he put both hands up in surrender. Once my cookies were no longer being threatened, I continued, hoping to make more sense. "What I meant was, in my experience, everyone leaves. Aren't you worried you'll wake up one day and change your mind? Or that Tierney will change hers? Aren't you scared you'll get hurt?"

Jack sat his spatula down and tilted his head, seeming to consider my question. I watched as he made the trek back to the fridge. He poured himself a glass of milk then grabbed a couple chocolate chip cookies and joined me at the counter, taking the seat next to me.

He broke a cookie in half and dunked it into his milk as he pondered. "That's a risk you always take with relationships, both romantic and not," he finally said. "It's like this." He took my hand and made a fist. "You can live like this, small and closed off, but at some point, you're going to get tired from the effort it takes to maintain that."

I watched as he opened my hand and continued. "But if you open yourself up, let other people in, it's easier. You run the risk of getting hurt, of course, but you also open yourself up to a lot of good things." With that, he dropped a cookie into my palm and grinned.

"At least that's how I look at it," he continued. "And with Tierney, of course there's a chance of getting hurt. I mean, have you met her? She could very possibly snap and kill me in my sleep one night."

I laughed and Jack raised an eyebrow. "It's cute how you think I'm kidding." He took a drink of his milk, then added, "I guess what love really is, is trusting someone enough to *not* kill you in your sleep."

I studied him for a few seconds before tearing my eyes from his. "Huh," I said as I took his words in. "Huh."

"Glad I could clear things up for you," Jack said with a smile, getting up from his seat. He laid a hand on my shoulder as he passed me, and I returned his smile.

I studied the cookie in my hand, the wheels turning in my mind. If I stopped being so closed off, I'd open myself up to lots of good things. Like cookies.

And sweet guys with dimples...

Maybe Jack had a point.

Taking a bite of the cookie, I hopped off the stool and headed back into the living room. Bitches were gonna stop getting handsy.

24: Donuts & Airplanes

———

"Well, that was interesting," I said as we drove back to the motel a while later.

"Yep." Jude glanced out the window. A passing streetlight illuminated his face.

After my talk with Jack, I'd gone back into the living room and planted myself squarely between Jude and his latest admirer. "Hi, I'm Cat," I said, extending my hand.

She blinked her giant blue eyes and took it. "Lola," she said. "Can we help you?"

I wiggled deeper into the couch, ignoring the sparks shooting down every inch of the leg that came into contact with Jude's. How long had it been since we'd been this close?

Didn't matter.

"Well, see, there's a bit of misinformation being passed around tonight." I linked my arm through Jude's and smiled. "This guy here? He came with me."

"Oh." Lola blinked. "I'm sorry. I was told he was single."

"Yeah." I leaned my head against his shoulder. "We had a wee little fight on our way here. But we have since realized that we just can't bear to be apart." Tilting my head up, I batted my eyes at Jude. "Isn't that right, schnookums?"

Jude's lips twitched, but he stayed solemn. "It sure is, pookie." He dropped a kiss on my forehead, then sent Lola an apologetic smile. "I'm sorry. I should have told you."

With an outraged squeak, Lola stood and tossed her long, dark hair over her shoulder. On the other side of Jude, the cute blond gave a timid smile and followed Lola from the room.

"Sorry," I said once they were gone. Sliding over, I put some much-needed distance between us. "I mean, if you wanted to make out with her, you could have—"

"No, no." He rubbed a hand over his face. "You showed up just in time. She spent the entire time you were gone talking about her soon-to-be ex-husband, and how he 'just didn't fulfill her needs.'" Shuddering, he peeked through his fingers at me. "Hard pass."

Now, back in the car, I wanted to reach over and cover Jude's hand with mine, to reclaim that closeness we'd had briefly back there. I wanted that more than anything. And yet both hands remained tight on the steering wheel.

Jude reached over and my heart skipped and then sunk as he turned on the radio.

Stupid heart.

The music did little to drown out the thoughts in my head. I sighed and shifted in my seat, pressing on the gas. I needed to get out of this car as soon as possible.

"You're speeding," Jude murmured, his voice soft.

I glanced at him, then back to the road. "Sorry." I let off the gas.

And then we fell back into heavy silence.

"So," I said after a few minutes. "That girl was on you like a drunk chick on prom night."

"I don't know." Jude turned the radio down just a smidge. "My prom night wasn't nearly that terrifying."

I laughed. "Oh, yeah?"

"Yeah." He shifted in his seat so that he was leaning my way. "A bunch of us rented a limo, then hung out at the all-night diner in Hope Falls after. It was a good time."

"Huh." I glanced over. "Mine sucked."

"Why?"

I peeked his way, a smirk on my lips. "Little known fact," I said, inching the volume even further down. "I was a nerd in high school. Big ol' nerd. Chess club, debate team, Mathletes."

"No way."

I laughed. "Yes way. When prom night came around, I was dateless. Ended up driving a couple of the kids from Chess Club from prom to some skeevy motel. There was a lot of gross, geeky making out in the backseat that night, and I had no part in it." I shrugged. "For the best. Brett Rink was *so* gross."

"Huh. Never would've guessed that," Jude said, and I could feel his eyes on me.

"What about you?" I turned the car left. We were nearing the motel, and just when Jude and I had worked passed the weird silence. Figured.

"Me? I...uh..."

"Let me guess: all-star football player, prom king, voted Most Popular?"

"Yeah," he sighed. "Except it was basketball."

"Gah! A *jock!*" I groaned.

"What's wrong with jocks?"

"Nothing, except you were the bane of my existence in high school." I glanced over. "Name calling, pranks, humiliation. You guys are assholes."

"Hey, hey, hey. I may have been a jock, but I was *not* an asshole. I'm a nice guy."

"Eh." I waved him off, feeling weirdly vulnerable. I didn't talk to anyone about this. "You're all right."

"Thanks. And for the record, I'm sure you were a very cute nerd."

A smile pulled at my lips and I gave in to it, stopping at the corner to look over at him. His teeth flashed white in the dark. "Thank you. I really wasn't, though. Braces, frizzy hair, glasses...I was a mess."

"Doubtful."

I smiled back and turned into the motel parking lot. "Your palace awaits, sir."

Jude shifted in his seat and cleared his throat, making a show of undoing his seatbelt. He gripped the door handle, then pulled back. "So..." he started, drumming his fingers against the handle. "Want to come in? For a bit?"

My breath quickened. *No,* I thought. *Bad idea.* But when I looked over at him, with the streetlight shining in, catching the hopeful glint in his eyes, I heard Jack's voice in my head. *When you open your-self up, good things happen.*

Well, I was ready for something good.

Turning off the car, I smiled. "Sure."

———————————

TWO HOURS LATER, WE found ourselves sitting cross-legged across from each other on Jude's bed, a spoil of vending machine treasures between us, as we talked. Just talked. About everything from traumatizing high school experiences—like marching band for me, when they tried to teach me the tuba and I could barely lift the thing, to Jude's first girlfriend dumping him in the school cafeteria in front of everyone.

Conversation shifted after that. I tore open a package of powdered donuts and held it out to him. "So," I said, glancing around the room. "You ready for the rest of this jungle-circus-wedding thing?"

Jude shrugged, chewing then swallowing his donut. "I think it's nice. I mean, a whole weekend to celebrate two people promising to spend forever together. But I'm a sap. Don't mind me." He took another donut and shoved it into his mouth, leaving powdered sugar on his lips. I wanted to kiss it away.

"H-have you," I started, tearing my eyes away from his mouth to pick at the nail polish on my thumbnail. "I mean, the only thing I've ever been in love with is this donut." I held it up for Jude to see and then popped it into my mouth.

Stupid, I thought as I chewed. I'd just been about to ask the stupidest thing ever.

He rubbed the back of his hand over his mouth, removing any trace of sugar, and I stared, disappointed. "Have I ever been in love?"

I shrugged and tore my eyes from him. "I could really go for some pizza right about now."

I could see Jude smile from the corner of my eye. I shifted on the bed, shoving the pile of junk food aside to lay my head on the pillow. I didn't want to have this conversation. Not one cell in my body wanted to talk about this.

Except for one cell. One pesky little cell somewhere around my heart that was just *dying* to know the answer to the question: Had Jude ever been in love?

Jude laid down facing me, his eyes meeting mine. "Once," he said, unflinching.

For some reason, my stomach sank, cold and heavy. I closed my eyes, counted to five, then opened them. "Huh," I said, hoping my voice didn't betray the tornado of stupid, dumb emotions that tore through me.

What did it matter if Jude had been in love? It wasn't like I wanted him to fall in love with me. Quite the opposite, actually. He needed to run. Far, far away.

"What was it like?"

The question fell from my lips before I could stop it. My eyes found his again and I swallowed tightly, bringing my hands up to tuck under my cheek. My heart rattled around my chest like a restless bird in a cage as I waited for Jude to answer.

He seemed to think about it for an eternity. Seconds ticked by on the clock, the only sound that filled the room. Finally, he took a breath and answered.

"Like jumping out of an airplane, not sure whether your parachute will open. You see the ground coming right at you, and you know that if you pull that cord and nothing happens...*splat*. But if it opens, if the other person feels the same, it's like you're flying, above everything. You're invincible. Because that person loves you back." He stopped, clearing his throat. "Or something like that."

I closed my eyes, picturing it. Me, jumping out of a plane, pulling the ripcord, praying hard for my chute to open.

"Jesus, that sounds terrifying," I whispered. "Why would you want to do that to yourself?"

I could feel Jude shrug. "You either jump and risk it or sit on the plane all by yourself."

I let that linger in the air, too afraid to ponder it. My eyes remained closed, and I just listened. Listened to the sound of Jude breathing, slow and steady, to the beat of my heart and his, like a lullaby.

"What happened?" I whispered sleepily, snuggling in closer. "With the one?"

Jude sighed heavily and rolled onto his back. I opened one eye and watched him stare at the ceiling. "We got divorced."

"Wait, you were *married*?" This new tidbit rendered me cold with shock. "How did I not know this?"

"We haven't really done a lot of talking thus far." There was a smile in his voice, with a touch of something else. Regret, maybe? Sadness?

"Right, right. Continue." I closed the distance between us and rested my head in the crook of his shoulder, my cheek against his chest. His arm closed around me and I sighed, warm and cozy.

"We met in college, dated all throughout," he continued, his voice vibrating against my cheek. "We were married for five years."

The powdered donuts turned to rocks in my stomach. I didn't like where this was going. "What happened?"

"She fell out of love."

He said it so bluntly. Matter of fact. But below the words, a not-quite-forgotten hurt simmered. "Woke up one day and realized the life we'd planned wasn't what she wanted anymore. At least not with me."

"God," I whispered, tears prickling behind my eyelids. I closed them so he couldn't see. "I don't even know what to say to that."

"You don't have to say anything," Jude said, his fingers brushing my hair away from my face. "It happens. Sometimes you jump and it doesn't work out. But you pick yourself up and you try again."

As he said that, I thought of my mother. Of all the times she'd hit the ground with a *splat*, and all the times she'd gotten back up to try again. I wasn't sure if that made her brave or stupid.

"What about you?" Jude asked, his voice quiet, his hand gentle in my hair. "What's your story, darling, daring Cat?"

"Not much to tell," I said, burying my face in his t-shirt. "I've never been in love. Never even been close."

"Why not?"

It was such a simple question. Just two tiny words that shot right through me like arrows to the heart.

What could I say? Fear? Stubbornness? Independence? What was it, really?

I took a breath, unsure of how I'd answer. When I started to speak, the words were not what I thought they'd be.

"I ever tell you my mother has been married four times?"

"You may have mentioned it," Jude said, his fingers moving from my hair to caress the bare skin of my upper arm. I shivered and nestled closer.

"My dad was her first husband. First-class douche nozzle. I haven't heard from him since they divorced when I was six. I just really remember my mother, lying in bed for days, weeks, maybe months, sad and quiet. I was a kid. I didn't understand why she wouldn't get up and play with me." I shrugged, the memory cutting me to the marrow. I hadn't thought of it in years.

Before Jude could speak, or show sympathy, I continued. "Next divorce came when I was sixteen. That was the hardest. She married Arthur when I was nine, and he was so amazing. He loved me like I was his own, and so did his parents." I smiled softly, thinking of my grandmother. "Hazel is the best thing to come out of my mother's marriage misadventures."

"I'm glad," Jude said, steadily stroking my arm. "I'm glad you have her."

"Me, too." I moved in closer, soaking in as much of Jude's body heat as I could, suddenly freezing. "I don't even know why they divorced. Arthur adored my mother. He adored me. He was a good guy."

"Sometimes, things just don't work out," Jude said, and I knew he was trying to be helpful.

"Yeah, but...she was devastated. It was worse with Arthur than it was with my father. She cried all the time. Stopped eating. Shut down. I was sixteen, and suddenly I was responsible for taking care of my mother. I just..." I cut the sentence short, turning my face into Jude's shirt. "I have never understood what happened between them. Maybe I never will." I moved my hand under Jude's shirt, wrapping my arm around his bare midriff. The skin-on-skin contact soothed the parts of me left jagged by the memories.

A ghost of a voice asked me what I was doing—lying so close to him, telling him things I didn't tell anyone. Was this a good idea? Shouldn't I move? Get in my car and drive away?

I pushed it down and let Jude's arm tighten around me.

"Then, divorce number three," I said, keeping my eyes closed. "Then four. By that time, I didn't even bother getting to know the guys. What was the point? My mother was just going to leave them, any-way."

The next sentence fell out the easiest. I'd been holding it in for almost two months now, never finding the right time to talk to anyone about it. Not Tierney, not Hazel. But, for some reason, now, with Jude, it felt right.

"She's dating Arthur again."

Jude's fingers stilled on my arm. "How do you feel about that?"

The fact that this was his first question...well, I couldn't stop the flash of heat inside my chest. Burrowing in closer, I answered. "It sucks. A lot. Seeing him has brought up all these old memories that I would rather forget."

Jude was quiet, soaking in this new information, probably realizing just how fucked up I really was. Maybe he was planning his escape from the bathroom window.

I wouldn't blame him.

"He's just going to leave again," I said, my body growing heavy with sleep. "They all do."

25: Ferris Wheels & Falling

———

The next day passed in a blur of naps and talking, and daytime TV. Jude and I stayed in his motel room until we were forced to get up and function for Jack and Tierney's rehearsal dinner. We made a quick trip to Tierney's parents' house so that I could pick up my things, then back to the motel to shower and change.

The rehearsal dinner was much less eventful than the night before had been. Probably because there wasn't booze. Afterward, I went with Jude back to his room, where we did nothing but hang out and watch TV.

I could have gone back to the Chandler house, to crash in the spare room, alone. But something had happened last night with Jude. A barrier had fallen. I wasn't ready to put that distance between us again. Distance meant the fear would burrow its way back in. And I rather liked feeling fearless.

If only for a little while.

I crept out of bed the next morning, careful not to wake Jude, who looked so peaceful when he slept it was ridiculous. Gathering my things, I tiptoed to the bathroom and turned on the shower.

The wedding wasn't until later this evening, but there was so much to be done. Tierney had a monopoly on my time, as her Maid of Honor. I would be abandoning Jude for the better part of the day, and I felt sort of bad about that. Hopefully, the residents of this wacky town would take it easy on him.

Once I finished showering and got dressed, I tiptoed back into the room. Jude still slept soundly. I smiled and walked to the door.

About thirty minutes later, I made my way back, breakfast in hand. Junk food was great and all, but something told me that Mr. Six Pack didn't make a habit of binging on such things all the time. And so I'd gone to the diner down the street for something with a little more sustenance.

When I walked in, Jude was awake and sitting up in bed, his chest bare and glorious. My mouth watered, and it had nothing to do with the food I'd brought with me.

"Good morning, sleepy head," I said, kicking the door closed behind me, along with my libido. "I brought breakfast."

"Look at you, Suzy Homemaker," he said, his voice still husky with sleep. I tingled as I moved closer, climbing onto the bed.

"Don't read too much into it, man. I bought it down the street. I can't even boil water."

"That's all right," he said, reaching for the bag. "As long as you know how to dial a phone and use a menu, we should be good."

At the realization that I wanted his words to mean something deeper—something more than this friendship we'd been cultivating—a bolt of terror shot through me.

Jude dispelled it with a single smile, and I joined him on the bed. "So, I got you an egg white omelet—which sounds disgusting, by the way—with whole grain toast."

"Sweet," he said, opening the takeout container. "Thank you."

Once we finished, I turned toward him, an apologetic smile on my face. "So, this is where I leave you. So much wedding to be done."

"I'm a big boy, I'm sure I can entertain myself for a few hours. I'll see you at the wedding later."

———————

I MET TIERNEY AT HER parents' house. She sat in her childhood bedroom, staring off into space when I walked in.

"Hey, Tier." I sat next to her. "What are we looking at?"

"I'm going to be married in, like, seven hours," she said, her voice low, monotone.

"Yes, you are. You lucky broad. That fiancé of yours is *hot*." I smoothed her crazy waves away from her face, sensing that she was on the verge of one of those bride-zilla meltdowns I'd heard so much about.

Back away slowly.

She glanced at me, a wobbly smile on her lips. "Yeah. He is."

"Just think, you get to wake up to that every morning. Pretty cool, right?"

"Right." She looked down, studying the fraying sleeves of her century-old college sweatshirt. Silence stretched over us then, and I waited, sensing there was something else on her mind.

Finally, she spoke. "What if this doesn't work?"

My hand froze. *Shit.* I wasn't equipped to handle this. Where was her mother? Her mother would know the perfect thing to say. I didn't—

"Sometimes, it doesn't work, Cat." Her eyes were still trained straight ahead as she spoke, but she reached for my hand. "Sometimes, people get divorced. What if Jack and I get divorced?" She looked at me then, and tears swam in her bright green eyes.

I squeezed her hand. "You love this guy. I've never seen you so happy. And he clearly adores you. You'll be fine." I said the words I knew I was supposed to say, but they felt hollow coming out of my mouth.

"But what if we aren't?"

Pulling my eyes from hers, I studied our clasped hands. I had to say something. I had to come through for her. I had to comfort her, make her feel better, help her see that taking this leap with Jack was—

"Love is like jumping out of an airplane, Tier." Jude's words echoed in my brain, and I sent him a silent *thanks* as I repeated them back to my best friend. "You don't know if your parachute is going to work, but you have to take the risk." I shrugged, smiled, and warmed at the memory of Jude's breath stirring my hair as he spoke those words to me. "What's the point in staying on that plane all by yourself?"

Tierney's eyes held mine. I could see the wheels turning in her head. Finally, after a few seconds, she nodded. "When did you get so smart?"

"Someone much smarter than me told me that once." Standing, I held my hand out to her. "Now, let's get this show on the road, sister."

―――――――――

HOURS AND A VERY EXHAUSTING list of tasks out of the way, I stood behind Tierney, putting the finishing touches on her hair.

She was the most beautiful bride I'd ever seen, and it wasn't the dress that did it. It was the flush on her cheeks, the glow in her eyes, the smile—the radiant, radiant smile—on her lips. This was a woman in love.

And, for the first time ever, I envied that.

Shoving that thought aside, I weaved cherry blossoms into her dark curls. "Jack isn't going to be able to keep his hands off you," I said as I finished up and stepped back.

Tier took in her reflection, lips curving. "That's the idea."

"The car is downstairs," her mom said, opening the bedroom door. "Your dad is waiting outside."

Tierney and I went downstairs and out the front door, finding Mr. Chandler—a bulky, kind-eyed man, at the car.

"You look beautiful, Pumpkin Patch," he said, holding the door open for Tierney.

She reached up and placed a soft kiss on his cheek. "Thanks, Dad," she whispered, and I looked away, giving them their moment.

A few minutes later, we were on our way.

Beside me, Tierney reached over and took my hand. "I can't believe I'm about to be a married woman," she said, her eyes light with excitement.

"Me, either," I said, and I meant it. All the years we'd spent together, all the bad dates and even worse TV we'd endured, it never really registered that maybe someday Tierney would get married.

I should have known, though. She'd always been wired differently, didn't get as much enjoyment out of the dates and the nights out and the freedom of singlehood. No, she was always meant to settle down.

Along with that thought came a sense of sadness. If she was always meant to settle down, what did that mean for me? Perpetual single girl enjoying the bar scene would get old. Already was, actually. So...lots of late night TV binges and ice cream and probably cats.

I'd be the crazy cat lady.

The car came to a stop before I could explore that line of thinking any further. Good thing, too. It was depressing.

The wedding was being held outside, on the fairgrounds toward the edge of town. There were tents set up toward the back, one for the bride, another for the groom. Beyond that, there was a much larger tent, where the reception would be held. There was also a carousel, a few carnival games, and some food vendors. In the center of it all, stood a Ferris wheel.

I didn't quite get it, but hey, whatever made my best friend happy.

We headed for the bridal tent, where we would spend another indeterminate amount of time gussying up. While Tierney's mom took my place in front of her daughter, checking her makeup, I snuck outside.

I knew the moment I stepped out of the tent that I was looking for Jude. I had arranged for Tierney's brother to pick him up from the motel and bring him to my car so that he could meet me there. I'd glimpsed my car in the parking lot, so I knew he was here somewhere.

My eyes searched the ever-growing sea of people, looking for him and coming up empty. I'd resigned myself to the idea of not seeing him till after the ceremony when someone tapped me on the shoulder.

I spun around to find the most beautiful man I'd ever seen, dressed in a light gray suit, white shirt, no tie. Tierney was right. This guy killed it in a suit.

"H-hi." My skin flushed. "I was just looking for you."

"You found me." He reached down and took a loose strand of my hair between his fingers, tucking it behind my ear. "And you look beautiful."

I looked down at my toes, painted pink and showcased by a pair of simple silver sandals. "Thanks. You, too."

Why did I suddenly feel like a nervous teenager on her first date? That made zero sense. I'd seen this guy naked. A lot. I shouldn't be nervous.

Taking a gulp of air, I lifted my head. "What did you do with yourself all day?"

"You know, the usual." Jude shrugged. "Watched reruns of *Until the End of Time*, ate bon-bons, and painted my toes."

I laughed. "That sounds perfect. Wish I could have been there. I would have painted your toes for you."

"Next time, for sure." He smiled and my heart skipped like a bad CD.

"Looks like things are getting started," he said. "You better get back." And then he leaned down and kissed my cheek, a gentle kiss that shot right through to the center of my being. I stumbled back, surprise zipping through my veins. Before I could respond, he moved toward the crowd. "I'll see you later."

His name found itself on my lips before I could think about it. He turned around, and the early evening sun flowed over him like honey. My throat went dry.

"I, um..." I started, pushing myself forward. "Here." I reached into my hair and pulled out a cherry blossom, tucking it into his lapel. Standing on my tiptoe, I put my lips next to his ear. "Keep your eyes on me."

Before I could retreat, he brought his hand up to rest on my cheek. "That's not going to be a problem," he whispered back, leaning down to press his lips against mine, soft and sweet.

And then he dissolved into the crowd.

I watched until I couldn't see him anymore, then felt behind me for the tent flap, stumbling backward. That kiss shouldn't have done things to me. I'd had much more explicit kisses and felt less. But—

"Mom, no. I'm not wearing a veil." Tierney's voice cut into the fog. "Could you please just lay off for one second?"

"But, sweetie, you'd look so much more...*wedding-y* with a veil. Don't you think, Cat?" Mrs. Chandler turned to me, her brows arched.

"I actually think Tierney looks very wedding-y." I moved forward and readjusted the blossoms in her hair. "I mean, if that's not the face of a blushing bride, I don't know what is."

Tierney grinned and I knew she was resisting the urge to stick her tongue out at her mother. "Thank you," she whispered as her mother turned away.

About twenty minutes later, everything was in order. The music started—Jack and Tierney were walking down the aisle to some 80's hair band power ballad—and the tent flaps opened. The space between the guys' tent and ours had been lined with a white carpet that lead all the way to the altar.

Luke, Jack's best man and brother, stepped out of the tent and our eyes locked. I hadn't spoken to him since our brief encounter a couple years back. Even at the rehearsal dinner last night, I'd done a bang-up job of avoiding him. Having Jude with me had helped. Nothing said *off-limits* like a six-foot-four masterpiece.

Now, though, I didn't have a choice. Time to suck it up.

Giving me an uncomfortable smile, Luke offered me his arm. I took it and we started down the aisle. "So, um. This is awkward."

"Little bit," he replied, his blue eyes trained straight ahead. "I apologize for avoiding you. This isn't a situation I've found myself in very often."

My lips twisted. "You mean, you don't run into your one-time hookups all the time?"

He glanced at me. "I don't usually do the hookup thing." We progressed down the aisle, and he added, "The boyfriend factor certainly isn't helping."

"He's not my boyfriend." The response was automatic, and I wanted to take it back as soon as I said it. *And say what?* I thought. Jude *wasn't* my boyfriend.

"Really?" Luke looked my way, interest lighting his eyes. "In that case, I might have to ask you for a dance later."

I started to tell him not to bother, I wasn't interested, but we'd reached the end of the aisle. Parting, we took our spots at the altar.

Standing at the front of the crowd, my eyes found Jude immediately. He grinned and waved and he looked so damn good in his suit that my pulse pounded loud in my head.

Just then, the crowd got to their feet as Tierney and her father started down the aisle. She looked radiant, a vision in lace. A smile curved her lips and lit her eyes, which never left Jack.

I looked over at the groom, the man my best friend had chosen to spend her life with. His blue eyes were trained on Tierney, so warm and filled with love that something inside me ached, heavy and hot.

When she reached him, she took his hands in hers and blinked as her eyes filled with tears. She leaned forward and whispered something I couldn't hear, and Jack smiled, cupping her cheek in his hand.

I swallowed, blinking back tears of my own that I wasn't even sure I could explain. As the minister launched into his spiel, I turned my head away, focusing on the swarm of people in front of me.

Jack and Tierney exchanged vows as the sun sank low in the darkening sky. As the minister announced that Jack could kiss his bride, a soft summer breeze blew over us, ruffling Tierney's hair. He brushed it off her cheek with his hand and then lowered his lips to hers in the most beautiful kiss I had ever seen.

The crowd applauded and somewhere in the back, someone flipped a switch, igniting the fairgrounds with the multicolored lights of the Ferris wheel.

As the minister presented Mr. and Mrs. Jack Elliott to the crowd, there was no more blinking away the tears. I let them slide down my cheeks freely, so happy for these two people. They stopped kissing long enough to load into a cart on the Ferris wheel, and we all watched as they launched into the air. Tierney waved her bouquet, looking absolutely ecstatic. As the Ferris wheel lifted them higher, her eye caught mine and she tossed her flowers down. I caught them and then glared at her, but she was already too lost in her husband to notice.

Sniffing the mix of lilacs, cherry blossoms, and lilies, I smiled. I'd been to a million of these things—at least it seemed that way, as many times as my mother had gotten hitched—and none of them had made sense to me. I couldn't understand the reason why people got married.

After watching my best friend, someone I'd watched fight it all—the falling in love, the letting love go, and finally fighting to get it back—I got it.

You either jump and risk it, Jude's voice rang in my head again, and my eyes found his and held. *Or you sit on that plane all by yourself.*

Jack and Tierney chose to risk it. And even the cynic in me believed they'd fly.

26: Wedding Shenanigans

———

"**T**his is probably the coolest wedding I've ever been to," Jude said later, as we headed into the reception tent. "I mean, who expects to win one of these things at a wedding?" He held up a bright pink elephant that he had one in a game of ring toss.

"To be fair." I took the elephant from his hand. "You're, like, a ten foot tall moose. All you had to do was drop the rings onto the bottles."

"But I didn't." He took the toy back, fake-outrage on his face. "I tossed those rings like a pro."

I shook my head, a smile on my lips. "You're like an overgrown five-year-old," I muttered, even as I looped my arm around his waist and lead him through the maze of tables.

Inside the tent, colorful paper lanterns hung from the ceiling, in keeping with the carnival theme. Twinkling white lights lined the perimeter of the tent, giving the space a shimmering glow. The centerpieces were varied stuffed animals, much like the one Jude had won, holding balloons and assorted fair prizes. It was so cute I simultaneously wanted to squee and barf.

"My childlike wonder is damn charming," Jude said as we reached the front of the tent. "Ooh, elephant ears!"

"You're right. *So* charming," I drawled, holding the stuffed elephant up. "I'm going to escort Pinky here from the area so she doesn't have to witness the horror of you devouring what possibly used to be her mother."

"You're so wrong." Jude shook his head, even as he reached for one of the greasy, sugary treats. "Sick and wrong."

"All part of my allure, buddy." I winked and walked away, hoping to find Tierney. Dinner started in ten minutes and I hadn't seen the newlyweds since they finished their Ferris wheel ride. They were probably off somewhere, celebrating their nuptials like horny teenagers.

"Hey, there."

I turned to find Luke smiling at me. The twinkling lights highlighted his absurd good looks, and, for a second, I saw what Old Cat had seen before.

But I was not Old Cat anymore.

I didn't know when that happened, but there it was. And Old Cat did not want to bone Luke. Old Cat didn't want to bone anyone for the sake of boning anymore.

It had to mean something at some point, right?

Realizing I hadn't said a word to Luke, I waved. "Hi."

"So, I know the dancing hasn't started yet, but I was hoping you'd like to grab a drink. Maybe have an actual conversation?"

Oh, so *he* wasn't looking to bone, either.

Huh. Weird.

Tilting my head, I smiled. "Listen, Luke," I started. Even if he *didn't* want to hook up, I didn't have it in me for more. At least not with him.

My eyes trailed away from Luke to find Jude standing at the dessert table, making conversation with Dottie Daniels. The older woman seemed to be keeping her hands to herself this time.

Maybe...

I didn't get to finish the thought. Luke cleared his throat, bringing my attention back to him. "You don't do serious." He lifted a shoulder. "Tierney tried to tell me, but I figured it was worth a shot."

"Oh." I blinked. "No, that's not—"

"It's all right." He smiled and reached into his pocket, he pulled out his business card. "I'd love to take you to dinner sometime. You know, if you change your mind."

I took the card and watched him walk away, my brain trying to process what just happened.

"Please, don't turn him down on my account."

I glanced over to find Jude next to me, a fresh elephant ear in hand. His face was cloudy as he held it out to me. "I'm a big boy. I can keep myself occupied."

I took the elephant ear. "That's not...I don't..."

Before I could complete my thought, Tierney and Jack entered the tent to a round of cheers and applause. When I turned to tell Jude, in no uncertain terms, that I did not want to take Luke up on his offer, he was gone.

ABOUT AN HOUR LATER, the reception was in full swing. People had eaten their share of carnival foods and had begun to crowd onto the dance floor. Between my Maid of Honor duties and general wedding-y stuff, I hadn't been able to pin Jude down.

But when one of *Boy Toyz'* biggest hits piped through the speakers, I knew this was my chance. I kicked my shoes off under the table and made a beeline for Jude. He'd somehow been roped into dancing with a group of six-year-olds—which, *squee.* I quelled every ooey-gooey reaction inside me and tapped him on my shoulder.

Stopping mid-Robot, he looked my way.

"I believe it's my turn," I said with a smirk.

I was met with a chorus of groans from the wee girls.

"You did not say *please*," Tierney's niece said, her hands on her hips as her dark eyes glared at me.

"You are so right." I put my hands up. "Will you *please* dance with me, Jude?"

Jude grinned. "Sorry, ladies," he said, looping his arm through mine. "I can't resist those manners." Once we'd moved a few feet away from the girls, he added, "But I'm totally singing along."

I narrowed my eyes on his face, going for a serious expression. "Okay, but very quietly. We don't need to cause a scene here, and I think a teenage girl trapped inside a grown man's body just might do that."

Jude laughed, twirling me around. "Deal," he said as he pulled me back against him. I hit his chest with a thump and stumbled. His arms tightened around me, and his eyes caught mine. We swayed to the music as he sang, very quietly, resting his chin on the top of my head.

The song was up-tempo, its pop beats reverberating through the tent, and yet I held onto Jude, letting him choose the rhythm. Closing my eyes, I rested my cheek against his chest and listened to him sing the cheesy lyrics.

"This song is not very good," I murmured a minute later. "Why do I like it so much?"

"Cute guys who sometimes take their shirts off," Jude replied.

I smiled against his shirt. "You know me so well."

We swayed aimlessly for the entire song. As it transitioned into something else upbeat, I lifted my head. "So, listen. About Luke—"

"You don't need to explain yourself." He didn't meet my eye as he said it. "We're friends, right?"

The words felt like a sharp jab under the ribs. My steps faltered and he caught me. "R-right."

But is that all you want from me?

Just then, Tierney came over and threw her arms around me, squishing me between her and Jude. "Get a room," she muttered, smacking a kiss on my cheek.

"Shouldn't you be driving your new husband slowly insane right now?" I asked, reluctantly moving away from Jude to look at her. She was flushed and grinning like a madwoman. It looked good on her.

"I just thought I'd tell you how ridiculous you two look, slow-dancing to *Boy Toyz,*" she said, patting Jude on the cheek. "I can request something more appropriate, if you'd like. 'Let's Get It On,' maybe? A little 'Feel Like Makin' Love?'"

"Asshole," I grumbled as Jude laughed. "Go be happy somewhere else."

Tierney grinned as she practically floated through the crowd to Jack.

Within seconds of her departure, a new song filled the atmosphere. I immediately recognized the opening lines.

"Seriously, Tierney?"

Jude threw back his head and laughed, the sound vibrating my body. I stepped back and crossed my arms over my chest, trying not to notice how utterly delicious he looked. "Do not encourage her."

"Come on. 'Pour Some Sugar On Me'?" Jude's shoulders shook with laughter.

I took his hand and marched through the sea of people till we reached Tierney and Jack. They sat at their table, nose to nose, being all lovey-dovey and gross.

"Listen here, lady," I said as she looked up. The corners of her mouth twitched as she fought off a smile. "Jude and I are going to hit the road. And just for that little stunt you pulled, we're taking this with us." I held up a delicious-looking cherry pie I'd pilfered from the dessert table on the way over.

Tierney lifted a shoulder. "All right. Word of advice, though. The filling will stain your sheets. You may want to lay some plastic down before you...eat it."

Jude snorted and I glared at both of them before turning to the groom. "Jack, dear boy, you be good to my best friend, okay? If I stay a minute longer, I just might make you a young widower." I leaned across the table and kissed Tierney on the cheek, then Jack. "Congrats, you two. Enjoy your honeymoon."

27: Tumbling Down

———

"Okay, so we don't have any plastic," Jude called from the bathroom a while later. "But we do have an extra shower curtain." He came out holding up a package, wriggling his brows suggestively.

I tossed a pillow at him from my place across the room. "Not happening, buddy," I said around a mouthful of pie. "I don't believe in wasting good food."

"Worth a try." He tossed the shower curtain aside and joined me on the bed, reaching for his fork. "This pie *is* pretty good."

"Exactly." I licked my fork clean and set it aside. I hadn't changed out of my bridesmaid dress, and he still wore his suit, minus the jacket. We probably made quite a sight, sitting in bed in our fancy clothes, sharing an entire pie.

"So." I pulled my knees up to my chin and watched as he took a bite of pie. We'd avoided this conversation long enough. "About Luke."

Jude paused mid-chew. "You don't have to explain, apologize, or whatever you're going to do."

"But I do." I squeezed my knees tighter, trying to squish the butterflies flapping around in my stomach. "Luke and I slept together. Once. Like, a couple years ago." The words tumbled out and I watched Jude's face closely as they hit him. His shoulders tensed, but he kept chewing. So I kept talking. "But there's nothing between us now. Nada."

He shrugged, an attempt at casual that didn't quite stick the landing. "You don't owe me anything." His fork delved into the pie. "Like I said earlier, we're friends."

"Are we, though?" The words fell out of my mouth before I could catch them. Too late. Couldn't take them back. My arms tightened around my knees and I added, "Friends, I mean."

His eyes flew to mine. "Well, yeah." He dropped his fork into the pie plate and sat it aside. "You don't think so?"

"No, what I mean is..." My stomach somersaulted. Mistake. This conversation was a mistake. Time to backpedal. "Yeah. You're right. Friends." Giving him an *everything's fine* grin, I went for the pie.

He reached out to stop me. I looked up to find his eyes on me. Burning, intense. "What are you trying to say?"

I swallowed, suddenly feeling vulnerable. Tearing my eyes from his I stared at the sparkly pink nail polish I'd just put on that morning. My heart pounded, slow and hard, inside my chest. *I can't,* it said. *I can't, I can't, I can't.*

Jude's fingertips tilted my chin up, bringing my eyes back to his. "Just say it," he whispered, and there was a need in his voice that matched the way I felt inside.

"I...I thought we could do the friends thing," I started, studying the yellowing striped wallpaper. "But the more time I spend with you, the more I realize that I can't be your friend. Because..."

"Because?" Jude prompted, and I could feel him leaning in. I turned to find his eyes on me, all warm and gray-green and sweet. "Say it, Cat."

Words were elusive, but I knew how to show him what I meant. My breath hitched as I got to my knees, facing him. I put my palm against his cheek, feeling the harsh rub of stubble on my skin. He leaned into my touch, and I watched, fascinated, as he closed his eyes and his brows furrowed. Slowly, I moved my hand from his face to lace my fingers through his hair.

"Because you make me want to jump off that plane," I whispered.

Jude's eyes opened and, before I could process what was happening, he buried his hands in my hair, pulling my mouth to his.

It was a kiss wrought with so much emotion that I was afraid to identify. And so I didn't try. Leaning in, I threw myself into the flames that had been licking at my heart for days, weeks, months, and I welcomed the burn.

His hands left my hair to land on my waist, pulling me onto his lap, fingertips exploring all the skin left bare by the tiny dress, his lips drawing from mine like they longed to hear secrets I'd never told anybody.

And I wanted to tell him every single one.

My hands shook as I reached for the buttons on his shirt. He broke our kiss and watched me work on them, his chest rising and falling at a rapid pace. When I finally reached the last button, I spread my hands over his bare chest. His heart pounded against my palm like thunder and I closed my eyes, letting the intensity rush through me.

Reaching up, he brushed a strand of hair off my forehead and I opened my eyes, meeting his heated gaze. He leaned in then, one slow inch at a time, until his lips were on mine. He eased the zipper of my dress down. I let it fall to my waist, taking my bra with it. Then, he pulled me hard against him, naked flesh against naked flesh.

A shudder ran through my entire body as I pushed his shirt off his shoulders and ran my hands over his back.

I tore my mouth from his and trailed hot kisses down his neck and over his shoulders, cherishing each inch of skin I tasted, until Jude groaned and pushed me onto my back.

My eyes flew open. I watched, breathless, as his eyes roved over my body, followed by his hands. He reached for the dress, still at my waist, and pulled it down my legs, taking the rest of my clothing with it, until I lay before him, naked.

"You're beautiful."

And something in the way he said it, the way he looked at me, crumbled a little more of that wall inside me. Tears stung my eyes and I blinked them away, reaching for him.

"What's wrong?" he asked, his lips hovering above mine.

Instead of answering, I closed the remaining distance, crushing my lips to his. I kissed him with a hunger, a desperation, an edge that was so unfamiliar to me, yet so exhilarating. "Nothing," I whispered when we parted. "Absolutely nothing."

I reached for his pants, then, and fumbled with the belt, until Jude reached between us and disposed of the last articles of clothing separating us. Then, both of us equally naked, equally exposed, he pulled away.

"What—" I started, but the question halted on my lips as my eyes fluttered open to find Jude hovering above me. We lie there, skin on skin, heartbeat against heartbeat, eyes locked. The air between us thickened and suddenly I was just so tired. Tired of being tough, of being distant, of keeping people out.

After a while, those bricks I'd built higher and higher had gotten so heavy. I just wanted to put them down for a while.

And so I met Jude, kiss for kiss, touch for touch, until there was nothing left but this moment. This moment and us.

Alarm bells clanged in my head, warning me that these feelings, the way that Jude was looking at me, had disaster written all over it.

The tears I had fought off seconds earlier trickled down my cheeks, and Jude leaned in to kiss them away. The bells faded into the distance, leaving behind only the sounds of our hearts beating madly against our chests.

"Cat?" he whispered, and he pushed the hair away from my face and gazed at me, concern in his eyes.

"I'm okay," I said, then pulled Jude's lips back to mine, kissing him until the tears subsided, replaced by heat and fire and the frantic need to be known, really known, by another person.

And then, brick by brick, that wall inside me came tumbling down.

28: Do the Thing

―――

Morning came, its golden light drifting into our room until it was impossible to ignore.

"We should get up," Jude murmured, even as his arm tightened around me. "We have to check out soon."

"Mmm," I groaned, burying my face against his chest to shield my eyes from the sun. "I don't wanna."

Laughter rumbled beneath my cheek and I smiled. That laugh of his...got me every time.

"I don't want to, either," he said, his fingertips moving up and down my spine. "I would like nothing more than to stay in bed with you. For days and days. But we have to be grown-ups now. When we get home, though..." He trailed off, his hand sliding over the side of my breast, causing all kinds of reactions in my body.

I shivered and moved away. "You do *not* play nice, buddy." Sitting up, I let the sheet fall to my waist. I glanced over my shoulder, my hair falling into my face. "You're so going to pay for that."

Jude watched, eyes darkening, as I stood and walked naked across the room to the bathroom. "What are you doing?" he asked, and I stopped long enough to toss a smile over my shoulder.

"Taking a shower. And you are *not* invited." With that, I closed the door behind me and turned on the water. *Five, four, three, two...*

"You sure you don't want some company?" Jude asked, peeking his head into the door.

I turned and let my eyes move from the dimple in his cheek, over his bare shoulders, those ridiculous abs...

My stomach tightened and heat flooded through every inch of me. "Well..." I started, only to be cut off by Jude's lips against mine.

Together, we tumbled into the shower, where we stayed until the water rained down cold over us.

———

THE DRIVE BACK TO PORT Agnes was a blur of hand-holding, cheesy boy band sing-alongs, and conversation. As I parked my car at the curb outside Jude's apartment, I turned to him, a smile on my lips. "I had a really great weekend, Jude. Like, a lot."

He tucked a strand of wind-blown hair behind my ear, his fingers lingering on my jaw. "Me, too," he said, that damn dimple making an appearance. "Like, a lot."

I laughed and swatted his hand away, reaching for the door handle. "You hungry?" I asked as I got out of the car.

"Sort of." He came around to the back and opened the hatch. "But something tells me you're famished." He pulled out his bag, dropping it at his feet.

"Always." I grabbed him by the unbuttoned flaps of his plaid shirt. "Want to put your bag inside and go get some grub?" I wasn't ready for the weekend to be over. Partly because it'd been so wonderful, partly because I knew that once we parted ways, fear would get the best of me and I'd second-guess everything that had happened over the last forty-eight hours.

As if he could hear my thoughts, Jude wrapped his arms around me and pulled me snug against him. "Sounds like a plan," he said, his chin resting on the top of my head. We stayed that way for a couple seconds before he spoke again.

"Listen, I've been thinking..." he trailed off, hesitance in his voice.

I pulled away and looked up at his face, my stomach dropping to my toes. "Yes?" Anxiety gnawed at me. Was this the part where he changed his mind? Where he said that he liked me, but I wasn't really the kind of girl he wanted to date? I couldn't—

"Next weekend is Sunny's birthday, and we're making a trip home to celebrate...I was wondering...wanna come?"

Well, that was unexpected.

"I...uh..." I stammered, my hands flying up to twist the ends of my hair. My heart hammered faster and my face burned.

You've already broken Rule Number Three, a voice sang in my head. *A couple times.*

Dammit.

I dug around in the recesses of my mind for a reason, any reason, why this couldn't happen, but the moment I looked at Jude's face, the moment my eyes met his, so hopeful and nervous, I knew my answer.

"Sure, that sounds fun," I finally said. My stomach did flips as a smile broke out across his face. If all it took was four tiny words to put that smile there, well, I'd say those four words a million times over.

"Great." Jude pushed his hand through his hair. "Awesome. Sweet. Thanks." He shifted from foot to foot, looking ridiculously adorable.

I laughed and pulled him to me. "You're welcome," I said before standing on tiptoe to press my lips to his. "Now, about that food..."

A FEW HOURS LATER, after I left Jude at his apartment, I found myself pacing the floor of my own place. Back and forth, back and forth, twisting my hair into a braid, then undoing it, like a possessed hairdresser.

What had I agreed to?

Did I really give the okay to meeting Jude's family?

What was I thinking?

"Oh, God," I muttered, plopping down on the couch only to get back up again. "I can't. I can't. I can*not*."

I had to cancel. Tell him I changed my mind. That I just found out I had some horrible, terminal, contagious disease and I didn't want to give it to his family.

Cowardice was a disease, right?

I reached for my phone, then stopped, balling my hand into a fist. "Stupid," I said. "Dumb, dumb, dumb."

Before I could change my mind, I picked up the phone again and dialed a number, chewing on my thumbnail while it rang.

I got an answer after the fourth ring. "Hello?"

"Tierney! Hey! Thank God! I need you! I may be having a breakdown!" I winced as exclamation points escaped my mouth like bullets from a machine gun.

"Cat? You do know I'm on my honeymoon, right? In Greece. It's, like, four a.m. here."

"I know, I'm sorry," I said, sitting on the arm of my couch. "I didn't know who else to call. I...I'll be all right if you want to...get back to honeymooning." I squashed the surging panic inside me at the thought of Tierney hanging up, even as I said it. I was not equipped to deal with this alone.

"No, no. It's okay." She sounded groggy from sleep and guilt chewed at my insides. "What's up?"

"Never mind. False alarm. I'm fine," I said, tossing myself onto the couch. "Just being neurotic. The usual."

"Cat, you did not wake me up in the middle of the night on my honeymoon for a false alarm." I listened as Tierney murmured something to Jack and move away. "Out with it."

"It's Jude." I moaned, throwing a hand over my face in true drama queen fashion.

"You don't say." Tierney's voice was flat and I could picture her, bedhead and sleepy eyes, waiting for me to get to the point.

I ignored the sarcasm and forged ahead. "It was supposed to be casual. You know? Started out as one night, then it turned to two, then three, until we were both saying 'Just one more night.' Before I knew it, we'd been sleeping together for months. I have rules, Tier. Rules that must not be broken. And Jude has broken three of them. Three!"

"My god. You and your rules," Tierney muttered, but I continued talking.

"I didn't want anything serious. He didn't, either. So then we tried friends. It seemed to be working. Until..."

I chewed my fingernail, trying to figure out what to say next. How could I verbalize the torrential emotions rushing through me?

Tierney waited a few more seconds before she spoke. "Okay, so the friends thing seemed to be working until...?"

"Until it wasn't," I said. "I don't know exactly when things changed, but they did. Then, suddenly, I wanted more. I wanted to *date* him. I missed him when he wasn't around. *I took him to meet Hazel.*"

"Whoa. Wait a damn minute here," Tierney said, sounding all kinds of offended. "It took you *three years* to introduce me to Hazel!"

I smiled, despite the serious subject matter. "Sorry, Toots. I had to make sure you were going to stick around. Do you know how many flaky friends I had before you showed up with your awesomeness?"

She pretended to think about it, then said, "Well, if you put it that way, it makes perfect sense. You gotta be awesome to meet the grandma."

"Right. And...well, Jude is. Awesome. A lot." I shoved myself off the couch and headed into the kitchen.

"So, what's the problem?" Tierney sounded genuinely baffled. "He's awesome, you're awesome. Go be awesome together."

"It's not that easy and you know it." I pulled a pint of Ben and Jerry's out of the freezer and grabbed a spoon. After shoving a heaping spoonful of fudgy goodness into my mouth, I added, "He invited me to meet his family."

Nothing but silence came from Tierney's end. I started to think she hung up on me when a low whistle emanated from the phone. "That's...something, isn't it?"

"Why do you think I'm freaking out?" I almost yelled. "It's huge. It's monumental. It's enormous. It's—"

"It's great, Cat."

I stopped cold, mid-bite. "Wh-what?"

"Really. You two are fantastic together. I saw it. Jack saw it. Pretty much all of June Lake saw it." Her voice softened as she added, "Just enjoy it, sweetie. Stop freaking yourself out."

"Have you not met me, though?"

"Listen, I love you, but I—" Tierney started, only to get cut off abruptly.

"Cat? Hey, it's Jack."

"H-hey," I said around the spoon in my mouth. "Sup?"

"You remember what we talked about the other night? The night of the maple pecan cookies?"

"Yes," I replied slowly, shoving the ice cream aside. "Those cookies were amazing."

"Thanks." I could practically hear his grin through the phone. "But that's not the point. You remember the part about opening yourself up to good things?"

I recalled Jack unfolding my fist and dropping a cookie into my palm and I nodded. "Yeah. I remember."

"Good," he said, his voice raspy with sleep. "Do that. Do the thing." And with that, he hung up, leaving me staring at the silent phone in my hand.

"Huh," I said slowly, putting the lid on the ice cream. *Do that.*

Wandering back to the kitchen, I put the ice cream back in the freezer and let Jack's words sink in. The more I thought about it, the more sense it made. This time next week, I'd be meeting Jude's family.

I was going to do the thing.

29: Good Old-Fashioned Indigestion

The panic came and went throughout the week. It took three more phone calls to Jack and Tierney, four pints of Ben and Jerry's and five consecutive hours of *Kill Radius* to keep me from backing out.

When Jude showed up at my place Saturday morning, I was wired on Mountain Dew, chocolate donuts, and sheer stubborn will.

"Let's get this thing on the road," I said as I swung the door wide open.

"Whoa, good morning to you, too." Jude entered my apartment, iced coffee and a bag of breakfast sandwiches in his hands. "I'm thinking you don't need another caffeinated beverage."

"Hey, now. I can always use another caffeinated beverage." I took the drink from his hand. "You're made of all things that are good."

"Are you talking to me, or the coffee?" Jude asked as he sat the food on the counter.

"Um..." I dipped my finger in the whipped cream. "You. Of course I'm talking to you."

"Uh huh," Jude said, his eyes lingering on my mouth as I licked the whipped cream from my finger. "Sure you were."

"Aww, I'm sorry." I sat my drink aside and closed the distance between us, grabbing the lapels of his jacket. "Did I bruise your ego?"

"What do I get if I say yes?"

I smiled, standing on my tiptoe. "What do you want?" I asked, dropping my voice low as I gazed up at him through my lashes.

Jude groaned. "We don't have time for what I want. We've got to get on the road."

"Oh, well. Sucks to be you." I twirled away to reclaim my iced coffee. "Let's get going."

"You're an evil, evil woman. You know that?" Jude bent to pick up my overnight back and headed for the door. "Out," he said, motioning for me to exit ahead of him.

I gathered our breakfast and walked out the door, laughing as Jude swatted my ass. "Hey, now. Keep your hands to yourself, mister."

He closed the door behind us and checked that it was locked. "You don't mean that," he said with a smirk.

I returned his smile and skipped down the stairs. "Oh, I mean every word." I pushed open the lobby door. "Hands. Off."

I no sooner got the words out when Jude spun me around, pinning me against the brick building. "All right," he murmured, his breath hot next to my ear. "Have it your way." He leaned in, his hands holding our coffee cups, while he trailed his lips down my neck.

My heartbeat sped up like a Maserati. "This only works if you *want* to keep your hands to yourself," I whispered, dropping the paper bag with our breakfast in it to tuck my fingertips into the waistband of his jeans. I tugged him closer and raised my mouth to his, stopping millimeters away from touching. "And something tells me that's not what you want."

Arching away from the wall, I pressed my body into his. "Not even a little bit," I finished, watching his eyes darken with need. He groaned and I wriggled away, reclaiming our breakfast from the sidewalk. I threw a wobbly grin his way as I headed toward his car—a billion-year-old beater he drove for long trips and winter, when his bike wasn't logical. "I win."

Jude huffed out a breath and dragged his hand through his hair. "I'm so glad we have a long drive ahead of us."

I laughed and pulled open the passenger door. "Plenty of time to cool off?"

After dropping my bag in the trunk, Jude joined me in the car, his eyes raking over me. "No, plenty of time for paybacks." He hit the automatic locks with a devious grin.

"Oh. Oh, no. Someone help me." My voice was monotone as I gave him a wide-eyed look. "This isn't a game you can win, buddy. I suggest you wave that white flag right now."

Jude's grin widened as he pulled on his seatbelt. "You know? I believe you. Something tells me I haven't begun to see all the tricks you have up your sleeve." He started the car and pulled onto the street before adding, "We're going to see my parents. The last thing I need is to show up, uh, all excited."

An unexpected laugh escaped my throat. "Yeah, no. That probably wouldn't be the best first impression to make. *Hi, I'm Cat, the chick responsible for giving your son that enormous—*"

"All right. I'm pretty sure you don't need to complete that sentence."

I smirked, but didn't finish. A couple minutes down the road, Jude reached over to take my hand in his. He pulled it to his lips and something tightened inside my chest. "You nervous?"

"Pssh." I shifted in my seat. "I don't get nervous. I'm one cool cat." I paused, wriggling my brows at him. "You see what I did there?"

Jude squeezed my hand then let go, shaking his head. "You keep making lame jokes like that, I just might change my mind about this whole thing," he said, half a smile on his lips.

"Ooh, really?" I asked, sitting up straighter. "Let me see...knock, knock."

"Nice try. Eat your breakfast," he said, ignoring me, even as amusement flickered across his face.

"Your line is, 'Who's there?'" I reached into the paper bag and pulled out a sandwich. Unwrapping it halfway, I handed it to Jude, then pulled out one for me.

As I settled into my seat, something warm radiated from my chestular region. *Indigestion,* I told myself, taking a huge bite of the sandwich Jude had thoughtfully provided. *Good, old-fashioned indigestion.*

JUDE'S HOMETOWN WAS about an hour forty-five away. Not far from June Lake. I actually found it surprising that he and Tierney hadn't known each other growing up. Didn't all people from these small towns know each other?

"Are we there yet?" I asked as we got off the highway and began weaving our way through the back roads.

"Almost," Jude said as we exited a town called Handford. A few minutes later, we passed a sign that read *Now Entering Wangton.*

"Wangton?" I choked back a giggle. "Wait, wait. Handford is right next to Wangton? What's next? Buttville? Are *you* from Buttville?" I turned to Jude, unable to stop the laugh from escaping. "Please tell me you're from Buttville!"

Jude's lip twitched. "Sorry, doll," he said, flicking on his blinker. "Wangton, it is."

"That is amazing," I murmured as we entered the town, which was basically just three buildings.

The center of town consisted of a tiny store literally called Wangton Country Store, a shoebox-sized gas station and a single, solitary diner. "Porker's Pizza, huh?" I murmured as we drove past. "You guys really hang out with your Wangtons out here, don't you?"

"You know it." Jude made a left onto an almost-invisible dirt road. "Sometimes, we even invite the folks from Handford and things get real crazy."

Reaching across the car, he squeezed my knee. "I ever tell you that I find your pre-pubescent sense of humor endearing?"

I grinned and put my hand over his. "Glad to hear it. Because the wang jokes haven't even begun." I ignored the sudden roar of nerves washing over me as we began passing houses. We'd reach Jude's soon, and then I'd have to meet his parents. Why had this seemed like a good idea, again?

"Is it too late to jump out of the car?" I asked, my hand covering Jude's.

He laced his fingers through mine and slowed the car, pulling to the side of the road. "All right," he said, and I raised my eyes to his. "We can turn this car around, go back home, and forget all about this meeting the family crap. No big deal, some other time." He paused, reaching over to push the hair from my forehead.

"Or," he continued. "We could drive the remaining hundred feet, pull into the driveway, and go inside, where I'll show you my old room, complete with the porn stash under the mattress. I might even still have a Super Nintendo, somewhere..."

"With Super Mario Bros.?" I asked, my anxiety lowering to much more manageable levels.

"And Donkey Kong."

"Okay." I unbuckled my seatbelt to move closer. Jude lifted his arm and I slid in, resting my head on his shoulder. "I'm sort of freaking out, you know."

He kissed the top of my head. "I know."

We sat like that for a couple minutes before Jude spoke again. "So, my mom's name is Edie. She's a sixth grade English teacher. Dad's Dave. He's a retired factory worker."

I moved back to my side of the car. "Okay. What else do I need to know? I feel like these are the things we should have talked about on the way here."

"Well, *someone* was too busy making penis jokes," Jude said as he put the car in drive.

I shrugged. "Hey, man. Penii are funny. Now, continue. Tell me about your family."

Jude talked for the next couple minutes as we completed our journey down the bumpy dirt road. We pulled into a long, paved driveway and I took in the modest split-level house nestled away from the road.

It had yellow siding with black shutters and a red brick walk leading up to the door. A well-used basketball hoop hung from the garage and I could picture teenage Jude shooting many a hoop here.

As Jude turned off the car, I took a deep breath and wiped my hands on my knee-length cotton skirt—not typical Cat gear, but I wanted to make a good impression.

"Relax," Jude said, opening his car door. "You already met Sunny. *She's* the crazy one." And with that, he got out and came around to my side.

Here we go.

30: Crash, Boom, Bang

———

Jude's family was unlike any family I'd ever met.

Granted, my familial experience was rather limited, but the whole "loving, supportive" thing sort of threw me off.

Edie, Jude's mom, had a contagious laugh, always accompanied by the smile she'd passed on to all of her children. Her dark hair was worn to her shoulders, with bangs that brought out the twinkle in her eye. Dad Dave was a tall, lanky man, with a firm handshake and his son's good nature. Birdie, the youngest Oliver offspring, regarded me with the same narrow-eyed speculation I'd gotten from Sunny the first time we met. It wasn't till Jude cleared his throat behind her that she smiled and introduced herself.

Sunny arrived a while later. She'd ridden with Ben and seemed annoyed by his mere presence, but she greeted me with a sort-of smile, anyway.

Now, a couple hours later, we were gathered in the dining room, an elaborate meal of homemade mac and cheese with chopped-up hot dogs mixed in, on the table in front of us.

"One of these days, Sunshine will outgrow this dish," Ben said as he piled his plate high with steaming pasta. "And move on to a *real* favorite meal. Like pizza. And beer."

Sunny snarled in his direction. "I don't remember inviting you to my birthday dinner, asshat."

"You kidding, sweets? I'm family. I don't need an invitation. Besides," he continued, handing the dish to Jude. "I brought you a kick-ass present."

"Is it your sweet, sweet silence?" Sunny shot back as she stabbed a hot dog with her fork.

I watched the exchange with amusement. Sparks burned hot between these two. How long had they been shacking up?

"Anyway," Jude said, seemingly oblivious to the verbal foreplay going on around him. "How about them Lions?"

A smile touched my lips as I filled my plate. Was this what normal families did? Share giant bowls of pasta and bicker back and forth?

Around me, everyone else began eating. Sunny set about antagonizing Birdie and I shoveled a few bites into my mouth. It was an oddly delicious combination. Hazel had made me many random things as a kid, but I'd never had this particular dish.

At the thought of Hazel, a brief memory flashed through my mind. About a billion years ago. Mom, Arthur, Hazel, Zeke, thirteen-year-old me, all seated around Hazel's modest kitchen table. I had just competed in the final round of a Mathletes competition, and that was all everyone wanted to talk about.

Arthur had presented me with a dozen roses and a silver bracelet with a protractor charm hanging from it. I still had it tucked away in a drawer somewhere.

My eyes burned now as I thought about that. The pride in Arthur's eyes meant more to me than any gift could...

My food suddenly lost all flavor. I sat down my fork and tried to clear the memory away. Oxygen burned in my lungs and, with it, tears sprang into my eyes. I needed to get out of here.

Leaning over to Jude, I whispered, "I-I need to use the restroom."

I hurried down the hall before anyone could notice the stupid tears. Ducking into the bathroom, I closed the door behind me.

What was I doing here? I was far too screwed up for this scene. *Normal* people did family dinners. *Normal* people with parents that didn't abandon them or judge every little thing they did or wish they were someone else.

I didn't *do* family. I had Hazel. I had Tierney. Big family dinners, well they didn't exist in my world. I didn't know how to navigate that world.

What was Jude thinking, bringing me here?

A knock on the door jarred me from my thoughts. I pulled it open a crack, expecting to see Jude standing in the hall.

"Hey, Foxy." Ben raised his hand in a half-wave. "How's it going?"

I leaned against the doorframe and let out a huge sigh. "Blergh."

He laughed, his brown eyes sympathetic. "It's weird, right? The big, happy family thing."

"How—" I started, surprise widening my eyes.

"Let's just say, this ain't how my family does things." He pushed the door open further with his foot. "Follow me. I know what'll help you relax." And then, he took my hand and dragged me down the hall.

"Uh, sorry to tell you this, dude, but you're not really my type."

"No worries." He glanced down the hall, toward the dining room. "You're not my type, either."

Oh, I bet I'm not, I thought as he pushed open a door to our right.

"Ahh, here we are." We entered a room and Ben flicked on the light. "May I present to you, teenage Jude," he said, his arm sweeping wide.

I took in the full-size bed, basketball trophies and posters of hot chicks. "Huh." I entered the room and looked around. "Exactly what I thought it'd look like."

"I know, right?" Ben plopped down on the bed. "Our boyfriend is so predictable."

"He's not my—" The denial died on my lips as I caught sight of a picture on the dresser, peeking out from a pile of random magazines. Pulling it out, I studied it. A tuxedo-clad Jude, his hair much shorter, his dimples the same, next to a tall, gorgeous woman with a cascade of blond hair, in a sapphire blue dress. I turned toward Ben and held it up.

"The infamous Leslie." He joined me at the dresser. "Some lame-ass sorority dance, I think." He took the picture from my hand and glanced at it before tossing it aside. "Woman crushed him like a bug. A sexy, sexy bug."

I watched the picture flutter back to the dresser. "What was she like?" I heard myself asking as Ben picked up the TV remote and pointed it at the screen. I winced. *Dumb question. Dumb, useless question I didn't really need an answer to.*

I didn't need it. But I wanted it.

"Leslie?" Ben glanced at me, then turned on the gaming console. "She was all right. Sort of uptight. Tense." He shrugged a shoulder then threw me a controller. "Ready to get your ass kicked?"

"Oh, not a chance." I tossed my hair back and met his eye. "I've made teenage boys in Tulsa cry into their Mountain Dew with my badassery."

"That was mighty specific." Ben raised his eyebrows. "Are we talking about anyone in particular?"

I rolled my eyes, annoyance creeping over me. "Some punk named *diezombiebitch12*. I play him once a week or so, and he talks so much smack I just want to drop kick him."

Ben nodded. "You are intense," he said as the game started. "But I still think I can take you."

"Oh, you're on." My competitive edge did the talking for me. "Show me what you got, big boy."

We played in silence for a couple of minutes. I should've left it that way. But curiosity ate at my insides. I had to know. "What happened with the bug-crusher ex?"

Ben's eyes shot my way briefly. He didn't answer right away. Maybe he was hoping I'd tell him to forget it. Never mind.

I didn't.

Finally, he spoke. "You know how there are women that collect things to make them look good? Like, thousand dollar purses or squeaky little lapdogs to put in said purses?"

I frowned. "Yes?"

"That was Leslie." Ben jammed his thumbs over the controller's buttons, decimating a zombie or two. "She was all about image. And Jude...well, *you've* seen him."

"Right..." I halfheartedly swung my machete at a horde of undead.

"But the thing about Jude is, he ain't just pretty." He kept his eyes on the screen, actively navigating the course. "He's got goals, you know? Goals that don't include playing dress-up for his wife's fancy events. Or taking a job that will make him unhappy just because it makes him—and by association, her—look good."

My brain immediately called up a conversation I'd had with Jude about his job—how he wasn't happy where he was. How he had his eye on something else. Something he *really* wanted to do.

"The deejay job..."

"Leslie's idea." Ben shot to his knees, frantically smashing the buttons. "Dammit, die. *Die!*"

I went quiet as the new information sunk in. It made sense now, the fire in his eyes when he told me about the other job opportunity. He'd been sidetracked by his wife, by trying to make her happy. And now was his chance to do what *he* wanted.

A smile touched my lips. I couldn't wait to see him get that new job.

"So, what are you two doing, anyway?"

Ben's question brought me abruptly back to the moment. I glanced over. "What do you mean?"

Ben returned my look. "Not to be an asshole, but Jude isn't a casual guy. And from what I've gathered, that's...kind of your thing." He paused, then added, "No offense."

My cheeks heated. I kept my eyes straight ahead. "None taken."

"I'm just asking because he's into you." He also stared at the screen in front of us. "And I don't want to see him get hurt."

I froze. Hurt him? I had been so consumed by the potential of my own pain that the thought had barely occurred to me. But now, armed with the story of his heartbreak...the pressure weighed heavy on my shoulders.

Swallowing hard, I pushed my response passed my lips—the only true response I could give Ben in this moment. "It's not my intention to hurt him."

Ben dropped the controller to his lap and turned toward me. I did the same. Leaning forward, he squinted, studying me. After a few long, uncomfortably intense seconds, he nodded. "Good." Then, he picked up his controller and turned back to the TV.

"Sorry to interrupt."

We swung our heads to find Jude peering into the half-open door-way. The floor shifted sharply beneath me, and my controller fell to my lap. "Hey," I said, attempting a smile. How much had he heard?

"Hey there, stud." Ben stood. "I was just kicking Cat's ass at *Kill Radius*."

"The hell you were," I shot back, letting him help me to my feet. "Is it time for cake?"

Jude laughed, pushing the door open wider. "It is. And Sunny has been eyeing that present you brought her all night. She may snap of curiosity soon if we don't let her open it."

"Oh, yeah!" I crossed the room with a few quick skips. Jude wrapped his arm around my waist as I passed him, pulling me close. My heart sputtered. I searched his eyes for any indication that he'd heard Ben and I talking. If he had, he hid it well.

"Sorry for disappearing," I murmured as Ben slid by us and started toward the dining room.

"I mean, I'm not gonna lie," Jude responded, his lips against my temple. "I was a little afraid you and Ben ran off together to found a zombie apocalypse army."

I laughed. "If I ever do, you're coming with me."

Jude's chest vibrated with a laugh as he steered me down the hall. "Have a change of heart, did you?"

"Well, yeah," I said right before we reached the dining room. "What's the point of surviving the zombie apocalypse without you?"

Jude's eyes flickered and he leaned in for a kiss.

"Guys, come on! I've got a pile of presents that Mom won't let me touch until everyone is in the room," Sunny called, bringing an end to our conversation. We walked into the dining room and joined everyone.

"You constantly astound me with your patience." Jude wrapped his other arm around his sister. "Open mine first."

Sunny darted across the room and picked up the present wrapped in skull and crossbones paper, turning toward Jude with raised brows.

Jude nodded and she tore into it. I watched, intrigued. This was the most excitement I'd seen from Sunny in...well, ever. "Ha!" she exclaimed, holding up a t-shirt. "This is *awesome!*"

"*WTF,*" I read aloud. "*Where's The Food.* Say, Sunny. Can I borrow that sometime?"

Sunny grinned and hugged the shirt to her chest. "Get your own, lady. I don't know you like that."

"Fair enough," I conceded. "Open mine next." I pointed to the plain white box. "You might change your mind."

With a raised brow, Sunny picked up the box and pulled off the lid. "Oh, *my God!*" she exclaimed, her eyes widening. *This* was officially the most excited I'd ever seen her. "You got me pie!"

"Not just any pie," I said, crossing the room to join Sunny. "Jack pie."

"I don't know what that means." Sunny looked from me to the pie, suspicion wrinkling her brows. "But I am intrigued."

I laughed. "My best friend's boyfr- er, husband has a restaurant in Port Agnes. Best desserts ever."

"Ooh, how have I not heard about this place?" Sunny said, taking the pie to the table. "I must have you now."

"You're, uh, talking to the pie, right?" Ben cut in, smirking. "Because I'm down, either way." He waggled his brows, looking from me to Sunny then back again.

"Stop being gross," Sunny snarled with more hostility than usual.

I suppressed an eye roll. *Oh, would you two just bone already?*

Ben took a step back, brows raised in alarm. "My bad," he said.

Sunny finished opening her presents, we had cake—and pie—and then Edie and Dave retired to bed, leaving us kids alone.

"Well, it's been fun," Birdie said as she shoved away from the table. Her tone was a touch less snarky than Sunny, but I got the feeling she was holding back. "But I'm going to my room. I'm all nerded out."

I glanced over at Jude as she made her exit. How had he ended up so...*nice*?

"Love you, too," Sunny called to her retreating back. "Don't know who she's calling a nerd."

"So, uh," I said as Jude put his arm around my shoulder. "Pretty sure I was promised Super Mario Bros."

"Dude!" Sunny exclaimed, jumping up from her chair and grabbing my hand. "This must happen!"

She dropped my hand as we reached the room and headed straight for the TV. Ben followed right behind her, and they began bickering over who got to go first. I turned to Jude, but whatever I'd been about to say slipped away the moment I met his eyes.

"Everything okay?" he asked, and he did that thing where he pushed the hair from my face.

Crash, boom, bang, went my heart, and suddenly I felt like I was freefalling.

"F-fine," I managed, moving away from him to join the others. "Just fine."

And I didn't know if I was talking to Jude or myself.

AROUND THREE A.M., we wrapped up our impromptu gaming party, but only because Ben had passed out in Jude's bed somewhere around two.

"Come on, sugar lips," Jude said, nudging Ben with his foot. "Time to go to your own bed."

"But I wanna stay here with you." Ben nestled deeper into the bed. "We can snuggle and talk about our dreams and aspirations."

"You've got the wrong girl." Jude yanked the blanket away from him. "I'm the love 'em and leave 'em type."

Ben sat up, his dark hair all askew. "You give and you give and you give," he grumbled, standing. "And you still get replaced by some fiery little redhead who probably does that thing you won't do."

"Hey, now," I said, giving him a shove toward the door. "I don't do that thing, either."

Jude heaved a sigh as he remade the bed. "I just can't win. No one will do the thing."

At that, Sunny stood from her spot on the floor. "I can't listen to any more of this." She walked to the door. "If I hear the word 'thing' one more time, I'm gonna kill you all."

A few minutes later, Sunny and Ben were gone and the whole toothbrush-ing and pajama-ing routine was out of the way. I returned to Jude's room and found him lounging on his bed.

Sudden shyness skittered through me. I eased around the bed to the empty side. Jude pulled back the blanket and patted the bed. "So, about that thing," he said, a suggestive smile on his face.

"Ha. Not a chance, man." I snuggled in next to him. "I'm on a hardcore caffeine crash. Plus, you know, I'm just not that kind of girl." My eyes closed as Jude's arm wrapped around me.

"That's all right," he said, his voice leaden with sleep. "I still like you. Sort of."

"Sweet." I yawned, gentle waves of sleep tugging at me. "Hey, Jude?"

"Yeah?" He reached over to turn off the bedside lamp.

"I sort of like you, too."

"Mmm." His arm draped over my waist, pulling me against his warm body. "Good."

Closing my eyes, I nestled closer. "Hey, Jude?"

"Hmm?"

I lay there, listening to his heartbeat and our breaths syncing up. Everything about this moment felt...right. Real. Concrete and safe and...

"I think I'm ready to jump," I whispered just as a soft snore emanated from him. "Please don't let me *splat*."

31: Jump

———

The next morning, I awoke in Jude's bed alone. In the distance, I could hear talking and laughter, and glorious smells drifted in under the closed door. I stretched and rubbed my eyes, flickers of the night before flashed through my head and I smiled. Burying my face in my pillow, I breathed in the scent of fabric softener and Jude, something niggling at the back of my mind.

A moment, the briefest of seconds, Jude's arms around me, the feeling—the absolute certainty—that he'd catch me if I let go. If I jumped out of the plane.

Please don't let me splat.

Had I really said that? And did Jude hear me?

I sat up. What if he heard me?

What *if* he heard me?

My heart slammed. I threw my legs over the bed and started across the room and opened the door, following the sounds until I reached the end of the hall. I found everyone in the kitchen, and I hung back, watching the scene.

Edie and Dave stood at the stove, side-by-side, flipping pancakes and frying bacon, respectively. Sunny stood at the island, chopping fruit, and Ben was nowhere in sight. And Jude...there he was, breaking eggs into a bowl the way he'd been breaking down my defenses.

As if he could feel me staring, Jude looked up and caught my eye.

"Hey, sleepyhead." He abandoned his task to join me in the hall. He leaned down to kiss me and I covered my mouth with my hand.

"Morning breath," I said, letting him pull me in for a hug instead.

"For the record," he said, his lips against my hair. "I don't care about your morning breath."

"Oh, I wasn't talking about me." I wrapped my arms around his waist. "*My* breath smells like sunshine and bubblegum."

Jude laughed and backed us into the kitchen. "I'll let you have this one." He deposited me at the large center island before returning to his eggs.

"Anything I can do?" I asked, tugging at the wrinkled t-shirt I'd slept in.

Edie whirled around, her eyes crinkled with a smile. "Oh, no, sweetheart. We've got this under control. You just have a seat and enjoy. Do you need anything to drink? Coffee? Orange juice? Whiskey?"

"Actually." I climbed onto a stool. "I prefer vodka with my pancakes."

Laughing, Edie turned toward the fridge and pulled out a carton of OJ, sliding it across the counter. "I like you," she said, giving my shoulder a squeeze as she went back to the stove.

A grin found itself on my face. I glanced at Jude, who gave me the thumbs up before pulling a whisk from a drawer.

As I sat there, with everyone buzzing around me, one resounding thought played in my ears: *I could get used to this.*

But what about your rules? came another voice. *Rule Number Four: Don't get attached. This looks like* attached *to me.*

I ignored it and reached for a slice of bacon from the plate in front of me. Who needed so many rules, anyway?

———————————

THE REST OF THE WEEKEND passed in a pleasant haze of delicious food, late night video games, and family bonding time. The old me would have said it made me itch, it made me squirm, it made me sick to my very core. But that was not the case. It made me feel downright cozy. All warm and fuzzy and shit.

That feeling held as Jude and I drove back to Port Agnes, holding hands and singing along with the radio. Once we left the highway, Jude pulled my hand to his lips and said, "You sick of me yet, or you want to hang out for a while?"

I laughed. "I don't know. I *might* be ready to kick you to the curb after listening to you sing *Boy Toyz* all the way home."

"Please. I was killing it, and you know it."

"Fine, fine," I conceded. "You weren't so bad." I paused as he put the car in park. "And I'm not sick of you yet."

He looked over, a smile of pure contentment on his face. "Well, then let's get inside." He got out of the car, coming around to open my door.

"I just want you to know," I said as I took his hand and led him into the building. "That I had a really great time this weekend. Like, really. Your family is—"

"Crazy, weird, overwhelming?"

"Wonderful," I finished, pulling his arm over my shoulder. "I really feel like Sunny and I bonded over the last couple days. I mean, she didn't threaten to kill or maim me once."

"That's a pretty big deal. I've been friends with Ben since the second grade and Sunny threatens to murder him on a fairly regular basis."

I dug my keys out of my pocket. "What is *up* with those two, anyway?"

"What do you mean?"

"Come on, man." I looked at him in disbelief. "Either those two are scrumping, or they really want to scrump."

Jude's face went pale. "That's...they're not..." I thought for a moment that he was going to barf. "Please stop saying scrump."

"Okay. My bad." *Do not point out the obvious,* I thought. *Got it.*

Once we were inside, I kicked off my shoes and plopped down on the couch. "There's ice cream in the freezer."

"And potato chips?" He grinned and joined me, laying his feet across my lap.

My insides warmed at the intimacy of the gesture. Smiling, I gave Jude's big toe a pinch. "Of course I've got potato chips, Sir Stinky Feet."

Jude slid his foot from my reach. "Hey, now. Not all of us can smell like bubblegum and sunshine."

I nodded solemnly. "It truly is a gift."

He laughed, then opened his arms. "Come here a minute, will ya?"

He didn't have to ask me twice.

I crawled into his lap, resting my forehead against his. "Here I am," I whispered, looking into his eyes. My heart thudded hard, reverberating throughout my entire body. "Now what?"

His hand cupped my face. He ran his thumb over my bottom lip and my eyes drifted closed. Gently, he pressed his lips to mine.

His touch was tender, fingertips tracing along my jawline. My lungs fought for oxygen as he took my chin between his thumb and forefinger and moved his lips from mine.

"What?"

"Nothing." He tucked my hair behind my ear. His smoky hazel eyes melted into mine and he smiled. Everything around us faded to a dull shade of gray. "I'm ready to jump, too."

So he'd heard me the other night. My heartbeat faltered, then flared to life. He heard me, and he felt the same.

I waited for the inevitable stab of fear to follow. It didn't.

And, man, was that liberating.

Somewhere in the back of my mind, Rule Number Five screamed to be heard: *Do Not, Under Any Circumstances, Fall In Love.*

I ignored the warning that clawed at me like a demon starved for souls. Instead, I clung to the warmth, the realness, the certainty shining in his eyes. I took a deep breath, and the words I exhaled were the bravest ones I'd ever said:

"So what are we waiting for?"

And then there were no more thoughts, no fears, just feelings. The feel of Jude's hands in my hair, his pulse pounding against my chest, the heat of his skin under my fingertips, the fire in his kiss. Slowly, so slowly, the kiss shifted. Gone was the softness, the sweetness, replaced by a need so strong I gripped tight to Jude's shoulders for fear of losing control.

As if he sensed my fear, he wrapped his arms around my waist, holding me close to his chest. The steady thump of his heart against mine was like a lullaby, putting to rest the very last demon screaming in my mind.

And then I jumped.

32: Fall

―――

"**Y**our kitchen makes the whole *breakfast in bed* concept rather difficult."

Jude's voice woke me from the most scrumptious sleep I'd had in a long time. I groaned and rolled over to find him standing in my doorway, wearing nothing but his Spiderman boxers.

"You could serve me rocks and twigs and I wouldn't care, as long as you served it looking like that."

"Well, luckily, I found some things slightly more edible than rocks and twigs." He crossed the room and presented me with a tray. "Toaster pastries, frozen waffles, and string cheese."

"String cheese?" I picked one up and unwrapped it.

"Like I said, limited options." He sat on the bed across from me, and I drank him in. My mind replayed moments from last night in long, lingering snippets, and something bloomed warm and bright in my chest. I waited, bracing for the cold, the screeching of brakes, the howling warnings to run, to hide.

Silence.

I smiled, a sigh of relief melting through me. Peeling a piece of cheese off, I held it out to Jude. He leaned in, catching it in his mouth. I laughed. "This is very sweet of you."

Jude gave an adorable shrug as he finished off the cheese. "Yeah, well, I figured if I was going to wake you up, I better not do it empty-handed."

"Good call." I pulled back the blankets beside me and patted the bed. "Get in. You're probably freezing."

He cocked an eyebrow but obeyed, his chilly feet finding my toasty warm ones. I squealed, moving away.

"What?" He slid his hands under the blanket. "You don't want to warm me up?"

His hands, while not frigid, were still pretty cold as they slid over my naked, sleep-warmed skin. I shivered and tried to wriggle out of his reach, but he pulled me closer, until we were nose-to-nose.

"Hey," he said, his eyes both warm and wary. Probably awaiting the freak out.

Couldn't blame the guy. I'd gotten good at freaking out.

I nestled closer. Not today. "Hey," I whispered back. His arms closed around me, and I rested my forehead against his shoulder. "Do you know that last night was the first time—ever—that I let a boy stay over?"

His fingers trailed over my back. "Yeah?"

"Mmm hmm." My heart beat slow and steady. I raised my eyes to his. "I'm glad it was you."

The smile that broke across his face could've powered up the entire city. He closed the distance between us and kissed me, sending an electric charge straight to my toes.

I looped my arms over his neck and kissed him back.

An obnoxious buzz filled the air, followed by another. And another.

Jude's lips stilled on mine. "Ah, dammit," he muttered as his head spun to locate the sound. Stretching, he grabbed his phone from the nightstand. "Sorry, babe," he said as he sat up. "It's work." Swinging his legs over the side of the bed, he answered the call.

I drank in the sleep-mussed hair, the smooth lines of his shoulders, the delicate edges of the tattoo cascading over the back of his arm. Last night, I'd let go of everything that held me back. I let go and trusted that Jude would catch me.

And he had.

Every mushy cliché jogged through my mind and, for once, I did not curl my lip in disgust. Instead, I couldn't stop smiling.

Feeling my eyes on him, Jude glanced over and smiled back. He reached out and brushed a piece of hair from my forehead. I leaned into his touch and closed my eyes.

Goodbye, Old Cat.

"Right, right. I understand." Jude retracted his hand, and the bed shifted as he stood. Peeking from one eye, I watched him pace the small space. "That's what I was thinking." Tilting his head, he listened to the person on the other end respond. With a look my way, he eased toward the door and covered the speaker with his hand. "I'll be right back."

As the door closed behind him, I snuggled deeper into our cocoon of blankets and pillows. My body still ached from his touch, but my heart...my heart had never felt this good.

So, this is what it feels like to fly.

My reverie was interrupted by an enormous growl emanating from my stomach. Oh, right. Breakfast.

I sat up and reached for a silver-wrapped toaster pastry. As I tore it open, I sent a subliminal message passed the closed bedroom door. *Get back in here,* it said. *Get back in here and hold me.*

As if he heard me, Jude pushed the door open. "Hey." He smiled as he crossed the room. "Sorry about that."

I smiled back and pulled my pastry from its wrapper. "Everything all right with work?"

"Yeah." He put his phone on the nightstand and sat on the edge of the bed. "Yeah, everything's fine."

I tossed the blankets aside and slid across the space between us, wrapping my legs around his waist. "I certainly hope they apologized for yanking you away from the completely undressed chick in your bed."

He laughed. "I didn't get an apology." His hand ran along the top of my thigh. Little sparks of desire threatened to start a full-on inferno.

I rested my head against his back and resisted. "Rude."

His fingertips slid to my calf, but he didn't say anything.

I lifted my head and watched him make a return trip to my thigh. While my every cell leapt to attention, Jude's touch didn't seek anything more. His heartbeat thumped faster against my chest. I leaned forward to see his face. "You sure everything's okay?"

Jude glanced over, eyes like a partly cloudy sky. Before the sun could peek through, he looked away. "Yeah. Just..." His hand paused at my knee, and his thumb drew patterns across my skin. "I didn't get an apology, but I *did* get a job offer."

I gasped and pushed to my knees. "Jude, that's amazing!" Looping my arms over his shoulders, I smacked a kiss on his cheek. "Tell me everything!"

"It's a huge opportunity." His eyes flickered again, the clouds stubbornly staying put. He didn't look like a man on the verge of his dream job. "Everything I've been working for."

There was an invisible ellipsis at the end of his sentence. An impending *but*. I provided it.

"But..."

His gaze dropped to his hand, still on my knee. "It's in L.A."

"Oh." The weight of his words dropped me to my knees. I shivered from the loss of his warmth. "I didn't know you applied for a job in L.A."

Jude swiveled to face me. "It was months ago." He took my hand in his. "Before you and I..." His eyes fell to our intertwined fingers. "I didn't think I'd get it."

I pulled my hand back. *Distance*, came the familiar refrain. *There was safety in distance.*

Looks like you're about to be real *safe,* a voice whispered back.

I ignored it, and the searing pain it brought with it. "Well, you got it." I pulled the sheet tight around my body. *Smile,* the voice continued. *Don't let him see you cry.*

Ahh, Old Cat. Didn't take long for her to reappear.

I obeyed her command, never more grateful for the glossy barrier between me and the world. "Congrats."

I picked up my abandoned breakfast, putting a big, fat period at the end of the topic.

Jude ignored it. "Cat." He waited until I looked up. "We need to talk about it."

My thumb traced over the sprinkles on my toaster pastry. "Mmm, strawberry."

He covered my fidgeting hand with his. "Cat."

"No." I dropped the pastry and looked him in the eye. "We had an awesome weekend. Can we just...hold on to that for a while longer?"

The clouds in his eyes had turned to fire. "If you're buying time to build your walls back up—"

"No walls here." Before he could insist we talk about the flashing fuchsia elephant, I crossed the chasm between us and straddled him. My breasts brushed over his bare chest as I leaned closer, my lips hovering over his. "No clothes, either."

This—the fire, the passion, the sex—was easier. Safer. I understood the way Jude's body responded to mine, and mine to his. Anything else...well, I didn't want to think about that right now. More than anything in this moment, I needed to be back on familiar ground.

I grazed his bottom lip with my teeth, taking satisfaction in the tremor that rushed through his body. No tenderness here. No feelings. Just the friction of skin on skin, the fire of desire. I didn't need anything else.

Jude's hands covered mine and moved them to his chest. His lips pulled at mine, gentle, cherishing. Fingertips, soft as rain, caressed my cheeks. Slowly, he kissed me until my knees shook. Until my heart slammed against my ribs so hard I thought it would break. The bed beneath us felt crooked and so I gripped Jude's shoulders tight.

Something inside me shuddered and then broke. A whimper escaped my throat, but it felt different. Not from a carnal place, but from somewhere else, somewhere deeper. My hands slid up to Jude's cheeks, the stubble against my palms sending shivers over my body.

No.

I needed to bring it back to my level.

I dragged his mouth back to mine and kissed him, my hands buried in his hair. He throbbed hard against me and I tightened my legs around his waist. "Jude," I whispered. "I need you. Now."

As he pushed me onto my back and reclaimed my lips, one thought echoed loud above the cacophony of noise in my mind. A thought I wanted to ignore. A thought that had the power to break my heart.

I wanted him to stay.

But he was already gone.

33: Splat

I f there were a competition for Most Creative Ways to Avoid a Conversation, I'd be the front-runner.

Over the next few days, every time Jude approached the subject of his inevitable departure, I'd suddenly find his lips irresistible. My clothes uncomfortable. His touch vital for my survival. I couldn't remember the last time I'd had so much sex, in so many different places or positions.

After day three of hot, exciting, subject-changing sex, Jude caught on. I had to reach deep into my bag of tricks for an old favorite to get out of The Talk.

I hadn't done *that* in years.

By day four, there was no distracting him. That left one other tactic: avoidance.

Which was how I'd allowed the girls from work to drag me out for Karaoke night that Friday. A decision I regretted more than ever as Beth-Ann rehashed her Dog vs. Bra story while a middle-aged man in a sweater vest serenaded us with an enthusiastic and off-key rendition of "Ice, Ice Baby."

"So we compromised." She raised her voice to be heard over the music. "I'll buy cheaper bras and he'll send his dog to obedience school."

Kylie frowned and leaned forward so that we could hear her. "That's not a good compromise at all." She pulled the cherry out of her froufrou drink and popped it into her mouth. "If the dog is going to obedience school, why should you have to give up your underwear?"

"I thought you dumped that dude," I said and immediately wished I could take it back. I didn't want to be involved in this inane conversation.

I didn't want to be involved in any conversation.

But this conversation was better than the one Jude wanted to have.

At that thought, I leaned forward and rested my hand on my chin, the picture of attentiveness. I'd sacrifice all my brain cells to this inane chatter to avoid *that*.

"I did." Beth-Ann replied. "But he's so cute when he grovels."

"As cute as the dog with your bra in its mouth?" Kylie cut in. "I find that questionable."

Onstage, Sweater Vest ended his song, and a plump, graying woman in glasses took over. The opening chords of "Wind Beneath My Wings" started and I exhaled slowly. This night just kept getting better.

Across from me, Beth-Ann pounded back the rest of her drink. "You girls ready?" she asked once she finished.

My head shot up. "What?"

Kylie daintily sipped from her glass. "Ready."

Then, before I could process, both girls were on their feet, arms linked with mine, as we headed for the stage.

Stilettos were good for a lot of things—leveling height differences, improving any outfit, making the menfolk go crazy—but they sucked for traction. I tried to stop, but my feet just slid across the floor. "I don't sing," I said as we neared the stage. "Not even a little bit."

"Oh, come on!" Kylie gave me a final pull, and I stumbled to a stop in front of the songbook. "It'll be fun!"

"I don't think you know what that word means," I said as I eyed the sanctuary of our abandoned table. "Because this ain't it."

My protests went unheard as they poured over the song list. Kylie's hand did not drop from my wrist, preventing any attempt at escape. Once the wind was no longer whooshing beneath the older woman's wings, she left the stage to make room for us. Seconds later, the bar was filled with the beat of a vintage Britney Spears number.

As the song barreled into its first chorus, Kylie took the lead, leaving Beth-Ann and I in the background. Fine by me. I swayed mindlessly and sang the words, trying not to wince when Kylie butchered the high note.

Our performance came to its merciful end, and we made our way back to our seats, collecting high-fives and cheers from our fellow Karaoke enthusiasts. Clearly, their standards weren't very high. Once we were back in our seats, Sweater Vest sent a fresh round of drinks our way.

As I lifted my glass to him in thanks, I leaned in to Beth-Ann. "You should get his number. I bet he's a cat person."

Her eyes widened. "I've got a boyfr...huh." She gave him a once-over, then turned back to us. "You think?"

I shrugged. "'Course, he probably still lives with his mom. So, ya know. Win some, lose some."

Kylie laughed and speared the cherry in her glass with the straw. "At least your bras would be safe."

Beth-Ann looked back at Sweater Vest, who tossed a grin and a wink her way. "Do you think he wears the vests when he's..."

A snort shot from Kylie. "Oh, he totally does."

As they continued to discuss his potential sexual habits, Sweater Vest took the stage again. A familiar melody floated over the room.

Boy Toyz.

The song hit *Play* on the memory bank in my brain. Jude, singing along in the car, shamelessly attempting the high notes. At Tierney's wedding, resting his chin on the top of my head as he serenaded me. And later...

I squeezed my eyes shut and stopped that memory before it could fully form. Good memories were not helpful right now. Not when, as soon as I gave him the chance, Jude would tell me he was leaving.

The thought stabbed at my insides. How long could I avoid that talk? How long before he sat me down, took my hand in his, and told me he'd made a decision. That he'd taken the job.

How long before he walked away?

I took a hearty gulp of my drink and signaled the waitress for another. There'd be no thinking tonight.

"I LOVE YOU GUYS *so much!*" I leaned forward and peered into the front seat of Kylie's Fiesta. "You are *such* a good singer!" Reaching in, I booped her nose.

Kylie laughed as Beth-Ann peered around her. "You need help getting upstairs?"

"Me?" I straightened and waved her off. "Pssh. No, I'm good." Taking a step back, I tripped over the curb and caught myself. "I'm fine!"

Beth-Ann frowned. "Are you su—"

"I'm sure. I'm good!" Leaning down, I waved. "We should do this again! Soon!" I straightened and headed toward my building. "See you at work!"

As I pulled open the lobby door, I hummed the chorus of the last song we'd performed—"Lady Marmalade" had never sounded better—and dug into my purse for my keys. My veins buzzed from the fourth...or fifth...drink I'd downed at the bar. I couldn't wait to crawl into bed and sleep a long, dreamless sleep. No more thoughts of—

"Hey."

I froze. Jude stood outside my door, his smudgy eyes lighting up on my face.

Dammit.

I shook my hair away from my already-heated face and tried to hide my surprise. "*Heeey*."

"Sorry to just show up, but I finished work early, and I..." he trailed off and rubbed his hand over his face. I inched toward the door. Maybe I could sneak inside before he—

"We need to talk."

Double dammit.

I dangled my keys from my fingertips and looked up.

I need to tell you I'm leaving.

He didn't say the words out loud, but he didn't have to. I could feel them in my bones. And I wasn't ready to hear them.

I brushed passed him and shoved my key into the knob. Or tried to. "Just give me five minutes to stretch." Tossing a flirty smile over my shoulder, I tried the keys again. Success. "And we can try that thing again." Pushing open the door, I stumbled inside.

"No, Cat." He steadied me. "We need to *talk*."

A long groan left my lungs. "But, why?" I leaned against the door-frame and closed my eyes. "I don't want to."

"I know." He pushed a piece of hair away from my face. "Believe me, if I could keep letting you use sex as a distraction, I would. I mean, that thing you did the other night..."

"Good, right?" My fingers grasped the open flaps of his jacket and I pulled him closer. "There's more where that came from."

His eyes flickered briefly, but serious Jude took the reins before he could give in. "Cat..."

"I *know*," I groaned. "We need to talk." Pushing away from the door-frame, I entered the apartment, Jude close behind. I cast a wistful look down the hall. *Oh, bed*, I thought. *I can't wait to be inside you.*

Instead, here I was. About to have the conversation I'd been doing my best to avoid for days. Shouldn't a girl be able to put off her own inevitable heartbreak?

"Go on." I tossed my purse onto the couch and walked into the kitchen. I couldn't do this alone. "Get it out of the way." As I spoke, I yanked open the fridge, locating the half-empty bottle of Cabernet from Tierney's last visit.

Jude followed me. "How much have you had to drink?"

"Not enough." The stopper skittered across the counter, and I lifted the bottle to my lips. After a long swig, I met his eye. "Now, go on." Alcohol ran hot through my veins, leaving a soothing numbness behind. "Tell me you're taking the job."

Not numb enough.

I took another swig. "Tell me you're leaving." My eyes found his, and I blinked back the sting of tears. "Just like everyone else."

Jude flinched. "I—"

I pushed passed him and bent to remove my shoes. Wine dribbled from the bottle, splashing on the carpet. "Oops!" I laughed as I straightened, and watched the liquid soak in. "*This* is why I should only drink white."

He didn't even smile. "I'm not everyone else."

"See, but." I leaned against the couch and cradled the wine bottle against my chest while I worked on the second shoe. "You kinda are."

He crossed the room and stood in front of me, towering like an old pine. "I didn't come here to tell you I'm leaving."

"But you will." I tilted my head back to see his face. The room spun around him. Wasn't he dizzy? "You'll get my hopes up, make me love you, and then you'll leave." I stood and stumbled passed him. "They all do."

"Goddammit, Cat." Jude steadied me, his hand on my arm. "Would you listen to me?"

"Why?" I yanked my arm from his grasp and staggered backward. "What's the point?" I peered up at him. Was he getting taller?

"I should've known better. Should've stuck to my rules." I tucked the bottle into the crook of my elbow and glared. "But you had to go and break them. You...you damn tree." I pushed passed him toward the hall. Bed. Bed was down there somewhere.

And Jude wasn't.

Except that he was following me.

A growl rumbled through me as I faced him again. "What do you want?" I threw my arms wide. The wine bottle clunked to the floor. "Why won't you go away?"

"Because I—" He stopped. Looked at the wine at our feet, then back to me. "I don't think now's the best time for this conversation."

"Why not?" I crossed my arms, defiant. "You wanted to talk. Let's talk."

Instead of replying, he bent and picked up the bottle. I watched as he walked into the kitchen, returning seconds later with a wad of paper towel.

Irritation flared inside me. "You don't need to do that." I reached for the towel, but he moved away.

He knelt and began mopping up the mess. Without looking up, he said, "I'm going to head home. I'll be back in the morning, and we can finish this conversation then."

"Fuck that."

His head shot up. "What?"

"I don't need to wait until tomorrow, Jude." My eyes burned, but I went on. "If you're going to get on that plane, you can goddamn tell me tonight."

He stood, abandoning the mess. "I haven't made a decision yet." Conflict etched itself across his face. He wanted to take the job. I could see it.

Well, I wasn't going to be the reason he didn't. I wasn't going to be that person. He'd already been through that.

"Take the job."

"Cat, I—"

"Take the job, Jude." I lifted my chin, holding his gaze with mine. "It's what you want. And I won't be like Leslie."

At the mention of his ex-wife, Jude frowned. "This has nothing to do with Leslie. This is about me and you."

I shook my head. Leslie was tangible. Right there, in my grasp. The reason he would walk away. Even if he didn't see it yet.

So I had to make him see.

"It's not, though." I shoved my fingers through my hair. In my chest, my heart rattled loud, begging to be heard. Begging me to shut up. Begging me not to do this.

I ignored it.

"She held you back. I won't do that."

"That's not what—"

"It is." I stepped backward. "And that's not me." I met his eye once more as I reached my bedroom door. "Take the job."

And before he could say another word, I disappeared into my bedroom, closing the door behind me.

Once inside, all air hissed from my lungs and I sank against the door, sitting on the floor. Hugging my knees tight to my chest, I squeezed my eyes shut as my body started to tremble. I could still hear Jude outside my door. I pictured him, hand raised to knock before changing his mind. He'd drag his hand through his hair, huff out a breath, eye the door once more, and then he'd walk away.

I listened for footsteps, but they didn't come. Why wasn't he walking away? Everyone walked away. *Everyone.*

"Walk away, Jude," I whispered. "Prove me right." As I said the words, my heart thumped an entirely different wish. My heart begged Jude to stay. To hold his ground.

He hadn't moved yet. I leaned my head against the door, listening to him shuffle back and forth. Finally, he spoke. "Cat, listen," he said, his voice soft. "I know you're freaking out." He paused and my heart stopped with him. "There's a lot to consider. I... " He trailed off and I wanted to get up, open the door, and pull him close, ask him to stay. Instead, I pulled my knees tighter to my chest, a prisoner in my own body. All I could do was sit there, willing Jude to stay. To make a liar out of me. To show me that sometimes people *didn't* walk away.

Seconds ticked by, tears fell to the floor and I scrambled for the rubble around my heart, desperate for the safety of that wall.

"All right," Jude said, interrupting my thoughts. "I'll go. Just...I need you to trust me, Cat. Just a little bit." He sounded like I felt, torn and tortured. I placed my palm flat against the door, my heart fighting an epic war with my head.

Get up, Cat, I told myself. *Get up and open this door.*

I squeezed my eyes shut and willed my body to listen, but still I sat on the floor. I sat on the floor until it was too late, until Jude's footsteps sounded down the hall and he was gone.

And this time, I had no one to blame but myself.

34: Blue-Eyed Distraction

———

The sun scorched my eyeballs as I hit the sidewalk the next morning. I pulled my sunglasses from my purse and silently cursed the big ball of happy in the sky. Why was it that the weather never matched my mood? It should've been rainy and gloomy.

Apocalyptic.

The memories hadn't returned until I found the wine stains. Soaked into the carpet so deep they'd never come out. Might as well have been my blood.

Take the job, Jude.

I swallowed the bitterness that filled my mouth. Why had I said that?

Because you meant it, a voice replied. *Because you knew it was the right thing to do.*

Reaching beneath my sunglasses, I rubbed a gritty eye. In the light of day, things were usually clearer. Made more sense. Or, at times, were mortifying lessons in Drinking Too Much. This morning's memories fit none of those categories. No, they came with a hefty helping of *What the hell did I do?*

Sober Cat wanted to call him. To tell him she'd made a mistake, that she was sorry, and to please stay. But the lingering doubts remained. Doubts I'd done a good job of avoiding for days. Doubts that came roaring to the surface last night.

Drunk Cat had a point: Jude's ex-wife had held him back. Kept him from the things he wanted. If I asked him to stay, how was I any better?

I wasn't.

So I couldn't ask him.

And I couldn't go with him.

The thought had occurred to me somewhere around 4 a.m. It was promptly followed by thoughts of Hazel and Tierney and, yes, even Mom.

I couldn't leave.

So *goodbye* was the only answer.

A surge of nausea rushed through me, and I squeezed my eyes shut. I gave myself thirty seconds of self-pity before forging ahead.

Down the street, my favorite food truck was serving up the greasiest, most delicious burgers. The final ingredient in Cat Keller's Hangover Cure. At least I could solve *one* of my problems right now.

The other...well, judging by my silent phone, it seemed to have solved itself.

As I stood in line, I idly eyed a group of kids watching their dad light up the fuse on a packet of firecrackers. Oh, yeah. Fourth of July. Fireworks. Freedom.

Whatever.

"Now, that's not the face of someone who's about to enjoy the best burger in town."

I turned to find a pair of blue eyes sparkling at me.

Luke.

I mustered up something resembling a smile, and my already-raw insides twisted. Just seeing him brought back memories of Tierney's wedding reception, and everything that followed. Little did Luke know, he'd been the catalyst for so many good things.

And some not so good.

"I don't like to be kept from my food," I muttered as I turned back to the shrinking line in front of me.

"Understandable." He shifted behind me, and I could tell he wasn't sure if he should continue.

Good, I thought. *Go away.*

He didn't.

"You doing okay?"

I turned to find his eyes on my face. The genuine concern in them caught me off guard, and I had to choke back a surge of emotion. *Hangover side effect,* I told myself. *Nothing more.*

"Oh, yeah," I said with a wide, fake grin. "Just fine."

"I don't believe you." Luke narrowed his gaze on me. "But I also don't know you well enough to call you on it."

For a brief flash, Old Cat came out to play. "Well, what are you gonna do about it?" I grinned, and it was like trying on an old favorite pair of shoes, only to find your feet had grown.

"Next!" the guy in the window called, and I jumped, guilt spilling over me like a bucket of ice water.

I practically ran to the counter. "Hey," I said with too much enthusiasm. *See?* I told myself. *I'm friendly with everyone!* "How're you?"

"Doing good," the cashier replied, unmoved by my friendliness. "What can I get for ya?"

I rattled off an order big enough to feed three people, acutely aware of Luke still standing behind me. I wanted to rewind, go back, undo that weird flirty moment. I did not want to flirt with Luke. I didn't want to flirt with anyone. I just wanted to go home and eat greasy food and pretend the last few months had never happened. Pretend last night had never happened.

Hell, even pretend the last five minutes had never happened.

"Ugh."

The cashier's eyes widened. "Excuse me?"

"No, no. Not you." I waved a hand. "Sorry. Just...sorry."

He nodded slowly as he handed my card back. "Your food will be right up."

"Thanks."

I stepped aside and busied myself putting my wallet back into my purse. Home. I really needed to be home. Away from people. Away from everything.

"I think you threw him off." Luke took the empty spot beside me after placing his order. "Maybe even turned him on a little bit."

I snorted. "Yeah. That's kind of my schtick." Yanking the zipper closed on my purse, I readjusted my sunglasses and stared straight ahead.

"I've noticed." There was a smile in Luke's voice, and I looked over to see if it made it to his face. It did. "So," he continued once he had my attention. "I was thinking—"

"Listen, Luke." I faced him. "I'm gonna be real up front with you."

"Uh oh." His blue eyes sparked. "I'm listening."

"You're a nice guy, but I'm not in the best place—"

"I think you're misunderstanding me," he cut in. My mouth snapped shut, and he continued. "I'm not asking you on a date. You've made it very clear you're not interested."

"Okay..."

"You seem kind of down, and I just figured it'd be a shame to sit home alone on a holiday, when everyone else is out enjoying themselves."

"What makes you think I'm going to be home alone?" I growled, silently urging my food to cook faster. Maybe I shouldn't have ordered the second burger. I could've already been on my way home...

"You got me there." Luke smiled—looking remarkably like his brother—and continued, "Anyway, on the off chance you'll be alone, there's a huge thing at the park tonight. Food, music, fireworks. I thought I'd check it out. You should come along."

My immediate reaction was to turn him down. Of course I would turn him down. After everything with Jude...well, a warning sign should've been flashing over my head. *Hazard Ahead,* it'd say. *Turn Back Now.*

This guy didn't seem to notice the warning signs, though.

I crossed my arms and looked him up and down, assessing. He really *was* a good-looking guy. Any other time, I wouldn't have even hesitated to say yes. In fact, I *had* said yes once before. This wasn't any other time, though.

But why *wasn't* it any other time?

A pair of gray-green eyes flashed through my mind, all warm and caring and *abso-fucking-lutely* terrifying. My heart seized, tight and burning, and I gritted my teeth, refocusing my attention on Luke.

His eyes were bright and blue and not at all terrifying.

Why the hell not?

35: Boom

———

Hope River Park was packed with people. The annual Fourth of July barbecue was in full swing. As we entered the mass of people later that night,

Luke tossed a smile over his shoulder. "Hope you're hungry," he was saying as we weaved through the crowd. "This year's barbecue features a hot dog bar with all the fixings—*and* ice cream."

My tummy rumbled at the thought. "You mean, I could have a hot dog with mustard, chili, *and* a cherry on top?"

We reached an opening with two rows of tables loaded with food. "I mean, if that's what you really want, I'm sure we could rustle up a cherry." He held a plate out to me.

I took it. "Hopefully, they've got potato chips for the ice cream."

The moment the words were out of my mouth, my mind shot to a night a few weeks back, with a marathon of *Until the End of Time,* and ice cream sundaes. A smile pulled at my lips, even as I shoved the memory away. Jude was the past. There would be no more TV marathons or dimpled grins.

A heaviness settled over me and no matter how I tried to shake it off, it lingered. What had I been thinking, agreeing to come out tonight? This was a dumb, stupid, horrible idea. I needed to go back home and think about what I'd done.

Numbly, I loaded a plate with food, my stomach full of rocks. And guilt. Rocks and guilt and hurty things.

As we reached our seats, Luke's eyes narrowed on my face. "You all right over there?"

I forced a grin and plopped down in my chair. "I'm fine." I picked up my fork and stabbed my potato salad. "Spectacular, even."

Taking the seat across from me, he grabbed his own fork. "You're a terrible liar," he said as he pushed his baked beans away from his potato chips. He didn't look up from his plate, but he continued talking. "So, why are you alone this weekend, anyway?"

I could hear the unspoken question—what happened with the guy? And I didn't want to answer it. I stared at the ketchup swirl on my hotdog. "Why are *you* alone this weekend?"

Luke laughed. I looked up in time to see his eyes crinkling at the corners. "Fair enough." He sat his fork aside and folded his hands in front of him. "I got stood up."

"What?" I leaned forward, scrutinizing him. "How? Who? *Why?*"

The strands of lights draped overhead caught a glimmer of something less-than-happy in his eyes, and I immediately wanted to take back my interrogation. "Bad timing?" he replied, shoulder lifting. "Old flame. Changed her mind."

Sitting back, I studied him. His tone was casual, body language relaxed, but I wasn't buying it. I wanted to push, to find out more, but I wasn't prepared to reciprocate, so I picked up my hotdog and too a huge bite instead. "Sucks, man," I said. "I'm sorry."

"Me, too." He smiled. "For whatever reason it is that you're alone." Holding up his hotdog in a mock toast, he took a bite.

Once we finished eating, we headed toward the Riverwalk Café, which had a balcony overlooking Hope River. The seats on the balcony were the best place to be for the fireworks display. Or so I'd heard. I'd never actually been there. Reservations for those seats were pretty pricey.

We got settled in on the balcony just as the show started. Splashes of color shot over the river, lighting up the sky and reflecting off the water. Luke settled in beside me and let out a whistle. "Hell of a view, huh?"

"Oh, yeah." I leaned in to be heard over the fireworks. "You sure know how to show a girl a good time."

He laughed. "Yeah, when they show up."

"Aww, man." I looked over, but the rest of my reply died on my lips as my eyes locked with the person standing twenty feet away.

Jude.

"Shit." I jumped up from my seat. "*Shit.*"

Luke frowned up at me. "What's wrong?"

"I'm sorry, I just..." My head swiveled. Where did Jude go? "I...I have to go."

"All right." He stood, confusion crinkling his face. "Well let me at least drive you ho—"

"No, no." I backed away from our seats and squinted through the dark. I couldn't see him. He had to be here somewhere. He didn't just disappear. "I'm sorry, Luke. I just...I've got to go."

I didn't wait for him to respond. Couldn't wait. The longer I stayed here, the further away Jude was getting, and I needed to find him. I needed to find him and tell him...

Tell him what?

That I'd gotten drunk and dumped him, only to go out with a new guy the next night? *He* didn't know this wasn't a date.

My heart slammed hard against my ribs as I maneuvered through the crowd, peppering my speech with *excuse me* and *I'm sorry.*

"*Fuckshitdamn*," I muttered, slipping sideways through a crowd of overly-enthusiastic teenagers. Where was he?

I reached the exit without a sign of him, and so, defeated, I went down the stairs and sat on the bench just outside the restaurant. Fireworks shot over the water, each boom reverberating through my body with every beat of my ragged heart.

"You know, we never said we were exclusive."

I looked up to find him standing in front of me. My eyes drank him in hungrily, from the tips of his sneakered feet to his red t-shirt to his cautious, storm-gray eyes. I started to stand, but he motioned for me to stay seated.

"We never had that discussion," he continued. "So, maybe I don't have the right to be upset about this." He waved a hand toward the restaurant, indicating Luke. I opened my mouth to explain, to tell him it wasn't what it looked like, but he spoke again before I could utter a syllable. "But you didn't even give me a chance, Cat." Shoving a hand through his hair, he sat down beside me. "You didn't give me a chance to stay."

I glanced over at him, pulling my ponytail over my shoulder to twist the ends. My chest tightened as I took in the kaleidoscope of emotions on his face. "Jude, I—"

"What are we doing?" he cut in. "Because I thought we were heading somewhere good."

"We were." A lump formed in my throat as he turned his head toward me. The multi-colored lights from the fireworks glowed on his face, and I didn't think he'd ever been more beautiful. He'd never been more out of reach, either. "But you're going to leave."

His eyes flashed hot. "Goddammit," he ground out. "You can't keep going through life thinking everyone is like your father. Like Arthur."

"What do you want from me, Jude?" I spread my hands out in front of me. "I'm fucked up."

"Don't pull that shit with me." He gaze didn't leave mine. "Everybody's fucked up. Not one person makes it through life unscathed." He paused. His next words came out slowly, deliberately. "Not everyone uses their issues as an excuse to hide from the world, either."

I flinched. "That's not—"

"You can't just choose not to feel anything." He dragged a hand through his hair. "You can't pretend you didn't feel anything between us."

I leapt to my feet. "That's just it, Jude! I didn't want to *feel*." My voice cracked, but I pushed passed it. "This was supposed to just be sex. Then somewhere along the way it got all mixed up, and now the lines are blurred, and I...I can't do it."

"Why does everything have to be so black and white with you? All or nothing. Love or fucking. Stay or go." He shoved his hands into his hair and let out an exasperated breath. "You ever think there's more to this—to *us*—than that?"

My eyes filled and I looked away. Part of me, the broken, sick, beating part of me wished I could end this fight, throw myself into his arms and say, *Yes. I want this. I want you. Whatever it takes, I want you.*

But a voice screamed loud above the whisper, told me to run, to rebuild the walls, asked me if I wanted to risk it.

Because, as much as I wanted to believe in us, there were no guarantees. Six months from now, a year from now, five years from now, we could crash and burn. He would realize what he'd given up to stay with me, and he would leave. And I didn't think I'd survive that.

"I told you I couldn't do it." My voice was husky with tears I refused to shed. "It's unfair of you to ask for more."

Jude's eyes burned into mine. His face was a stone mask, not a shimmer of emotion. Not the Jude I'd let crash through my walls. I shivered.

"I'm not asking for anything, Cat." His voice was nearly lost in the booming show behind him. "Not anymore."

And as the grand finale started, he walked away, leaving my heart in the dirt at my feet.

36: You Get Hurt Either Way

"Good morning, darling daughter," my mother sang as I reached her table. "You're looking...well."

I pulled off my oversized sunglasses to hit her with a laser beam glare, then plopped down in the chair across from her. "You're lucky I'm here at all."

I hadn't slept in the week since the breakup. At all. My nights were spent chasing visions of dumb boys from my mind and trying to convince myself that I should join a convent. Marry Jesus. That dude was nowhere near as complicated.

Mother pursed her lips. "You really shouldn't stay out all night, sweetheart. You're no spring chicken. You won't recover from your drinking as well as you used to. That's just science."

I bit back the bitchy reply on the tip of my tongue and eyed the empty seat next to her. "Where's Arthur?"

An ever-so-slight crack appeared in her glossy veneer. She straightened and pushed a lock of hair behind her ear. "I'm afraid Arthur and I are no longer seeing each other."

An onslaught of emotions rained down on me: concern, relief, self-satisfaction. A complete lack of surprise. I'd called it from the beginning. What I *didn't* call was the obvious misery on my mother's face. I hadn't seen her this upset since...

Well, since the first time she and Arthur broke up.

"What happened?" I asked, though my gut already knew the answer.

Her gray eyes found mine. I waited for the usual reply: *The chemistry wasn't right.* Or, *He clipped his toenails in bed.* Instead, she said, "He didn't want to keep hurting you."

Shock spilled ice-cold over me. I sat back and dropped my eyes from hers. Man, I was killing it lately. Everywhere I turned, I broke something.

"I'm sorry, Mom," I said, and I meant it. I didn't want to see Arthur, but that didn't mean I wanted her to hurt. "Is there anything I can—"

"Actually, yes." If the look on her face was any indicator, her next words were not going to be pleasant ones.

I sat straighter and prepared myself for the tirade: *Why couldn't you have tried? Must you always be so difficult?* And, my favorite, *When are you going to grow up, Catherine?*

Johnny the waiter chose that moment to appear, delaying my verbal execution a few moments longer. Pencil poised over his notepad, he said, "The usual, Miss?"

I started to answer before I realized he was talking to my mother. *Suck up.*

Mom sat her menu aside and smiled. "Yes, please."

Johnny nodded, clearly relieved to have pleased the beast.

"And for you, Miss?"

"I'm not hungry." I smiled up at him. "Thank you, though."

Silence descended upon us. I looked up to find both Johnny and my mother staring slack-jawed at me. "What?"

"N-nothing," Johnny stammered. "Just water, then?" I nodded and he backed away, leaving Mom and I alone.

"Not hungry?" Mom said, her delicate brow arching. "You've never uttered those words. Are you ill?"

"I'm fine." I picked the remaining bits of weeks-old polish off my nails. Fleck by fleck, I dusted the white linen with pink sparkles. "Just not hungry."

Mom's eyes lingered on my face for a few seconds before she gave a tight nod. "All right."

I savored the quiet that followed, closing my eyes to soak it in. Exhaustion seeped from my bones. I was tempted to use the basket of rolls as a pillow and snooze the meal away. If I thought that would keep Mom from un-pausing our conversation, I would have.

All too soon, the quiet came to an end. "As I was saying," she said, and my head jerked up.

Here we go.

"My first impulse when Arthur ended our relationship was to blame you—I couldn't understand why you wouldn't give him a chance. Why you wouldn't give *us* a chance." She toyed with the tines of her salad fork as she spoke, not looking at me.

I quelled my go-to response—a defense built of snark and deflection—and waited quietly for her to continue, no energy left to defend myself.

"But I spent some time thinking, and...well, I understand." *Tink, tink, tink* went her nails along the fork. "I didn't give you a particularly strong foundation to build your life on."

Sympathy—an emotion I hadn't felt for my mother in years—surged forward. "Mom, that's not true. You—"

"I don't mean materialistically." She lifted her gaze. "The way I handled the hard stuff—heartbreak, grief, vulnerability—well, I'm afraid I set a bad example."

I sat back in my seat, stunned. My mother had never been one to admit fault. Something outside of her was always to blame for the demise of her relationships. Every single time.

"I...um..." I trailed off, not even sure what to say.

In my silence, Mom kept talking. "I'm worried about you, Catharine."

The words fell out onto the table with a loud thump. My head spun around to see if anyone else had heard the racket, but I seemed to be the only one.

Bringing my eyes back to Mom, I said, "I'm fine. No need to worry. I've never been better." The lie was bitter on my tongue and I regretted not ordering something strong to wash it away.

Mother crossed her arms on the table and lifted her impeccable brows. "We're both adults here, darling. No need to lie."

Reaching into the breadbasket, I grabbed a roll and bit into it. It tasted like Styrofoam, but I kept chewing. "I'm not lying. I am seriously so awesome right now."

"You're wearing sweatpants."

I shrugged. "Comfy."

"And you didn't order your grease-soaked death sticks."

"I—"

Shit. She had me there.

"So what?" I tossed the roll back into the basket, earning a disgusted-but-subtle sneer. "You should be pleased. Between the food and the emotional dysfunction, I'm becoming more like you every damn day."

"That is the absolute last thing that I want."

The fire in her voice brought every syllable of sarcasm to a halt. "I've spent years wishing I could have a moment—just one moment—of fearlessness. Of certainty. Resilience." She paused for breath, and I didn't move, convinced that if I did, she'd revert back to the closed-off, reserved mother I'd known my whole life.

"Why do you think I've been married so many times?"

I opened my mouth, then promptly shut it. She wasn't looking for any answer, let alone the ones I'd give.

"I meet these men and they're nice and treat me well, but I hold my heart just out of reach. The moment they get close, I leave. I hurt them. I leave before they can hurt me."

She said it all so casually, like she was talking about the season's latest fashion trend.

"I loved your father," she went on. "Fiercely and intensely loved him. With everything in me. And he left. It didn't matter how much I loved him, he was always going to leave." Her shoulder lifted. So matter-of-fact. I leaned forward, trying to remember the last time she'd talked about the man who made up half my DNA.

It'd been *years.*

"Arthur was different." Her lips tilted in a soft smile. "He knew I was pushing him away. He knew and he didn't care. That man...he was determined."

Her eyes drifted off into the distance, dreamy and unfocused, and it was clear that she'd loved *him*, too. "Each year we spent together, he chipped away more of my defenses. Until..." Trailing off, she blinked.

Was she crying?

"Until?" My heart hammered. I had always wondered what happened with Arthur. They seemed so happy. He adored her. They were—

"Until I cheated on him."

"Y-you what?"

Blowing out a deep breath, Mom met my eye. "I cheated. He was so determined to show me that he could love me and not hurt me, to make me feel safe enough to love him in return, and..." Her voice cracked and a tear slipped down her cheek. "I ruined the best thing I ever had."

I watched as the tear soaked into the tablecloth, stunned. For years, I painted Arthur as the bad guy. As the evil man who left us without reason and didn't look back. But it turned out...

My bloodstream burned hot. "Why didn't you tell me?" I slapped my hand on the tabletop and the ice in our glasses rattled. Mom flinched. "How could you let me believe he...he just *left*? Do you know what that did to me?"

"I know." She hastily wiped a tear from her cheek. The gloss was gone. The pretense. "I'm sorry, Cat. I'm so, so sorry."

I clung to my anger like a scarf keeping me warm in the winter. "Years, Mother. I didn't speak to him for *years*. He was my dad!" My heart twisted like a wrung-out dishrag. All that time we wasted—all that time *I* wasted. How different would my life have turned out if she'd only told me...

"Dammit." I scrubbed away the tears stinging my eyes. "How could you do that?"

"I was scared," Mom whispered. The vulnerability in those three words stopped me cold. "I lost him, and I knew I'd lose you, too." Her lips lifted in a sad smile. "I lost you anyway, didn't I?"

I sat back, a silent laugh filling the space between us. "Self-preservation is a miraculous thing, Mother."

She met my eye and nodded. "I know." Her fingertips found the fork again. *Tink, tink, tink.* "We're the same that way."

I froze. "I'm nothing like you."

She shook her head. "You're *just* like me." Her eyes still shone with tears, but she blinked them back before they could fall. "We leave first, so we don't get hurt. Only...it doesn't work, Catharine. You get hurt either way."

A thousand thoughts rushed through my head as I held her tear-soaked stare. Among the loudest: my mother was human. Real and vulnerable and imperfect.

Scared.

Even now, she was scared. The truth she'd held onto for years could blow apart the fragile relationship we had. She could've kept holding it close. Could've held onto it forever. But she came clean. And that...well, that was something.

Looking at her now, her cheeks stained with mascara, eyes wide and vulnerable, always-steady hands shaking, my heart refused to shut her out. She'd risked everything to tell me the truth. Forgiveness was a long way off, but I had to acknowledge her bravery.

I stood and rounded the table, pulling her close. I hugged her hard. "I...I love you," I whispered, dropping a kiss on her cheek.

"I love you, too." Her arms wrapped around me, and I inhaled the fancy perfume I hadn't been close enough to smell for years.

We stayed that way for a few more seconds before Mom became Mom again. "I think people are starting to stare," she said, and that was my cue.

"Right, sorry." I returned to my seat and looked at my mother through new eyes. "Thank you so much for sharing that with me."

She nodded curtly and then flagged down Johnny. "Dear, would you bring my daughter a burger?" Then, after a quick glance in my direction, she added, "And extra napkins."

37: Amends & Oreos

On the way home, I called Hazel. I owed her one hell of a thank you—for the years she'd spent stuck in between her own son and me. She didn't owe me anything. I wasn't her flesh and blood. But Arthur was. And Arthur was the one who'd been wronged.

But she stuck by me, too.

I needed to thank her for that.

She picked up the phone on the third ring.

"Grandma?" My voice came out tiny and quiet as tears pricked my eyes.

Immediately, Hazel was on the alert. "What's wrong, Kitten?"

I laughed—a short, singular sound. "I just finished brunch with Mom."

"What did that woman say to upset you now?"

I was silent for a couple seconds, unsure of how I wanted to put my next words. Finally, I said, "How come you didn't tell me why Arthur left?"

It was Hazel's turn to be quiet. Closing my eyes, I listened harder, willing her to respond. Needing the ground to steady beneath my feet once more. My mother's revelation sent my entire world topsy-turvy. I needed to be on level ground again. Maybe Hazel could give me that.

"It wasn't my place," she finally said. "Arthur didn't want you to be angry at your mom for the divorce. Clearly, that didn't work out, but his intentions were noble."

"But, if I had known..." I squeezed my eyes shut as the pain of all those missed years hit me. "If I had known, maybe I wouldn't have shut him out."

"Or maybe you would have. People do weird things to protect themselves, Kitten." Hazel softened her voice, and I suddenly wished I were right there beside her, laying my head on her shoulder. "Your thing just happened to be locking yourself away in a tower where no one could reach you."

The image she painted struck something in me and I sat up straight. Walls, towers, planes. Everything that kept people away. Arthur, my mother, Jude...all kept at a safe distance, so that I wouldn't get hurt.

"The thing is, sweetheart," Hazel continued. "Eventually, you're going to have to come down. No one can lock themselves away forever."

"Stop making sense, please," I muttered, the interior of the car closing in on me as revelation after revelation rolled in.

"I'll do no such thing," she shot back. "It sounds like you've got some thinking ahead of you."

"Nothing good ever came from *thinking*," I grumbled as I headed into my building. "I much prefer avoidance."

Hazel chuckled. "A lot of good that's done you, dear." In the background, something beeped. "That's my casserole. I'm going to let you go, dear. See you Wednesday?"

"Yes. Please." I pushed open my apartment door and kicked it closed behind me. "I can't wait."

After Hazel hung up, I tossed my keys and phone onto the counter and dive-bombed the couch. The cushions cradled me in all the best ways and I sighed. Sleep would've been awesome. I hadn't done much of that lately. But with all the new information that had just been piled on top of the old stuff, there was no way I'd sleep.

Turning my head, I let my gaze rove over the room. Bookshelf, gaming console, TV, wine glass, empty potato chip bag, day-old pizza—ugh.

I couldn't live like this. My insides were a mess. Nothing to be done about that. But *this* mess? This mess, I could clean up.

Standing, I grabbed the pizza box and piled crap on top. I'd just reached for the empty wine glass when something caught my eye. A little white gift box that'd been half-tucked beneath the pizza. What was...

Arthur.

Immediately, my mind replayed the memory—Jude and I on the couch. Arthur at the door. My heart in shambles over Peach.

At first, I'd intentionally ignored the package. Why did I care what Arthur brought me? I didn't even care about Arthur. Screw Arthur.

But then, in all that had happened after, I just plain forgot about the thing.

Now, armed with new information, well...maybe a quick peek.

Setting the precarious mess back onto the coffee table, I grabbed the package. It wasn't very heavy, and it didn't rattle when I shook it. Good gifts rattled. At least from what I remembered from my childhood.

Then again, it was well-known throughout the adult community that gifts passed the age of eighteen were much more boring.

Sighing my resignation, I pulled off the lid.

And my heart dropped to my toes.

Inside the box, surrounded by white tissue paper, was a simple wooden picture frame, showcasing a tiny redheaded girl and her even tinier kitten.

Setting the rest of the box aside, I lifted the frame and ran my fingertips over the photo. This was the day Arthur brought Peach home. I recognized the sheer ecstasy on my face. And the terror on Peach's. Three hours after, we'd taken Peach to Hazel's.

But before that...

It'd been the best day of my life.

I blinked as a tear splashed onto the photograph, bringing me back to the present.

Despite how everything turned out—the divorce, the giant rift between us—there had been some good. There'd been lots of good. I'd spent so long focusing on the bad, I'd almost forgotten.

But that cheese-grinned kid in the picture remembered.

And I wanted to remember, too.

I wanted to feel like that again.

Sniffling, I pushed away from the couch and propped the frame up on the coffee table.

It was time to make that leap.

THE HOUSE LOOKED EXACTLY the same. Two stories with blue siding and a white wrap-around porch, with the waves of Lake Michigan in the background.

My heart seized as a brief memory shot through me. Eight-year-old me, chasing Arthur around the yard with a squirt gun.

The summer sun was hot, the water was cold, and I had never been happier. One of the many memories I'd blocked out after the divorce. It had hurt too much to think about the good times.

I could only imagine how much it had hurt Arthur, too. And I made it worse by shutting him out all these years.

I couldn't take that back, but I could try to make it better.

I pulled up to the curb and turned off the car, taking a deep breath. I didn't know what I would say once I entered that house. I'd just have to wing it.

Before Old Cat got the best of me, I flung open the car door and got out. Tugging the sleeves of my sweatshirt over my hands, I marched up the walk and knocked on the door. No going back now.

The thirty seconds from the moment I knocked to the moment the door swung open were the most excruciating of my life. By the time I came face-to-face with Arthur, I had indents in my palms from my fingernails digging in and my stomach had twisted into intricate knots.

"Cat?" Arthur pulled the door open wider. "Well, this is a surprise."

"I know. I'm sorry." I took a step backward. "If I'm interrupting something, I...I can come back," I twisted my hands together and backed toward my car.

Arthur put up a hand to stop me. "No, no. Please, come in," he said, holding the door open.

I gave him a half-smile and entered the house, gob smacked by the familiarity. We'd spent every summer here while Arthur and Mom were married. Almost everything was the same, from the gleaming hardwood floors to the sweeping staircase I used to race down every morning, anxious to get to the beach.

Moving further into the foyer, my fingers ran along the wall, adorned with various framed photos. A snapshot of me at seven, holding up a birthday cupcake, candle lit, toothless grin. Another of Arthur and I on his sailboat when I was around fourteen. An empty spot where the one of Peach and me had been.

There were a couple of Hazel and Zeke, too, but my eyes kept traveling back to one photo in particular. My college graduation. Cap and gown, cheesy grin on my face. It was about six years after the divorce. Arthur hadn't been there.

I rested my finger on the frame and looked at him. "Why this one?"

Arthur met my eyes, his crinkled at the corners. "Just because your mother and I divorced, doesn't mean I stopped caring."

At that, tears filled my eyes. I'd done so good keeping them at bay, but I couldn't stop them now. Arthur took a step forward, then paused, unsure if he should comfort me. I wiped at the tears and lifted my eyes to his. "I'm sorry." My voice cracked on the last syllable. "I...Mom told me what happened—the first time—and I'm so sorry."

Wringing my hands together, I headed for the kitchen, surprised I remembered where it was. I went to the fridge and pulled out a carton of milk, then grabbed a glass from the cupboard.

Arthur went to another cupboard and pulled out a package of Oreos, opening it as he headed to the table. I followed and sat down, reaching for a cookie.

"What happened between your mother and me had nothing to do with you," he said, grabbing a cookie for himself. How many afternoon snacks had we shared at this table? I wondered. Too many to count.

"You were my daughter from the moment I married your mom. You were still my daughter the day we got divorced." His voice was gentle, with an undercurrent of hurt, and I forced myself to look at him.

"I didn't know that." I tried and failed to keep my voice steady. "You left. What was I supposed to think?"

"I should have made sure you knew that nothing changed between us." His voice was heavy. "I should have told you I was leaving."

I looked up at him, his face blurred by the tears in my eyes as I recalled the way he hadn't said goodbye. He'd packed his bags and left my mother to tell me they were divorcing. "Yeah, you should have. I...it sucked to watch you drive away."

Arthur reached across the table and took my fidgeting hands in his. I immediately pulled back, not ready to let go of all the anger and hurt that had lived inside me for years. "I'm sorry," he said as he picked up a cookie and pulled it apart. "I reached out to you."

"I know," I said. "And maybe I should have reached back."

"You were a kid," Arthur cut in. "You did what you had to do to protect yourself."

"We both did," I said, meeting his eyes. "You couldn't have stayed with my mom, and I couldn't let myself trust you again." I lifted a shoulder. "It is what it is. We can't change that now."

"No," Arthur agreed. "We can't. But we can rebuild from here." He paused, his brows furrowing, uncertainty in his eyes. "Right?"

My heart thumped harder. Could I do it? Could I take this final leap? I looked up, Arthur's hopeful gaze steady on my face. One nod, a word, and I'd open myself up to a whole new hurt. If I gave him this chance, gave *us* this chance, and he left...

No. I'd come this far. I had to jump.

I nodded. "I'd like that."

Arthur reached across the table and laid his hands on mine. "Me, too."

The tears I'd been blinking back spilled over my cheeks. And I pulled back to wiped them away. Arthur handed me a napkin. Once I'd sopped up the mess, I said, "You have to take her back."

His brows furrowed. "What?"

"My mom." I shoved my hair away from my face. "She's devastated."

His head hung. "I know. I just didn't want to—"

"There's a time and place for the noble knight act, man. And now ain't it."

I paused, taking a deep breath. "I'm a big girl. And, yeah, I'm pretty shit at the whole *being an adult* thing, but I can take care of myself."

Grabbing a cookie, I bit into it. "Keep that in mind the next time you consider making a decision to protect me."

Arthur nodded solemnly. "Got it." And then he kept sitting there. Looking at me.

"What?" I mumbled through Oreo.

He smiled. "Nothing. I just missed you."

Tears stung my eyes. "I missed you too."

38: The Most Dangerous Words

———

For the next few hours, we ate takeout and caught up on all the missed years. The air was heavy with caution and awkwardness, but a thread of hope sparkled like silver.

It would take a while to get back to our former relationship, but my insides warmed with the certainty that we would.

As the sun sunk over the lake, Arthur decreed I was too exhausted for the two-hour drive home—possibly something to do with me nearly falling asleep in my fried rice—and offered up the guest bedroom.

With a sigh, I peeled off my sweatshirt, kicked off my shoes and climbed into bed. Exhaustion seeped straight to my bones. After the whole Jude thing and my mother's nuclear bomb, and now Arthur, all I wanted to do was pass out. And this bed was heavenly. Closing my eyes, I snuggled into my pillow and pulled the comforter up to my chin.

And then just laid there.

I stared at the ceiling, thoughts rolling in like the waves outside my window.

I'd been a shit individual these last few...well, basically forever. But more so recently than ever before. There were a couple people in particular I owed an apology to.

I rolled over and grabbed my phone. The glaring screen told me it was almost ten. It *felt* so much later. But that meant Jack and Tierney were still up.

They had returned from their honeymoon a couple days ago—the honeymoon I'd interrupted with my multiple panic attacks about meeting Jude's family. If I called now, I'd catch them before they went to bed.

Taking a deep breath, I dialed.

"I'm sorry," I said as soon as Tierney picked up.

"Oh...kay." Tier sounded baffled. "You're forgiven?"

"My life has been a train wreck lately, and you're a good friend for sticking by me through it all—even four a.m. calls on your honeymoon. Thank you."

"You're welcome," she replied, confusion still evident in her voice. "Is everything okay?"

I smiled to myself. For the first time in years, I didn't feel the constant need to maintain the mountain of snark I'd spent years building. And it felt nice.

"Yeah, I'm good," I said. "Or at least I'm well on my way."

After I recapped everything—finally telling Tierney about Arthur felt good—Tier had me on speakerphone while she and Jack regaled me with stories from their honeymoon. About ten minutes in, Jack let out an enormous yawn.

"Well, sounds like it's bedtime," I said with a laugh.

We said our goodbyes, and I thumbed through my contacts for another number.

After I called Luke—who'd also been on his way to bed, because apparently, both he and his brother were ninety years old on the inside—and made amends for my hasty departure last night, I hung up and stared at the shadows on the ceiling.

That left one more person I needed to talk to...

Unlocking my phone again, I pulled up Jude's contact information. His picture glowed at me in the dark room, all dimples and smoky eyes, and my insides went squishy. Without thinking, I hit the Call button.

And then I hung up.

Nope. Calling Jude would be a bad idea. A bad, bad idea. It was over. Finished. Done for. I'd burned that bridge real good. There could be no going back.

Sadness washed over me.

I threw my phone aside and pulled the blankets over my head, trying to block out the persistent voice that sang the two most dangerous words in the English language: *What if?*

What if I called him? What if I sent a text?

What if it was too late? What if he'd taken the job? What if I never saw him again?

What if I drove to his place to find out for myself?

And then I was kicking off the blankets and getting out of bed. I needed to try. I needed to see Jude. I needed to make things right. Or, if I couldn't make things right, I at least needed to apologize. I owed him that much.

Stuffing my feet into my shoes, I grabbed my sweatshirt and purse and headed out the door, colliding with Arthur on the way down the hall.

"Whoa, whoa," he said, his hand closing around my elbow. "Where's the pizza?"

I smiled in spite of my manic-ness. *Where's the pizza* was something Arthur used to say to me anytime I was in a hurry to go somewhere. "Because pizza is much better than fire," he'd say.

Was it any wonder I loved food so much?

Shaking away those memories, I looked at Arthur, who was dressed in his PJs—a KISS t-shirt and plaid pants. "I'm sorry, I don't mean to disappear in the middle of the night. There's just...something I have to do. I'll be back though, I promise." I threw my arms around him. "I love you."

The words stumbled out before I thought them through. I stepped back and blinked. *Take them back*, my mind said. *This isn't something you do.*

But then I looked at Arthur, and he was just as surprised as me. Surprised, and just so happy. My heart echoed that. So, instead of snatching the words back, retreating behind that god-forsaken wall, I smiled, lifted my chin, and said it again. "I love you."

"I—I love you, too." He pulled me in for another hug. "Don't be a stranger, Kit-Kat."

I squeezed him back. "I won't."

I never wanted to be a stranger again.

I MADE THE DRIVE FROM Hope Falls to Port Agnes like a madwoman, too afraid of changing my mind to let up on the gas. As I drove, I tried to figure out what I'd do, what I'd say once I reached Jude's place. By the time I took the Port Agnes exit, I was no closer to figuring it out. All I could do as I weaved through the streets was hope and pray that he hadn't hopped a plane before I could pull my head out of my ass.

I raised my fist to knock, then dropped it to my side, then raised it again. I could do this. I had to.

Blowing out a steadying breath, I raised my hand again, and this time my knuckles connected with the door.

As I waited for him to answer, I finger-combed my hair and twisted it into a braid, then brushed uselessly at the wrinkled clothes I'd been wearing for nearly two days straight. Maybe I should have stopped home first. Jude would be much more likely to listen to me if I at least *looked* hot.

But he had seen me in much worse shape, and he hadn't run away.

I squared my shoulders and knocked again.

The door swung open. Sunny greeted me with a sneer.

I stepped back. "Oh. Um. Hi."

"Hi." Her eyes narrowed. "If you're looking for Jude, he's not here."

39: No Parachute

———

I sank against the wall, my heart dropping like a water balloon at my feet.

I was too late.

Sunny looked at me like she was afraid I'd snap at any second. "He'll be back soon if you want to wait insi—"

I didn't wait for her to finish. I whizzed passed her and plopped down on the couch.

"Oh...kay." Sunny closed the door behind her and moved around the perimeter of the room, to the kitchen. "You need anything? Water? Vodka? Lithium?"

Oh, she was funny. "No, no I'm good. Thanks."

She grabbed a bottle of water from the fridge, then came around to lean on the island, never turning her back toward me.

The silence was heavy. Awkward. Sunny probably knew what had happened with Jude and me. Or, she at least knew the bare minimum.

Which would explain why she looked like she was mentally dismembering me at this very moment.

I tossed a smile her way. "Any idea when Jude will be back?"

She did not smile back. "He went to pick up food, so any minute now." Her arms crossed over her chest. "I know people, you know."

"What?"

"I know people," she repeated, her blue eyes like daggers. "People that could make you regret ever meeting my brother."

"Oh." I eased away from Sunny, squeezing into the farthest corner of the couch. "Thanks for the warning."

And the quiet again.

Somewhere in the apartment, a clock ticked. I was thankful for the steady noise—it gave me something to focus on. Something *other* than the borderline homicidal maniac across the room. Oh, and the possibility that, if Sunny or her *people* did not murder me, Jude would reject me.

If that happened, maybe I could convince Sunny to murder me after all. If I asked nicely.

Tick tock, tick tock, tick tock, said the clock. I closed my eyes and forced a breath from my lungs. Ignoring Sunny's glare, I tried to figure out what I would say to Jude once he arrived.

I'm sorry, obviously. For being a cowardly asshole. And, *You were right.* Maybe a little, *I miss you.*

Oh, and, of course, *I love you.*

That last one was the scariest. Because it meant freefalling. It meant uncertainty. It meant I could smash right into the ground.

But it also meant bravery.

I rehearsed the words in my mind. *I love you. I love you. I love y—*

"They didn't have any of that weird sauce you like, so I got a different kind. I hope that's—"

I leapt up from the couch as Jude pushed through the door. He stopped mid-sentence when he saw me standing in his living room.

"I love you."

The words tumbled from my heart, over my tongue, and landed on the floor at Jude's feet. His eyes flew to my face, wide with surprise, but before he could respond, Sunny broke the silence.

"That's okay. I didn't really need the sauce. And, actually, you know what just occurred to me? Food always tastes so much better if I eat it at my place. So I'm going to do that." She crossed the room, took the takeout bag from Jude, and headed for the door. "Thanks for dinner, bro. I'll talk to you later. Nice seeing you again, Cat." She waved at me with her free hand as she sailed out the door, closing it with a thud behind her.

I flinched at the sound, then wrung my hands together, giving Jude a nervous smile. "Hi."

Hedging around me, Jude entered the kitchen and opened the fridge. He returned a second later with a beer. "What are you doing here, Cat?"

That was it. No *I love you, too*, or even, *Do you want a beer?*

What are you doing here?

Well, what did I expect?

"I'm sorry," I started, determined to get through this without falling apart. Or, worse. Running away.

He leaned against the counter and took a swig of his beer. "Is there anything else I can do for you?"

I flinched. His tone held no warmth. No pleasure. This dude was *not* happy to see me.

And I didn't blame him one bit.

Swallowing the surge of tears that wanted to escape, I picked up the beer bottles and empty glasses from the coffee table and took them into the kitchen, ignoring his puzzled look.

Once I'd dropped the bottles into the recycling bin, I began maniacally tidying up the tiny space. I washed the glasses, then moved to the counter. When Jude joined me in the kitchen, I was scrubbing at an invisible spot with way too much elbow grease.

"Cat."

I stopped mid-scrub and looked at him. Then looked around his apartment for the first real time. No boxes. No bubble wrap. Everything was in its place. "You didn't take the job."

His answer was immediate. "No," he said, meeting my eye dead-on, "I didn't."

"Okay," I replied, relief, so warm and sweet, flowing through my veins. "Okay."

Turning back to the counter, I picked up the sponge again. Mid-scrub, I faced him, a rush of frustration coursing through me. "But, why?" Water dripped from the sponge onto my sneakered feet, but I ignored it. "It was your dream job."

He rolled the beer bottle between his hands, his eyes trained on it. "I got a better offer."

Elation propelled me forward, and I put my hand on his arm. "Did you get the job here?"

Jude withdrew his arm and backed up. I swallowed around the scorching dismissal and went back to scrubbing. I didn't think he was going to answer when he finally spoke.

"Remember Lia Frost?"

"Angry rock star? Called me a groupie?" I rolled my eyes. "Yep."

A ghost of a smile touched Jude's lips. "That's the one."

"Did you take her up on the threesome?" I ignored the jealousy that followed my question. He was a free agent. He could bone whomever he wanted.

Didn't mean I had to like the thought, though.

This time, a chuckle. "I don't think her husband would be into that." He finally looked up, and for the first time since he saw me standing in his space, a spark lit his eyes.

Too bad it wasn't for me.

"She offered me a job." He sat his beer on the counter and wiped his hands on his jeans. A smile—a real one this time—cracked over his face. "As her publicist. Apparently, she appreciated my 'bullshit filter,' as she called it."

I kept my expression neutral to hide the surge of worries whirling inside me. Celebrities usually lived in L.A., didn't they? How was this better than the other job? "Does that mean you're still moving?"

He picked the beer back up and lifted it to his lips. That was it. Nothing more.

Okay...

I grabbed the sponge and went back to scrubbing. My heart slammed so hard my teeth chattered. My face burned, my hands shook. Maybe I wasn't ready for this conversation.

Or maybe this is what it feels like to take a chance, a voice whispered, and then suddenly I stopped scrubbing.

I could do this. I had to.

Dropping the sponge onto the counter, I turned to find Jude standing a mere two feet away from me. "Uh," I started, fixing my eyes on his right bicep and the angel wing peeking out from beneath his t-shirt. "Cool tattoo."

Jude glanced down at his arm, then back to me. "Thanks." His eyebrows knitted together. "It's...not new."

"I know that." I picked up the sponge. "I just...that's not what I wanted to talk about." I tried again, finally looking him in the eye.

My stomach twisted into knots. I missed those eyes, and how they changed from blue to green to gray to a mixture of the three, depending on his mood. I missed the enviable ease with which he lived his life—nothing got to the dude. And when he loved, he loved hard. I saw it with Sunny, and Ben, and his parents. I saw it with me.

And, goddammit, I missed it.

"I miss you." I blurted the words and watched as the words registered on his face. Much like the *I love you* earlier, if he felt anything about it, he didn't show it.

He leaned his hip against the counter, face closed. "I don't have time for this, Cat." He took a swig of his beer. "There are certain things I'm looking for in a relationship—the most important one being someone that actually *wants* to be with me."

"I do. I just—"

"Well, you've got a funny way of showing it." Pushing away from the counter, he brushed passed me. "Look, we tried. It didn't work." He looked back at me, a shrug lifting his shoulder. "You don't do serious. I should have listened."

"But I *want* to do serious." I crossed the room to stand in front of him. A slow tremble took over my entire body. I didn't think I'd ever been this terrified in my entire life.

You can't stay locked in a tower forever, I heard Hazel's voice say, and then I straightened my shoulders and ignored the shaking.

Now or never. This was my chance to be brave. To break the cycle. It might end in heartbreak, but what if it was all I'd ever wanted?

One look into Jude's eyes gave me my answer: all I'd ever wanted stood right in front of me. I might have ruined it forever, but if I didn't try, I wouldn't know.

"It's like this," I started, fixing my eyes on a spot just over Jude's shoulder. "I've been running scared my whole life. Too afraid to get hurt. Too afraid of becoming my mother."

I brushed passed him and started to pace. "But the thing is," I continued, twisting my hands together. "I already *am* my mother. Do you know what I mean?"

"Uh..."

"Only, she marries all these guys, but breaks up with them before she gets hurt. But my way is almost worse. See, I don't even let anyone get that close. I keep this giant-ass wall around me that no one can climb over, because if someone got over it, then they could hurt me. And I don't want to be hurt. Do you get what I'm saying?"

I stopped pacing and looked at Jude, his face a mask of complete confusion.

"Maybe?" he said, his brows furrowed as he tried to understand my blabbering. "You don't want to get hurt, so you hide behind a wall."

"Right. Only, it didn't work. Because you got behind that wall. Actually, you smashed it to pieces, caused all kinds of damage. Broke all my damn rules, too."

I met his eye and held it. Blowing out a slow breath, I continued. "That night in the motel, after Tierney's wedding...that was the closest I'd ever felt to anyone. And then I met your family, and I liked them, and I liked you, and...it scared the hell out of me." Tears stung my eyes. "*You* scare the hell out of me."

"Cat—"

"No, I have to finish. You deserve the truth."

"All right." He tilted his head. "Go on."

"You scare me, Jude. And that's why I ran. I didn't want to get hurt, and you had so much potential to hurt me. I needed to get away from you. And fast. But the thing is..." I paused, taking a huge gulp of air. My feet wanted to pace again, but I stopped, determined to look Jude in the eye as I said this next part.

"The thing is," I continued. "I got hurt anyway. Somewhere along this jacked-up journey we've been taking, I...I fell for you. And then I pushed you away. I hurt you. And I'm sorry."

Seconds of silence stretched over us. When Jude finally spoke, it wasn't what I wanted to hear. "So, that other guy was what? One last fling to see if you were ready to settle down?" Anger flashed, turning his eyes steely.

"Nothing happened with Luke." I lifted my chin, holding his eye. "*Nothing*, Jude."

He held my stare, but didn't say anything.

"Fear has made me do a lot of stupid things," I continued, twisting my hair in my hands. "And I hurt a lot of people because I was scared. But what I did *not* do is shack up with some other dude to get over you." I took a step forward. "There's no getting over you."

The teensiest emotion flickered in his eyes. I took the opening. "I love you, Jude."

Bam. The careful reserve on his face cracked down the middle. But he didn't say anything.

I laughed, my heart hammering an uneven rhythm in my chest. "Before today, I hadn't said those words to anyone but Hazel, and now I can't stop saying them."

Balling my hands into fists to keep from fidgeting, I kept talking. "I went to see Arthur today. Marched right up to his door and everything." I paused and smiled—I still couldn't believe I'd done that. "And we talked. And cried. And hugged each other for the first time in thirteen years." I stopped. My eyes burned. It'd been a long, emotionally exhausting day, but it was just the kind of day I needed to get me to this moment.

I gulped in a breath. Every second of this day had led me here. I couldn't let it go to waste. I needed to be vulnerable. I needed to be scared.

I needed to be brave.

"I love you." I took the few steps that separated us, pulse pounding loud in my ears as I repeated the words slower. Surer. "I. Love. You."

Jude's eyes narrowed on my face, and I could see the indecision in them. "Love is scary, Cat." He sat his beer on the counter and crossed his arms over his chest. "How do I know you won't run the moment you get scared again?"

"You're right," I said. "Love *is* scary. Relationships are scary. And there's no way to know how it'll turn out." I splayed my hands in front of me. "But there's no one I'd rather try with more."

His eyes flared. He wanted to believe me. I could tell. But he didn't want to risk another faulty chute.

Turmoil rolled off him like a tidal wave. Thrusting both hands into his hair, he walked into the living room. "I'm glad you're working through your fears. Making amends with Arthur...that's great." He looked at me, and my stomach hit the floor. Fear, doubt, everything you *didn't* want to see in the eyes of someone you'd just professed feelings for. "But—"

I didn't let him finish. Crossing the room, I stepped onto the couch.

"What are you doing?" He followed behind me. "Cat, what are you doing? No shoes on the couch."

I ignored him, pushing to my feet on the arm of the couch. "You know, I thought I couldn't do it," I said as I stood. The room turned a little spinny. I extended my arms to keep my balance. "I thought I couldn't leave, you know?"

"Would you please get down?" His voice came from just behind me. "I'd be much more comfortable having this conversation if both your feet were on the floor."

I didn't look back. "But if you go, I go."

"That...that doesn't sound good. What are you—"

"I'm jumping out of the fucking airplane." I tossed a grin over my shoulder. "Do *not* let me splat."

"Cat. Don't—"

Before he could utter another word, I squeezed my eyes shut and launched myself from the couch.

"Wait, Cat!" Jude said, but I was already flying through the air.

"Oomph," he grunted as I collided into him. His arms wrapped around me, and we landed in a heap on the floor.

"Good god, woman," he grumbled, shifting beneath me. "What if I hadn't caught you?"

"I'd have survived." I rested my chin on his chest and met his eyes. "I was just tired of sitting on that plane alone."

At that, Jude untangled himself from me and sat up, his long legs stretched out in front of him. A weighted sigh escaped his lungs. "Cat..."

I sat up, too. "I know."

"What do you know?"

My fingers found a loose thread in my sweatshirt. I wound it tight around my index finger, the thin, blue line digging into my skin. The pain mirrored the feeling inside my chest. I forced myself to breathe. Too look at Jude.

"I know that love ain't no field of...marshmallows and chocolate, or whatever." I swallowed. My heart hit my ribcage like a hammer. "I know that it's going to be hard and scary and..."

I looked up, face stripped bare of any pretense. This wasn't the time for pretense. "And I know you think I can't do it."

Jude's brows drew together. "It's not that I don't think you can do it." He reached over, unwinding the sweatshirt thread from my fingertip. I looked down and watched our fingers intertwine. "We're going to fight, you know. And sometimes you'll probably not like me very much."

I turned my hand over and his thumb ran across my palm. "Oh, I know." I reached for a smile but only sort of hit the mark. "Sunny told me about your bathroom-hogging habit."

He scoffed. "I have two sisters. Even five minutes in the bathroom was too long for them."

"Excuses." I peeked up at him, tracing over every line, slope, and swerve of his face. My heart thumped fuller. "You'll probably not like me sometimes, too. But then, you'll realize the error of your ways, and we'll make up."

His cheek dimpled as he laughed, but as quick as it showed up, it disappeared. I looked into his eyes and saw my own fear reflected back at me. He wanted to be sure, and, for that, I could not blame him.

But behind my own fear, an untapped pool of bravery waited. And I was ready to dive in.

I took a deep breath. "I want to go with you."

"What?" He frowned. "Where?"

"L.A." I shrugged. "Antarctica. Wherever you end up."

"Cat—"

"I mean it." I pushed to my knees and faced him. "I don't want to be where you're not. And if that means leaving my life here, then I'll do it."

The clouds in his eyes finally—*finally*—parted. He smiled, and I swore the sky outside flared with light.

"Come here," he said as he tugged my hand. I crossed the chasm between us and settled into his lap.

I didn't speak. Just waited. Waited for the verdict. Would my leap from the couch pay off, or would Jude send me home, alone?

"I want to be the one that catches you when you're crazy enough to jump out of planes, or off couches, or whatever," he finally said as he pushed a lock of hair behind my ear.

Hope flared, then faltered. "Why do I hear a *but*?"

Jude's hand dropped. My heart fell with it. "I'm not going to L.A."

"Antarctica, then?" I sighed. "It's a good thing I like penguins."

A laugh rumbled through him. "I'm not going to Antarctica, either."

"Okay, well wherever you're going, I'm there. Just, you know, give me time to prepare. I'll have to research the wardrobes, the food, the—"

He pressed his palm to my cheek, his thumb brushing over my lips. "Cat."

"Yesh?" I mumbled.

"I'm not going anywhere."

"But you said—"

"I said I got a new job. A job that I can do from here." His hand dropped to link with mine. "Sorry, no penguins."

"Oh." I sighed. "I'd already mentally stocked my closet with the cutest coats and boots and—"

He cut me off with a kiss. I wrapped my arms around his neck and kissed him back with every fervent emotion rushing through me. All the years of running, of hiding, of roiling cynicism and fear dropped away, and I knew: this one would stay.

And nothing would change that.

Pulling away from him, I rested my forehead against his. "I love you."

He eased back enough to look into my eyes. I'd never seen his warmer. "I love you, too." Then, he pulled me tight against him, leaning in for another kiss. Once we came up for air, he added, "Just one night, remember?"

"Fine by me," I murmured, leaning in for another kiss. "One night, over and over and—"

He cut me off with a kiss that said what *just one night* really meant: forever.

The End

Note from the Author

———

THANK YOU so much for reading Goodnight & Go! I hope you had as much fun with Cat & Jude as I did!

GOODNIGHT & GO is the second book in the Breakaway series. The third book, Ready to Run, will feature some very familiar characters. If you wondered as you read just WHAT was going on with Jude's best friend and his sister, well...you're definitely going to find out!

If you're interested in some deleted scene goodness, character inspiration, and maybe some cute pictures of my pooch, be sure to swing by my website and sign up for my newsletter!

And if you enjoyed this book—hell, even if you didn't—please be sure to leave me a review!

Acknowledgments

Christina—Dude, you read that pre-breakup breakup scene approximately 50,000 times without complaining. I owe you all the Dean Winchester gifs and chocolate!

Victoria—thank you for reading and reading and reading this book, and for always giving me awesome feedback! The last scene is so much better thanks to you!

Alyssa & Louise—for all the coffee shop writing and encouragement and laughs and love. You're a couple of badasses, and don't forget it.

Mom, Dad, Donald, & Jay—ya'll support the shit out of me. Thanks for pimping my books and coming to my events!

My editor, Jessica, for your endlessly insightful feedback.

Jeannie, Erin, Sarah, David, Amanda, Charlie, Brittany, Kayla, Jessica, Jamie. Everyone at the day job, and all the awesome nerds in my writing community. Thanks for listening to me rant/whine/generally be neurotic, for showing up to events, for buying my book and for reading my book, and for being the most supportive people ever. You guys fucking rock. All of you. Keep that shit up.

About the Author

MEIKA USHER is a romance author, a puppy mama, and a lover of all things pizza. When she's not writing snarky, sexy, love stories, she can be found binge-watching Supernatural (she's a Dean girl), memorizing all the song lyrics ever (it's her superpower), or planning to see the world, one country at a time (Prague is next on her list). Meika can be found on the interwebz at meikausher.com[1]

---

1. http://www.meikausher.com/

Don't miss out!

Visit the website below and you can sign up to receive emails whenever Meika Usher publishes a new book. There's no charge and no obligation.

https://books2read.com/r/B-A-HJHF-CMRS

BOOKS 2 READ

Connecting independent readers to independent writers.